Praise for *Wolfbreed*

"This may be the werewolf book of the year . . . a fresh, page-turning take on werewolf tropes that is not to be missed."

—*Booklist*

"Lilly lives in a world so strange that even werewolves have to fight for survival, and I found myself rooting for her from the very start. Before long, I was falling for her, too! *Wolfbreed* is a thrilling yet deeply moving journey that I never wanted to end."

—ROBERT MASELLO, author of *Blood and Ice*

"A mesmerizing story that entertained me thoroughly and moved me deeply. *Wolfbreed* is an exciting nonstop action adventure involving the supernatural. More than that, though, it demonstrates how the human spirit, even when in a not-entirely-human body, can be transformed and redeemed by the power of love. I adored this book."

—MARY BALOGH, *New York Times* bestselling author of *A Secret Affair*

"S. A. Swann has written a spellbinding fantasy of the Teutonic knights and the great Northern Crusade, set in a little-known period of history amidst the gloomy forests of Prussia and Li[illegible]s, this one k[illegible]

—C[illegible]hor

"Swann turns opposing viewpoints into sympathetic perspectives, clearly painting the complex political and religious dynamics of the time."

—*Publishers Weekly* (starred review)

"Swann does an excellent job of worldbuilding, and the setting of medieval Prussia is an interesting choice, adding its own unique flavor to the tale. It's blessed with a good story and interesting premise."

—*RT Book Reviews*

"*Wolfbreed* is definitely up there for my 'surprise find of the year.' If you're after an engrossing slice of historical fantasy, or if you just like werewolves, then I don't think you'll go wrong with this one."

—Graeme's Fantasy Book Review

"Swann has given readers an empathetic, remarkably drawn character in Lilly. . . . In *Wolfbreed,* he's given readers engaging characters, a plausible conceit, and a greatly-paced story."

—SFFWorld.com

Also by S. A. Swann

Wolfbreed

Wolf's Cross

Wolf's Cross

S. A. Swann

BALLANTINE BOOKS
NEW YORK

A Spectra Trade Paperback Original

Published in the United States by Spectra, an imprint
of The Random House Publishing Group,
a division of Random House, Inc., New York.

Swann, S. Andrew.
Wolf's cross / S. A. Swann.
p. cm.
"A Spectra trade paperback original" — T.p. verso.
ISBN 978-0-553-80739-4 (pbk.)
1. Werewolves—Fiction. 2. Poland—Fiction. I. Title.
PS3569.W555L57 2010
813'.54—dc22
2010014575

Printed in the United States of America

www.ballantinebooks.com

2 4 6 8 9 7 5 3 1

Text design by Diane Hobbing

This book is dedicated to
Lynn and Lucy, for getting me started.

PART ONE

Anno Domini 1353

I

Brother Josef had thought he had seen Hell itself. He had seen it in the black swellings that plagued his father and mother, sisters and brother. He had seen it in the doctors who fled at the sight of him coming from an infected house. He had seen it in the faces of those who still dared walk the streets of Nürnberg, carrying smoldering bundles of aromatic herbs to chase the infection away, or at least mask the omnipresent smell of death. He had seen it in the piles of bodies left to rot for lack of men to bury them. And he had seen it in the blackened face of a woman he loved, abandoned to die alone in her family's house.

However, upon joining the Order, he had learned that Hell took many forms.

It was the will of God, and his superiors, that he serve his probation under the command of Komtur Heinrich, who headed a convent of warrior monks within the still barely tamed wilds of Prussia. Komtur Heinrich held a peculiar place in the Order, and his men bore a name within the Order that Josef had not heard before: Wolfjägers.

Even the device they bore had a difference from that of the wider Order: a severed wolf's head occupied the upper left quadrant of the Teutonic Knights' black cross.

The weapons borne by the Wolfjägers were different in character, as well. The smaller items, daggers and arrowheads, were cast of pure silver. Swords and axes were of more typical steel, but with edges clad in silver.

It was not his place to question his role, and it was not until he saw the first signs of what the wolf hunters actually hunted that he understood.

He knew that their foe was some sort of demon, but he was worldly enough to expect that the "demons" they sought would resemble men. In the depths of his self-doubt, he feared they might resemble Jews. He knew that Jews were not responsible for the pestilence that had scoured the land. During the worst of it, the synagogue at Nürnberg had stood as empty of life as the cathedrals.

But that hadn't stopped riots in the countryside, as panicked villagers burned Jews like the city folk burned incense, in a pathetic attempt to keep the death at bay. Even decrees by Pope Clement VI hadn't been able to halt the slaughter.

Josef didn't believe that the men of the Order, devoted to Christ and the pope, would be so readily deceived. But when Heinrich talked of demons who walked like men, it so much resembled the rhetoric Josef had heard during the worst of the death that he wondered—and chided himself for the doubts. His faith had led him to this point, and he did not believe his service to God would be so subverted.

Soon enough, God and his Komtur saw fit to give him evidence of the demons the Wolfjägers hunted, and they were not men—Christian or Jew.

He was unprepared when Komtur Heinrich stopped them outside an unnamed village whose fields had gone wild and unharvested. At first, Josef thought they had come across an outbreak of the pestilence finding a northern foothold. But Heinrich announced, "For those of you new to this service, observe well what we find here. We are close on the trail of the demon."

They rode forward in silence, and unlike the plague villages Josef had seen when he had finally departed his family's estate at Nürnberg, the first bodies he saw were those of animals. The corpses of sheep and oxen dotted an overgrown field, their bodies black with flies. Despite the decay, Josef could tell that the beasts had died by violence, not from illness. Parts of the corpses were scattered, so that an accurate census of the dead wasn't possible.

They stopped at a house with a splintered door. Blood splattered the threshold as if in mockery of the angel of death. Inside was chaos—blood, fragments of furniture, and a broken scythe whose blade was spotted with gore and tufts of blond fur.

There were no bodies.

"It has been here," Komtur Heinrich said, drawing attention to bloody prints in the dirt floor of the cottage, where the weather had not washed the marks away.

Pressed into the gore was the pawprint of a wolf, but a wolf that would have to be the most monstrous animal Josef had ever heard of. The gauntleted hand of a large man could barely spread wide enough to cover it.

"What manner of wolf made these prints?" Josef asked.

"Wolfbreed," Heinrich answered. "The spawn of Hell itself. The beast has the aspect of a wolf, but stands—and thinks—as a man. It can cloak itself in human skin as it wishes, and it will ignore all wounds but the instantly mortal from all but a silver weapon." Heinrich lifted the scythe and turned to Josef, and for a moment, in the darkness, he had the aspect of the angel of death himself. "This was a futile weapon, useless unless it took off the head of the beast with the first stroke."

"But where are the bodies?" Josef asked, afraid of the answer.

⊕

He had his unwelcome answer at the village's church.

At first, as they approached the small building, Josef thought that the window ledges, the roof, and the cross set in front had all been draped black in mourning. It wasn't until they got closer that he saw that the black moved.

Every horizontal and near-horizontal surface in the area was covered with crows. The evil birds stood so closely packed that Josef's eyes couldn't distinguish one from another. They became a single black mass with ten thousand heads and ten thousand beaks. As one, the mass turned its eyes toward the approaching knights.

Then, as if by some demonic signal, they lifted as one, with a deafening screech and a thunderous pounding of wings against the sky. For an instant, the sun went black. Then the hellish cloud dispersed, leaving the men to view the feast that had drawn the birds here.

All the bodies had been thrown into the church, before the altar. Although the carrion birds had left little of the villagers but bone and sinew, the stench in the church was as bad as anything Josef had endured at Nürnberg. Given the state in which nature had left the bodies, the scene could have been the remnants of another plague village—a particularly gruesome one.

If it wasn't for the drag marks.

The corpses had been killed elsewhere and methodically dumped in front of the altar. Perhaps most disturbing was the small painting of the Madonna and the Christ Child, where the faces had been clawed away.

Josef knew then that they did face a demon.

⊕

They followed the demon for three days, through the Prussian wilderness. Josef thanked God that they didn't run into another spectacular atrocity, but that in itself was troubling. It meant that their foe—this *wolfbreed*—didn't act randomly or in haste. It had planned the death of that village, and had methodically carried out that plan.

And, as they followed its trail, Josef was disturbed by the thought that the trail they followed was younger than the scene of carnage at the village, as if what they hunted had waited for them to catch up.

Even so, their tracking wasn't perfect, and right now they stood in the woods, waiting to decide on the direction of their hunt.

The woods are dark here, Josef thought.

He sat astride a horse with the other probationary brothers of the Order—a line of ten men with incomplete crosses on their tabards. Ahead of them, dismounted, stood three of the knights with Komtur Heinrich, holding a low discussion about their course.

The tracks they followed had led down a path in the woods that was now little more than a game trail. The woods here were not dense, and their horses could navigate through the trees, but it had reached the point where their movement was restricted. Just turning his mount around would be an ordeal, weaving past trunks and over deadfalls, and the whole party had slowed to no faster than a man could walk.

Now they had stopped.

Above them, the sun had nearly left the sky, and the trees had already wrapped them in twilit darkness.

Where are we? Josef thought, unwilling to voice the question in the unnatural silence. Around them, the woods were as quiet as a sepulchre waiting for a corpse. The only sounds were the low voices near Komtur Heinrich and the muffled scrape of horses' hooves against the dead leaves covering the forest floor. While they waited for word from Heinrich, Josef held a loaded crossbow in front of him. It had been close to half an hour since they had stopped, and his arms were fatigued from the weight in his hands.

After everything, have we actually lost its trail?

Even as a neophyte to the Wolfjägers of the Order, he had seen enough of what they hunted to question that such a trail could be easily lost.

The creature they hunted cared little for stealth or subtlety. Its path was marked with scraps of blood, hair, and bone. Its evil was written in the corpses of man and beast alike. It had not made itself difficult to follow.

We haven't lost it, he thought.

We aren't following it.

It's leading us.

Josef looked back and forth, but the woods around them had become impenetrable with the evening shadows. He called out, "Brother Heinrich!"

His mount pinned its ears back and let out a cry of pure terror. Suddenly all the hoses were spooking, and Josef's mount reared up. With both hands on his crossbow, Josef couldn't grab the reins or the saddle to keep himself and the crossbow from tumbling backward. Before he fell, his horse whipped its head to the side, showing a foaming mouth and one huge eye, white with terror.

Josef slammed into the ground, momentarily stunned. He heard a growl that seemed to come from everywhere at once, and he realized, *It's here.*

He fumbled for his fallen crossbow as, off to his right, he heard a man scream. Around him, the knights gained control of their horses, doing their best to turn outward in the confined space. Josef's own horse was lost past Heinrich on the narrow game trail.

On Heinrich's face was a look of surprise that even his normally stony expression could not hide. *He hadn't expected the thing to attack.*

Josef found his crossbow and brought it up to face the greatest sound of chaos, but one of his brothers' mounts was in the way. He saw the hint of something large moving impossibly fast; then the rider in front of Josef tumbled off his mount to fall at Josef's feet, a large part of his throat gone.

The horse reared at something, and that something howled—a hellish noise followed by a ripping sound that left the horse collapsing to its knees. Josef backed up, looking for a target as the horse fell dead in a pool of spreading gore.

It had moved behind him. Josef spun around at the sound of growling in time to have the body of another rider slam down on top of him. Josef fell under his groaning comrade and screamed at the heavens, "Where is it? *Where is it?*"

He rolled out from under his brother and came face-to-face with the answer.

A head taller than any of Heinrich's men, it bore a head twice the size any wolf's had a right to be. Its muscles rippled under gore-stained blond fur, and it stood on legs crooked like a wolf's. But it had hands—demonic clawed hands that flexed and reached for Josef as it leapt at him.

With a brief plea to God, he brought the crossbow to bear on the approaching monster. He exhaled and took the extra second to aim, even though every muscle in his body screamed at him to fire *now*!

He pulled the trigger after aiming square at one of the creature's glaring blue eyes, knowing he only had the one chance to save himself and his comrades. A bolt though the brain would finish this thing once and for all.

But nothing happened.

He only had a fraction of a second to realize that the bowstring had snapped in the fall from his horse. The bolt rested against the block, inert and useless.

Then the monster was on him, slamming him to the ground, tearing at his armor. The weight of it slammed into his lower body, pressing down on his legs as it buried its muzzle in his stomach. He screamed as if the beast had already torn into his entrails, even though a part of his brain knew that it was still tearing through his mail and the padding underneath.

That cleared his head of panic for a moment. He had to find a weapon, an attack, anything. He whipped his head around, looking at a world blurred by pain and tears. Praying to God for—

The crossbow bolt.

The dead crossbow had fallen next to him, the unfired silver-tipped bolt still nocked. He reached a gauntleted hand toward it as the monster found his flesh under the mail, and Josef screamed as he felt its teeth sink into skin and muscle. Every fiber of his being tried to pull away, his body ripping itself away from the insult as the creature lifted him, raising him partway off the ground. The beast's muzzle wrinkled as blood flowed, darkening its fur. Even through the pain, Josef felt the heat of its fetid breath against his skin.

I am dead, Josef thought in a moment of pain-sharpened lucidity. The burst of calm must have been divine in nature—the same grace that allowed the saints to face their own martyrdom.

It was with that sudden clarity that he grabbed the crossbow bolt, brought it up, and jammed the point into the creature's left eye with all the force he could muster.

The beast howled, letting loose its grip on his stomach. Josef fell back into the mud, feeling his life spilling out of the hole in his belly. Before he lost his grip on the world, he saw the monster retreat, the bolt sticking awkwardly out of its face.

Josef lost consciousness praying he had finished the beast.

II

Maria sang to herself during the two-mile-long walk from her family's farm to Gród Narew. Sometimes she would sing small snippets of hymns, but right now she was having a more daring moment. The song was one of the bawdier ballads she had heard the knights of the szlachta singing when she served them in the large dining hall at Gród Narew.

She started singing low, but as she walked through the dense woods, she unconsciously raised her voice with every verse. When she reached the lightning-blasted oak that marked the midpoint between her farm and the fortress, she completed the song, singing at full volume of the conquest of the virile knight over the reluctant maiden. When the words of their consummate act echoed back from the woods around her, she paused a moment with burning cheeks and an embarrassed smile.

Her father would definitely not approve. He was very strict and ever wary of the Devil and his attempts to intrude into their lives. Song was one of those avenues he saw as allowing the Devil in. Maria's hand unconsciously lifted between her breasts to feel the small silver cross she wore under her chemise. It was still there, still protecting her from the Devil.

She glanced up at the sky, gauging the advance of dawn. The sky above shone a light pink through the trees. She couldn't see the horizon, but a glow around some of the tallest branches showed that the sun had just peeked above the ground. Just as she started thinking that she had taken too long in her trek through the woods, she heard the clanging of the bell at the fortress, marking the first hour of the day.

She sighed. She should be *leaving* the dense woods crowding Gród Narew, and here she was barely at the halfway point. She had spent too long with her chores at the farm. Now she was going to reach the fortress just as the stable hands would start working the horses. She clutched her cross more tightly and said a short prayer that God would keep her safe not only from the Devil himself, but also from one of the Devil's more petty minions.

⊕

The sun had fully risen by the time she left the woods and walked the path up the conical hillside toward the looming timber walls of Gród Narew. She walked up past wide stone-walled fields where sheep and goats grazed. The best pasture, though, was closest to the fortress walls, and reserved for the horses of the szlachta.

She hurried past the mounts of the nobility, hoping to make the gate before anyone saw her. But she knew that she had failed to escape as soon as the smells of manure and rotten cheese advanced upon her. Her daily nemesis, Lukasz, came from whatever chores he was in the midst of and vaulted the stone fence, landing on the path directly in front of her.

"You wound me, my fair Maria." He gave her a gap-toothed smile and reached for her with a filth-crusted hand. She backed up so that he pawed air rather than her chemise.

"Wound you? You seem quite hale." Maria stepped to the side

to go around the man. She hated being a target for this brute, but there wasn't much she could do about it. He was the personal servant to one of Bolesław's knights, while she was only here to ease the burden of her family's debts to the lord of Gród Narew. While he supposedly held no more status or rights than she did, as a practical matter he was almost noble himself. He was also the type of man who didn't let anyone forget it.

Today, Lukasz seemed particularly amorous, and he reached out again, grabbing her arm as she passed. "In my heart, fair maiden. You wound my heart, passing without so much as a glance toward poor lonely Lukasz."

The sweetness of his words did not reach his eyes. They never did. He would recite them to any maid or widow unfortunate enough to cross his path, and all the time his gaze would traverse his victim, leaving stains worse than those made by his hands, and harder to wash off. She shook her arm free of his grasp and said, "I have work to attend to, as do you."

"No work so important that it cannot spare our efforts for a time. Wouldn't you care to share some of your charms?"

She actually tasted bile in the back of her throat, thinking of the petty troll Lukasz playing the role of the knight in her ballad. "Those are for my betrothed," she snapped at him in a low whisper.

"A lucky man, indeed. You should grant me an introduction." Lukasz laughed at her, and she felt a sick sense of despair that she was so plain and common at nineteen years that this brute was the only man to show such an interest in her.

In the dark parts of her soul, she thought that her desire for solitude at times led those more discriminating than Lukasz to question her chastity. She didn't know, but she suspected what the other women in the kitchen chattered about when she left to serve the knights.

She blinked back her tears and started walking away from him, promising herself that she wouldn't turn around.

"Someday, Maria, I will be a knight. You could be the betrothed of *Rycerz* Lukasz."

Maria balled her hands into fists and spun around. "A knight?" she shouted back. "On that day I will be far too old and feeble to hold your interest, and you'll be too senile to remember any favors I granted you!"

Her outburst was greeted by laughter from the other side of the stone fence. A trio of stable hands, all younger than Lukasz, were standing in the pasture and doing nothing to hide their amusement at Lukasz's expense. Lukasz's face lost all trace of the false humor he'd been showing her and his skin rapidly changed color, becoming a blotchy red. "You shall not make light of my service, woman!"

"We both have duties to attend to," she said. It took a supreme effort of will not to add, "Don't you have manure to shovel?"

She turned to walk to the gate.

"You will not walk away from me like—"

She tensed, waiting for him to grab for her, but he was interrupted by the sound of hoofbeats. She felt the approaching horses in the packed earth of the path beneath her feet before she saw them. First she looked back the way she had come, but her path just led back into the dark woods that stretched south of the fortress.

"Everyone, the river!" yelled one of the stable hands from the pasture.

North and west of the fortress, the river Narew flowed, separating the fortress from the last wooded frontiers of Masovia. Across the river were dense woodlands, and eventually Prussia—the Monastic State of the Teutonic Knights. Even after the Polish king Casimir had found peace with the Teutonic Order, very little had come from that direction except the occasional messenger headed south, toward Poland. Masovia itself was still an independent duchy. Even under the rule of Casimir's brother, it had yet to rejoin the Polish union, leaving it an uneasy buffer between Poland and the Order.

The black cross standard of the Teutonic Order fluttered above a score of horsemen as they drove their mounts across a ford in the river. The sight sent a shiver of terror through Maria's chest. She grabbed her cross through her chemise as she watched the invading knights: men and horses, moving as if the hand of God itself was whipping their backs.

Behind her, the alarm bells tolled within the fortress.

"We're under attack," Lukasz said, standing rooted on the path while his fellow stable hands ran off to retrieve the horses from the pasture.

Maria stared at the men as they crossed the river and said, "No, we're not." Then she vaulted the stone fence and began running across the pasture toward the river.

What she had realized, after the initial shock of seeing the Teutonic Knights in Masovia, was that their tabards were smeared with gore, half their men were draped across the backs of horses like so many sacks of grain, and even the horses showed wounds leaking blood down their flanks.

The carnage was worse the closer she came. Even the men who rode upright had bloody rips in their armor, arms held limp at their sides, bandages tight against heads and arms and legs. Several of the horses were riderless, splashing through the water next to their mounted fellows.

She ran, thinking little of where these men had come from or whose colors they wore. She had seen the wounded knights and the wounded horses, and she knew that these men needed assistance.

Ahead of her, the German knights had made it across the ford in the Narew and were drawing up into a ragged group on the southeastern shore, in the shadow of the Masovian fortress. The alarm bells still tolled in Gród Narew, and Maria heard the main gates open. She glanced back over her shoulder and saw a hasty party of horsemen erupt from the fortress. Four mounted men, less than a quarter of the strength of the German party, bearing the threefold cross of the clan Bojcza, the emblem for Wojewoda Bolesław, lord of Gród Narew.

Maria noted immediately from the dress and the armor that only the man in the lead was a noble of the szlachta. The trio with him, while armed, were mere footmen. They accompanied their lord as a show of authority, not as a fighting force. As they rode out of the gate, Lukasz and the other stable hands scrambled to bring the grazing horses back from the pasture.

Maria was halfway down the slope of the pasture, heading toward the river, by the time Bolesław's men passed in front of her, following the broad path from the fortress gate down to the river's shore. The Germans, seeing the men approach, drew themselves up in such a ragged line as they could. A man bearing the tabard of the Teutonic Order dismounted and took a few steps forward.

He stood tall and removed his helmet, revealing a creased face adorned with a sharp silver beard. The man held his helmet in the crook of his arm and waited for the horsemen to approach. Despite his calm attitude of command, he had not escaped whatever evil had befallen his men. A single trail of blood wept from a wound under his graying hair, which curved across his cheek to stain dark a spot on the left side of his beard.

Maria slowed her approach. While it was obvious that many of these men needed assistance, Maria forced herself to temper that impulse. These men, on both sides, needed to satisfy the will of Masovia and the Teutonic State before mere human needs would be considered.

She came to a stop as Bolesław's men rode up to face the

Germans. The distress of the German knights became stark in the contrast between the two groups. The men from Gród Narew were clean and well-rested, and rode fresh horses. Maria recognized the man in the lead as Rycerz Telek, Lord Bolesław's oldest nephew—a man as broad as the German leader was tall. When he dismounted, it was with a lightness that belied his girth, and he walked forward with a smile more good-humored than the situation warranted.

The tall German, by contrast, had an expression that never wavered from a stern seriousness. Behind him, his men sat on exhausted mounts that seemed on the verge of collapse. Their horses snorted from foamy lips, and their flanks were drenched with a foul mixture of sweat, gore, and river water.

Telek walked up, smiling, and said, "My uncle, the Wojewoda Bolesław, extends his greetings and wonders if you have perhaps lost your way?"

German muttering broke through the ranks of the Order, until the tall man snapped something that silenced his men.

Telek began to repeat himself, but the tall man said, "I speak your tongue well enough, sir."

"Then," Telek responded, "perhaps you might like a guide to assist you finding your way back to your own demesne?"

"On behalf of His Holiness the pope and Hochmeister Ludolf König von Weizau, I humbly request assistance from Wojewoda Bolesław. I have many injured men who would not fare well on any journey."

"This much I see. And who is it that requests aid from my uncle in the name of the pope and the Teutonic Order?"

"I am Komtur Heinrich von Kerpen, and these men are brothers in my convent and knights serving the Order."

"And how come you to be within the borders of Masovia?"

"We serve our duty to God and the pope."

"We all do, Brother Heinrich. What enemy did you face to be so ill-treated?"

"We are not permitted to say."

Telek paced in front of the line of Heinrich's men. "These are not your lands, Brother Heinrich, and we aren't some Prussian serfs subject to your authority. My uncle has the right and the duty, granted by the Duke of Masovia, to dispatch any invading forces as he sees fit. As yet he has no quarrel with you, but blood has been shed here. How? And with whom?"

"I can only say that it was an enemy of God and the Church—"

"You try my uncle's patience. We're quite aware that whomever the Order decides to raise a sword against is an enemy of God and the Church. I suggest that you answer my question, lest you find yourself an enemy of Wojewoda Bolesław and the Duchy of Masovia."

Maria felt the tension even from where she stood on the hill-side. The air between Brother Heinrich and Rycerz Telek seemed so charged that she felt as if the sod between their feet were in danger of bursting into flame.

Brother Heinrich lowered his head and said, "I am bound by my vows."

"As are we." Rycerz Telek placed a hand on the pommel of his sword, and Maria felt her breath catch in her throat. It had been almost ten years since the end of open war between the Poles and the Order, and she was about to see it start all over again.

"But," Brother Heinrich said so quietly that Maria barely made out the word.

Telek lowered his hand and repeated, "But?"

"Grant us a bishop for our confessor, and he can give us leave to speak of what we fight."

"A bishop?" Telek raised an eyebrow. "Not a cardinal? Or the pope himself?"

"Any of those could release our vow not to speak of our mission. However, a bishop will suffice."

Telek gestured and his men dismounted. Two came forward and walked up to the Germans while Telek said, "Then if you're to grant us the honor of accepting the hospitality of Gród Narew, I expect you to surrender your arms to us for safekeeping."

III

Rycerz Telek Rydz herbu Bojcza watched his men relieve the Teutonic invaders of their weaponry. With each sword taken, a small weight was lifted off him, though he exercised as much restraint in hiding his relief as he had earlier in hiding his apprehension. Despite the forced joviality he projected, he knew that no good thing could come from the presence of the Order's knights in Masovia. Christ only knew what carnage they had wrought on the far side of the river, or to what end.

But the last thing he wanted—the last thing his uncle wanted, and, for that matter, the last thing Duke Siemowit III wanted—would be a convent of dead knights giving the Order a pretext to resume the hostilities that had ended a decade ago, breaking a peace that had only just been ratified by a treaty between the Order and the Duke's brother, Casimir.

Whatever horror these knights had wrought across the river from Gród Narew, he couldn't help but think that the men he saw had fared worse than their opponent. The stench of defeat hung upon them like a shroud, and the fact that Brother Heinrich had come here and surrendered was testament to how badly things had gone.

Without direct confirmation from Brother Heinrich—and

Telek supposed he would have to wait for a bishop to receive that—he estimated Heinrich's original party as numbering at least a score of mounted knights. If Brother Heinrich had originally had a full convent of warrior monks with him, that would have accounted for about twelve of that number. The rest would be either probationary members who had not yet taken their final vows as monks, or more secular knights looking to buy a way to Heaven with the tip of a sword—though those were more often seen in the Order's periodic crusades against the pagan Lithuanians.

The survivors looked to be either knights of the Order or probationary members. The tabards were all white and black, and if Telek remembered his German heraldry correctly, the men who wore an incomplete cross were probationary monks who hadn't taken their final vows. What he didn't recognize was the wolf's head that marked the upper left quadrant of Brother Heinrich's tabard.

Telek guessed it was some obscure signifier of the monk's rank in the Order. Either that, or the Order had given up the one thing it shared with the Poles: a distaste for the chaos of personal devices that seemed to plague the German nobility. A black cross on a white field was good enough for all the members of the Order, just as the triple cross was good for all the families of clan Bojcza.

When his men had retrieved all the swords and crossbows, Telek raised his arm and gestured a circle above his head. The watch up on the fortress wall would let his uncle know that things had concluded peacefully. He turned to one of his men and said, "Ride back. Send down stable hands to take charge of these horses and a party to help tend to the wounded here, with a cart to carry them back up the hill." He glanced up and saw one of the servingwomen from the fortress standing on the hillside, watching them. He pointed to her. "You, woman: come down and assist us with the wounded."

⊕

Negotiating the transfer of fourteen knights from the riverside up into the fortress consumed the bulk of the morning hours. Telek supervised every detail, from the washing and binding of wounds, to walking the Germans' horses into a walled pasture, to loading the wounded into a hay cart.

By the time his uncle's guardsmen led the last of the knights back to Gród Narew, he was left by the river with sixteen swords, a half dozen crossbows, and a pile of random armor—damaged, gore-stained, and already attracting a host of flies.

He also had two corpses, men who had died in the Order's retreat from—

"From what?" Telek said.

"Sir?" one of his men said from behind him. Telek turned around and saw that the man had just finished loading the Order's weapons into another cart.

"What were those men fighting?" Telek asked.

"I don't care to know, sir. Deadly evil business it is." The man spat and gestured to ward off the evil the Order's men had brought with them.

"They'll only bare their souls to a bishop." Telek looked back at the bodies and the damaged armor. "Perhaps they rode through Hell itself."

"Sir, should you jest about that?"

Telek laughed. "Son, you sound like one of those monks."

"But their wounds. They're more like bites, claw marks..."

"They likely ran afoul of a mountain cat." Telek thought of the odd addition to Brother Heinrich's tabard. "Or a pack of wolves."

"Have you looked at these weapons?"

Telek shook his head and walked up to the back of the cart. With the swords and crossbows were a pile of daggers. He picked one up and drew it from its scabbard. The sunlight glinted from a wicked blade, ornately engraved with German script that Telek could barely read. He snorted. "A little ostentatious for someone who's taken a vow of poverty."

"Look at the metal, sir."

Telek squinted at it and frowned. "Silver?"

"And this." The man held up a quarrel for one of the crossbows. Telek sheathed the dagger and took the quarrel, looking at the head of the weapon.

It was silver as well.

"Is the Order so wealthy that they tip their bolts with precious metal?" He placed the quarrel and the sheathed dagger down in the bed of the cart and picked up one of the knights' long swords. He gripped the scabbard tightly and paused before taking the handle, suddenly feeling some of the apprehension that his man was showing.

He slowly drew the blade clear of the scabbard—only a handsbreadth, but enough to see. Apparently the Order wasn't wealthy enough to forge a whole sword blade out of silver, but the more common steel had been inlaid with the precious metal. The truly odd part of the design was the fact that the inlay was not on the flat, where most decorative engraving would go. It was on the edge. The sword blade was silvered a finger's width back from the cutting edge on each side.

Perhaps he shouldn't be talking too lightly of riding through Hell.

⌖

Telek was usually the largest and most intimidating figure in any gathering, except when that gathering included his uncle. Telek's uncle, the Wojewoda Bolesław, the lord of Gród Narew, was a bull of a man, nearly a head taller than Telek and probably three stone heavier. He carried a full beard that had gone half silver, and in some places completely white. Telek's uncle had not shaved in nearly fifteen years—not since, in a skirmish with their Teutonic neighbors, a mace had badly wounded the left side of his jaw. The beard covered the scars and the misshapen hinge of the badly healed bone.

As a consequence, Telek's uncle always spoke deliberately, and had no love for the German Order.

When Telek entered his uncle's chambers, Bolesław was standing by a narrow window, eclipsing the afternoon sun and plunging the room into shadow. "Our guests surrendered peaceably?"

"Yes, Uncle," Telek said.

"Good." Bolesław turned away from the window and stepped toward him. Suddenly the room brightened, both with the sunlight and with his slight, close-lipped smile. "A lack of drama and intrigue is always appreciated." He walked over to an ornate chair that had been a gift from the Duke. It was debatable what creaked more when Bolesław sat—the carved oak chair or Bolesław himself. He settled himself with a sigh and asked, "Why are they here?"

"They refused to say."

Bolesław grunted. "You accepted this?"

"They were willing to surrender their persons and their weapons. It seemed prudent to take them hostage and revisit the issue at a later time."

"Yes, I am sure. Though, in their state, it seems foolhardy to antagonize us."

"Unless the truth would be more provocative than their silence."

"God's teeth, I do not like this. The duchy might already be at war with the Order."

"We're on the frontier here. We would know."

"But what if Casimir and the Order are at odds again? The Duke is still a vassal of his brother."

"Uncle, they just signed a peace treaty."

"Good until some fool gets an itch for more land."

"I don't think war's at hand, Uncle. These men did not approach us as an enemy."

"They were in no state to."

"And, while they are currently silent as to their intent within Masovia, they gave conditions for revealing that to us."

"Indeed? Conditions? I thought arrogance was a sin."

"They require a bishop to give them leave to talk."

"A bishop? Are they serious?"

"I have no reason to doubt."

Bolesław closed his eyes and leaned back in the chair, which emitted an ominous creak. "No reason to doubt?"

"Their seriousness," Telek said.

His uncle opened his eyes and stared at the ceiling. "Who am I to stand between these Germans and God? They wish a bishop, we shall fetch one. There's a fine one in Warsaw. You can fetch him back after alerting the Duke of our troublesome guests."

IV

When Rycerz Telek had summoned her into the midst of the Germans, Maria had been caught off guard. Her initial impulse to help the wounded had been tempered when he had arrived to confront the invaders, to the point where she'd realized that she had overstepped herself. Fortunately, if Telek thought as much, he had kept it to himself.

Within minutes of Telek calling her down the hillside, she was one of a dozen servants of Gród Narew washing and binding wounds. Almost by accident, she became the center of the effort. For, thanks to her stepmother, she was the only servant who had a working knowledge of German.

After tending to the worst of those who still lived, she and the others assisted the recently disarmed Germans into a hay cart to travel up the hill to the fortress.

Sixteen men had crossed the river. Only fourteen had made it alive. Three more survivors were so badly wounded that Maria didn't expect them to last the day. The old man, Brother Heinrich, was not above treating his men or helping carry them into the wagon. Even so, Maria felt as if he watched the whole process with an uncomfortable coldness.

To Maria, it was overwhelming. She rode back with the wagon, and even if she didn't look at the wounded young men who filled the cart, the miasma of blood clung to every breath she took. Every time the creaking wheels of the cart found a bump in the muddy trail, it was accompanied by a chorus of groans from the men who were conscious.

She couldn't help but wonder what had attacked these men so savagely. The wounds were inhuman—flesh torn and bitten. Several men were missing hands or arms, and about half showed wounds to the face that appeared to be claw marks. None of the men spoke of what had happened to them; few spoke at all. The quiet infected the Poles who treated them, so the ride back to the fortress had the mournful character of a funeral procession.

She heard some whispers from her fellow Poles: speculation that the Germans had retreated bloody from some battle and then had had the bad luck to be set upon by a pack of wolves. That explained their horrible state, and their reluctance to talk. Even so, Maria thought that whatever had decimated the Germans was unquestionably evil. Even a wild animal attacked to kill. Many of these men had been maimed, it seemed, simply for the sake of the maiming.

Maria held her cross to her chest and silently prayed to keep the Devil at bay.

Through the afternoon, the population of Gród Narew worked to accommodate the new arrivals. The order from Wojewoda Bolesław was to provide the Germans with accommodations as honored guests. This meant that, instead of being housed in the common barracks meant for visiting knights, the ambulatory Germans were split up into twos and threes and given lodgings that normally served the residents. The severely injured were placed in a series of rooms by the stables, displacing grooms and other stable hands.

Maria wondered about it until she heard one of the guardsmen comment that Wojewoda Bolesław was not just being a gracious host but was preventing any large group of Germans from assembling to plan mischief. Apparently, their leader, Brother Heinrich, had the honor of staying in the personal guest chambers of the Wojewoda himself—deep inside the central stronghold, far from the stables and the other houses where his men were being kept.

Maria thought that the Wojewoda Bolesław should be more concerned about what had attacked the Germans than the Germans themselves.

Because she was one of the few servants to speak the German tongue, Maria was one of a half dozen who gained additional duties. Along with her normal routine of assisting in the main kitchens, she now had the task of tending to one of the badly injured knights of the Order.

The man's name was Josef—one of the men Maria hadn't expected to make it through the day.

The kitchens had been more chaotic than usual, with the extra mouths to feed and too many people—Maria included—coming to their jobs late because of their visitors. The sun was setting by the time she had completed her duties in the kitchens. When she brought a bowl of porridge to the rooms by the stables to attempt to feed her charge, she did not expect to find the man still alive.

She opened the door to the small room, then stood transfixed for several moments, staring at the young man who had been unceremoniously dumped on someone else's bed. His skin was pale, nearly translucent, in the fading evening light streaming in from the unshuttered window, and his face bore an expression of almost angelic sadness. Her heart caught and she found herself grieving for this man, cut down too soon—

Then she realized that Josef still breathed.

The sudden revelation struck her like a physical blow. She hastily placed Josef's porridge on a stool and ran to the side of his bed, more afraid now that his life might slip away as she watched.

Placing a hand on his neck, she bent her ear to his lips. His pulse throbbed strong and steady under her fingers, and while his skin was damp with sweat, he was warm, not chilled or clammy. She listened to his breathing; it was stronger and steadier than she had a right to expect—strong enough that the heat of his breath warmed her ear and brought a flush to the side of her face. It was a flush that deepened to embarrassment when he groaned and turned his head so that his lips brushed the side of her cheek.

She pulled away quickly and looked at the man, briefly convinced that he had feigned unconsciousness to take advantage of her. It was a vile trick worthy of Lukasz.

But one look at Josef showed that he feigned nothing, and Maria felt shamed for thinking ill of him. Even in slumber, this man was of nobler bearing than Lukasz could ever aspire to.

If only the same could be said of his smell.

Maria wrinkled her nose. As the initial panic gave way to relief, she realized that Josef not only lived, but had fouled himself. She looked at the unconscious knight and bit her lip, slowly realizing what her duty to this wounded man would entail.

"It is my duty," she whispered to herself. Then she retreated to fetch a bucket of water and fresh linens.

When she returned, she faced Josef with some trepidation, afraid that he might awake while she cleaned him. The trepidation vanished when she pulled aside the soiled sheets covering him.

Whoever had brought Josef here must have shared Maria's thought that he would not make it to nightfall. They hadn't bothered to do more than remove his armor. He still had on the torn, gore-stained padding he had worn under his mail, and his legs were still wrapped in hose rank with blood, mud, and waste.

She bit her lip again, holding her tongue for fear she might blaspheme in her anger. The Germans and Poles might not be friends, but there was no excuse for this. Even if Josef wouldn't make it through the night, it was petty bordering on cruel to allow him to suffer this kind of indignity.

She cast aside her own embarrassment, rolled up the sleeves of her chemise, and worked on stripping the filth from the young man. It helped to think of her father, and of caring for him these past few months. She focused on the mechanics of tending to someone bedridden and too weak and insensible to care for himself.

Thinking of this young man as a frail invalid kept her thoughts on a proper course while she did what needed to be done. At least until he began groaning words in slurred German.

The first time he spoke in his delirium, the washrag in her hand was uncomfortably far up his inner thigh. She snatched the rag away, suddenly realizing that this was no frail old man she tended to. Fortunately, Josef did not regain consciousness.

Maria took a few deep breaths as Josef continued mumbling. She should go and find someone else to attend to this man; she should ask to be relieved of this duty. Rycerz Telek obviously had counted this man as one soon to die, but had misjudged Josef's strength. Would they have given her this duty otherwise?

But what do I do, leave this poor man naked and half-washed because of my own modesty? What fault of it is his?

She sighed and took a new washrag to hand, doing her best to ignore the sounds Josef made. The only complete sentence he spoke came when she cleaned and replaced the dressing on the massive wound in his abdomen. As she brushed the still-raw edges of the wound, he sucked in a breath and said, "It is here!"

Maria heard the panic in the man's voice and instinctively turned to look for what had invaded the room. But there was nothing.

She laid the back of her hand against his cheek, and it felt like his flesh was burning from the inside out. Her own embarrassment at tending to him seemed small and petty, and she felt ashamed.

"You poor man," she whispered. He didn't know where he was, or who was with him. She made a silent vow not to abandon him, and lightly kissed his forehead. "I'll pray for you, so you can wake up and know that your nightmare is over."

She tried to feed him, but he didn't respond to her attempts. She had to satisfy herself with squeezing water into his mouth from a damp cloth.

She left the shutters on the small window open, to let out the air of disease. They were above the stables, but the smell of horses and manure was preferable to the smell of sickness that was rank in this room. And the night air might help cool his fever.

Outside, the sun was long gone, and a fat moon hung over the trees at the foot of the fortress's hill. She needed to go home.

⊕

The two-mile walk seemed longer than usual, the woods darker, the shadows longer. She glanced around every time the wind creaked a branch, every time something rustled in the leaves. The woods loomed to either side, shadowed and impenetrable.

Somewhere out there was whatever had attacked the knights of the Order, whatever had wounded Josef. It was something she should fear to meet. But Maria was more afraid that Josef would die from his wounds. More than anything else right now, Maria prayed that her charge would live.

She told herself it was because she had been given responsibility for him. It was because of the wrongness of such a fine young man meeting such an undignified end. She had seen many men take up sword for their household or their God, and all accepted death as a camp follower, but they expected to meet death quickly in the heat of battle, not to succumb to fever and infection, delirious in their own filth.

Few men deserved that end—not Josef, and not her father.

That's what she told herself.

But she still felt his breath against her ear and the accidental brush of his lips against her cheek.

When she reached the edge of her family's farm, she sucked in a breath. Hanna, her stepmother, was going to require an explanation for her lateness, and there was little reason for Maria to believe that it wouldn't be a long and unpleasant questioning. Her father and her stepmother always wanted a strict accounting of her activities beyond their sight.

She paused at the gate and looked at her family's cottage. She could see the yellow flicker of a lantern shining from between cracks in the shutters. The dim light shone on the flanks of an unfamiliar horse tied up by the side of the house.

Who's here?

Suddenly, she thought of her father. Had he...

"Papa!" she called out. She ran to her house, afraid that the horse belonged to a priest come to administer last rites or console her stepmother. "Papa!" she called again, and the door to the cottage burst open.

For a moment she felt a near-disabling relief as she saw her father push through the doorway. But it soon gave way to alarm at the expression of rage and terror contorting his face. He ran to her, clad only in a nightshirt, bellowing, "Maria!"

Maria couldn't find her voice. He was ill. He shouldn't be out of bed. His hair was wild in the moonlight, his eyes gleamed with some preternatural terror, and the skin of his face had flushed almost purple. He grabbed her shoulders, shaking her. "You took it off! You took it off!"

"Papa?" Maria cried.

"What did you do?" He stared into her face. "Why did you take it off?"

"I don't understand." She hugged herself as her father shook her. "Papa, you're hurting me."

What frightened her most was the fact that her father was crying. "It was to keep you safe. Why did you take it off?"

Keep me safe? Her father was delirious. He must be talking about her cross. She reached up and pulled it from under her chemise. "No, Papa, I didn't take it off."

Her father backhanded her. She fell to her knees in front of him, clutching her face and sobbing.

"Don't lie to me!" he screamed.

"I-I d-didn't," Maria sobbed into the ground.

"If you didn't—" He sucked in a shuddering breath and stumbled backward. "If you—"

"P-papa?"

She got to her feet as her father stumbled backward again, gasping for breath and shaking his head. Her stepmother ran from the doorway, calling to him: "Karl?"

He shook his head, his voice no more than a breathless wheeze, and fell backward into her arms.

Maria held the cross between her breasts and said, "I didn't take it off."

Her father kept shaking his head and slid down as if his legs couldn't support his weight anymore. Her stepmother's voice cracked as she said his name. "Karl. You can't leave me alone with this! Not now." She turned back toward the door, where Maria's three brothers stood. "Come, help me bring your father inside."

Maria stepped forward, but her stepmother turned to face her. "Please. Not now. He's too upset."

"B-but . . ." Maria stood transfixed in front of the cottage as her brothers ran out, toward their father. As they helped carry him inside, her stepmother watched her, eyes shiny with tears and an emotion Maria didn't want to understand.

What have I done?

The confusion and fear in her parents' eyes confused and frightened her. Worse was the sudden unfocused guilt that consumed her.

For the first time in years, she was too keenly aware of the fact that she was a bastard child. Her father's blood ran in her veins, but not his wife's. Did Hanna hate her for that?

Maria followed them to the doorway, and every labored breath her father took made her shudder and left her feeling as weak as if she were the one who couldn't breathe.

She stood in the doorway, suddenly a stranger in her own house.

Hanna and Maria's older brother, Władysław, eased her father back into his bed; the covers were still thrust aside, as if he had sprung from his sickbed in a delirium. Her two younger brothers stepped back. The youngest, Wojciech, cried silently, while Piotr, her middle brother, held his shoulders.

Near where Maria hung back, next to the doorway, a young man tried uncomfortably to stay out of the way. Maria recognized the curly hair and the patches of stubble on his chin that had yet to make a beard. He was one of the younger sons from a neighboring farm, and he held his hat in his hand, crushing the brim in his nervousness.

"Shall I fetch a doctor—" he began.

Maria's stepmother didn't even glance at the boy. "And a priest. Move!"

The boy ran for the door before Maria could collect herself to remember his name. As he shoved his way by her he said, "I'm sorry. I didn't know how he'd react."

He didn't even look back to see Maria's bewildered expression as he untied his horse and mounted to gallop the two miles back to Gròd Narew.

"Maria," her stepmother called, "fetch your father some water."

"Yes!" She scrambled to bring it. Her father had stopped struggling and lay still on the bed. When Maria reached his side, his eyes showed no rage or fear, only resignation. Something made her look to her stepmother for approval before raising the cup to her father's lips. Maria couldn't help thinking that her stepmother's approving nod was tentative, as if some unforgiven transgression still weighed against her bastard stepdaughter.

Her father took only a few sips, then shook his head. Maria removed the cup, and he looked up at her. As she bent over him, the cross fell free of her chemise and dangled down from her neck.

He stared at it, then up at her. Then he reached with an unsteady hand and pressed it back up, against her chest.

"I didn't take it off, Papa."

He nodded as if he finally believed her, and let his hand fall to his side. "Karl," Maria's stepmother said. "Hang on. We've sent for the doctor."

He looked up at his wife and very slightly shook his head: no.

"It's not time. Please, it's not your time."

He took his wife's hand and sucked in a ragged breath. "Keep her safe."

In the end, it was the priest they needed, not the doctor.

V

For Maria, the next few days passed in a haze. Even though the months of illness should have prepared her for it, she had somehow never expected her father to die. But worse than the loss, which was a sucking wound in her soul, was the sense that somehow it was her fault. For some reason she had prompted his last fatal exertion, and she didn't know why.

Now every look from her stepmother or her brothers seemed to carry a cold accusation. Several times after her father was buried she had been tempted to ask if they blamed her, if this was truly her fault, but each time the fear had stopped her. What would she do if they confirmed it? What could she do?

What if the only reason she could still live in her home was because she eased the burden on the farm by serving in Gròd Narew? It was an unbearable thought that, with his death, she had somehow unknowingly pushed the rest of her family away as well.

So she avoided the question by waking early and doing her few chores on the farm before anyone else was up. A happy side effect was that she arrived at Gròd Narew before dawn, and before Lukasz and his fellow stable hands were out with the horses.

And, while two more Germans died over the next three days,

her German, Josef, hung on to his life. At first, returning to care for him after her father's death, she'd resented his survival. Why did he still live while her father had died?

The flash of irrational fury at him was frightening in its intensity. The shame and horror it left in its wake proved much more persistent. Paradoxically, in the days before he regained consciousness, she treated him much more tenderly—knowing that, had she the means, she could have easily killed him for the sin of surviving her father.

On the fourth day of caring for him, while she washed his chest with cold water to help temper his fever, he spoke to her.

"Who are you?" he said, blinking against the evening light.

She froze. Again, the act of his speech fundamentally changed the nature of what she had been doing. Moments ago, she had been cooling the flesh of an invalid, and suddenly she was caressing a young man's naked chest. This was no delirium, though; his eyes had opened and looked upon her with puzzlement and loss.

She stared deep into those eyes and felt, instinctively, that he somehow shared her grief. He had suffered a loss just as deep, and as—

"Who are you?" he repeated, shattering her reverie. She pulled her hands from his skin, silently chiding herself for feeling embarrassment. This was no different from caring for her invalid father.

It *shouldn't* be any different.

But this man wasn't her father.

"I am Maria." She spoke slowly, her stepmother's German uncomfortable in her mouth.

He blinked and stared at her as if she had spoken gibberish. *Probably can't understand my speech,* she thought.

Then he looked away from her to glance about the room. "Where am I?"

"Gród Narew, under the protection of the Wojewoda Bolesław."

"Bolesław?" he repeated. He leaned back and closed his eyes. "That is not a Prussian name."

"You are in the Duchy of Masovia."

He nodded, wincing as he started to sit up.

"Don't. You're badly injured." She placed her hands on his shoulders and pushed him down. His skin was warm but no longer feverish, and while he had broad shoulders and a warrior's build, his wounds had left him little strength to resist her.

He stared up at her and muttered, "My brother knights?"

"They're here," she told him. "But you need to rest."

He nodded, and in his eyes she saw the weight of his efforts. Fatigue drew on every muscle of his face.

"What happened to you?" she asked him.

But his eyes had already closed and sleep had claimed him before the question left her lips. She let her hands fall off his shoulders and stared down at his sleeping face. It had a different character now than when he'd been unconscious from his wounds and infection. His color was better, and there was a new sense of a person behind the sleeping mask.

"I prayed for you, Josef," she whispered, brushing the back of her hand against his cheek. "Now I think God has seen fit to answer."

Though he still slept, she heard him softly whisper, "*Sarah . . .*"

She pulled her hand away and took a step back, suddenly feeling an intruder on something very private.

I am only a servant here, she thought with a wash of shame, pulling the bedding quickly around him and leaving him to sleep.

Josef jerked awake, naked and drenched with sweat.

Where am I?

The disorientation crashed over him in heavy, suffocating

waves. He gasped for breath, staring at the dark room around him. He tried to move and pain radiated from his gut, locking every muscle in his body.

His hands clenched into fists, but instead of digging into forest loam, they balled inside linens damp with his own sweat. His heart raced because his mind immediately latched onto the thought of burial shrouds, images of the dead and dying at Nürnberg...

I'm not in Nürnberg, or Prussia, he thought, as his mind forced some form of order on his thoughts. *I'm in Masovia.*

For several moments he didn't remember why he knew that. But it helped calm his fears, even when the memories returned. The battle was over, and Brother Heinrich and his Wolfjägers had sought refuge in a Polish fortress.

Gród Narew, his mind volunteered, along with the dreamlike memory of the woman who had spoken to him.

His breathing and pulse calmed as the sense of nightmare receded, leaving him with the reality of a single sickbed in a narrow room with a long window open to the cool night air. And, as long as he stayed still, the wound in his belly proved only a dull ache.

He gave a short prayer of thanksgiving. Then he said ten Pater Nosters for the dead. He had seen enough to know that some of Heinrich's convent hadn't survived. When he was finished, he added one more prayer.

He prayed that they had killed the thing.

But long after his prayers had faded, he still lay upon a narrow bed in a dark room. He didn't know how long sleep had claimed him, just that it had been long enough that it was loath to return. For hours he lay, alone and awake, and the emptiness of the dark room began to eat at him.

He had not slept alone since he had joined the Order. He hadn't taken his final vows, but in all respects he was expected to live the life of a warrior monk of the Teutonic Knights of the Hospital of St. Mary in Jerusalem. That meant doing everything in common with his brothers, and sleeping with them in rooms that were always lit against the concealment of sin.

Why would they separate him from the others?

Perhaps God wanted to test his commitment to the Order. Or, perhaps, the lord of this place—the woman, Maria, had given him the aggressively Slavic name Wojewoda Bolesław, though he thought "Wojewoda" might be a title, not a name—perhaps Wojewoda Bolesław wished to prevent Heinrich's men from congregating or conspiring. Relations between the Teutonic State in Prussia and the Poles had never run particularly smooth, swinging between suspicion and open war ever since the German Order had been invited in to subjugate the pagans in Prussia, a hundred and fifty years ago—invited by the then Duke of Masovia.

Ever since, the Poles had consistently tried to renege on the promises of land and support they had given for the suppression of the pagan threat on their border.

Josef rubbed his eyes. Whatever the intent was of either God or Wojewoda Bolesław, being alone in the dark with his thoughts and the ache of his wounds made him very uncomfortable. More uncomfortable than even being alone in a place that inspired a reaction somewhere between suspicion and hostility should warrant.

He was uncomfortable because of the woman.

The more he remembered, the more uneasy he became. Especially when he recalled her washing his chest. He thought of her face looking down at him, framed by raven hair, her eyes filled with such concern. He remembered the touch of her hands on his shoulders—a strength and gentleness that drew his soul unlike anything since he had abandoned his old home, his old life.

It wasn't proper. Even before he had joined the Order, being alone with a woman like that . . .

Like what?

He was bound by the Order's tenets. Obedience, poverty,

chastity. Even if he was too injured to act on such thoughts, God still was testing him. Much like the brothers of the Order, who made a point of clearly showing the probationers all the duties and privations of the Order, always with the implicit question, "Do you really want this?"

No man joined the Order in ignorance. Every man who took the final vows knew what he sacrificed, of the world and of his own will. Of those who had entered with him, only a third remained, and perhaps only a quarter would end up taking final vows. Even now, Josef could say to his Komtur that he did not have the vocation, and he would walk free with the Order's blessing.

It was a test. If he wished to serve God in the Order, he would serve Him in the world, not in a monastery. It would be the height of arrogance, and cowardice, if he tried to insist that he serve only where he was free of any temptation. How could he be a knight of the Order, how could he face the monstrosities Heinrich hunted, if he couldn't face his own human impulses?

If he could resist a lupine demon tearing at his gut, he could resist the temptation of one young woman.

When Maria came in the following morning, she found Josef awake. He was tangled in the sheets, groaning, one arm thrust off the side of the bed. She dropped the bowl of porridge onto the stool by the door and ran to his side.

"Are you all right?" she said, grabbing his arm and trying to ease him back into bed. When she realized she hadn't spoken his tongue, she repeated herself in the best German she could muster.

"Please, help," he said. His cheeks burned red with fever, and she thought she might be seeing the end of him.

Panic stole most of the German she knew, but after a few stuttered syllables she spat out, "Doctor?" She didn't even know why she was asking him. He was in obvious distress. Once he was back on the bed, she ran to the door so she could fetch help. She stopped only when he cried after her, "No!"

She turned around and saw him pointing to a small stand where a chamber pot sat. "I couldn't reach," he said.

"Oh yes, of course," she said, her words slipping into Polish. She drew the stand and the chamber pot closer to the bed, then picked the pot up and handed it to him.

"Thank you," he said, and she realized that the flush on his cheeks was embarrassment, not fever.

"I'll give you . . . " She fumbled to find the word for "privacy." "I'll be outside. Call me when you're done."

She stepped outside the door, shutting it just short of the latch catching. Then she breathed slowly, collecting her thoughts. Josef would recover; she was certain of it now. And she almost shuddered with relief.

He also insisted on eating without assistance, even though it appeared to tax his strength. In between spoonfuls, he asked again, "Where am I?"

She repeated that he was in the Duchy of Masovia, but he stopped her.

"No, you told me that. This room, where is it?"

"Oh. These are normally quarters for the stable hands."

He glanced at the window. "That explains the smell of horses." He took another spoonful of porridge. "Doesn't the Wojewoda Bolesław keep rooms for guests? Surely, this close to his borders, the Duke Siemowit III will often send troops to be quartered." He arched an eyebrow. "Or perhaps such troops are already here?"

Maria looked at him and decided no good could come from directly answering that question. "The lord of the house decided that it would be more appropriate to house his honored guests in their own rooms."

"I wonder if the word 'honored' in your language translates into 'troublesome.' "

She smiled and said, "You've not been particularly troublesome to me." The words were out of her mouth before she could think better of them.

He set down his bowl. "And who are you, Maria—one of the ladies of Wojewoda Bolesław's household?"

She was suddenly reminded that this wasn't some peasant she was talking to. Josef was a member of a holy order of knights. They were separated not only by vows, but by station. She couldn't speak to him as if he were the stable hand who normally quartered here—though she felt a sudden surge of loss at the thought. "Sir, I am only a servant. I labor for the Wojewoda Bolesław on behalf of my family."

He must have noticed the sudden sadness in her face, because he responded, "No shame in that."

"If I implied otherwise, sir, I misspoke." She stepped over to take the empty bowl, clamping down on her traitorous emotions, and said, "If there is nothing else you require, I have other duties to attend to."

"Just leave an empty pot within reach," he said, smiling weakly. "I feel I need rest more than anything else."

She placed a clean chamber pot nearby, and a bell should he find himself in distress before she returned with supper. Then she withdrew as quickly as she dared.

VI

She felt uncomfortable returning to him. When he'd been an unconscious invalid, she'd had no thoughts about their relative status. He had just been a wounded man she had been giving aid to. Even if she had stared at his sleeping profile, or been too aware of his warrior's build as she ran a damp rag across his chest, his arms, or his legs—

In the end, it only had been herself. The focus of her idle attention could have just as easily been a statue, a painting, or a particularly well-crafted piece of furniture.

But Josef was awake now, and she could no longer pretend that her thoughts concerned only herself. This was a real person she had been lavishing her attention upon. A person who would normally never have cause to speak more than a dozen words to her.

Worst of all, a wakeful Josef did nothing to discourage her wayward thoughts. If anything, his quiet endurance of his pain and the gentle tone he took with her—despite their difference in station—made her all the more aware of what her idle musings implied. It made them more explicit, and all the more impossible.

But it was still her duty, and she couldn't abandon it now. Though to be truly honest, she wondered if she continued because she didn't have the position to refuse any duty she was given or because she didn't have the heart to.

She finally told herself that she tended to Josef because the last thing she would want to do was displease her masters at Gród Narew. Her service here provided her with a refuge from the guilt that had shrouded her home since her father's death. If Gród Narew cast her out, she didn't think she could bear living in that house and facing her family's unspoken blame.

So she did her best to bring him his meals and check his wounds without saying anything too familiar.

Unfortunately, Josef didn't seem to have any such reservations. It was as if his time unconscious had allowed a mass of words to build within him, and when she returned with his supper, they came out in a torrent.

There was little she could do other than nod politely and try not to say anything that might prompt more conversation on his part. While he ate, she stood in the corner of the room, occasionally casting a wistful glance at the darkening sky.

"My family lived in Nürnberg. Every generation has pledged someone to service in the Church. I have uncles and cousins who are priests and bishops; my ancestors served in the Holy Land." His words accelerated as he spoke, making it harder for her to understand them. However, she got the meaning of most.

Where he lived, the plague had come four years ago. It had taken his father, his grandfather, his siblings, and the woman to whom he had pledged his heart. The only member of his family to survive was a maiden aunt who had retreated to a convent so strict that she was not even allowed to speak to her nephew.

It had been a sign. Josef had given his family's lands over to the Church and had taken on the mantle of the Order.

When he finished the story, Maria found that her breath had caught; she'd been thinking of the loss of her own father, along with the loss she had read in Josef's sleeping face. This man had known her own loss, and so much else besides. She wanted to somehow acknowledge their shared pain, but all she managed was a whispered "I'm so sorry."

Even that, she said in Polish.

He glanced up at her quizzically. "What did you say?"

She bent over and took his empty bowl. "It is time for you to sleep, sir. You still need your rest."

He leaned his head back and said, "Yes, I suppose I do."

⌖

Josef needed human contact. He might be devout, but being alone talking only to God and himself wore on his soul.

So when Maria had come with his evening meal, he had talked of his life, and everything that had led him to serve the Order.

As he talked, he thought it was a good thing that he had not entered a less worldly Order than the Hospital of St. Mary; he didn't have the strength of spirit to commit to an ascetic life filled only with the contemplation of God. It might be admirable, but he was not his aunt.

Talking to Maria also reminded him that he had pledged himself to God, and why. He needed the constant reminder, because in Maria's presence he had the uncomfortable habit of thinking as he had before he joined the ranks of the Order, when he could allow a kind word or a gentle touch to lead to thoughts of something more.

But nothing was as it had been before. Not himself, and not the world. If nothing else, he spoke to Maria about his past to remind himself of that. He told her of his callow youth and his expectations of a title and an inheritance, and he told her of the pestilence when it came to Nürnberg, and the devastation the plague wrought on his family and estates.

Yet when he spoke of that evil time, he saw his grief reflected in Maria's face, and he almost stopped for fear of further distressing her, afraid that if tears came he would feel the urge to comfort her—and knowing that, despite his vows, any comfort he provided would be more for himself than for Maria.

Sensing that within himself, he kept talking even more earnestly. Talking of the woman to whom he had been betrothed, to remind him of who and what he was, what he had lost, and to push this poor woman away. Sarah had been the daughter of a powerful Nürnberg family that would have added to his own line's wealth and power. The child he had been at the time was smitten with her. Sarah was a young beauty at sixteen, always with a smile or a kind word for him, whatever dubious adventure he had become involved in. He had long ago convinced himself that Sarah would always be the limit of his earthly loves. Losing her was the final event that made him turn to the Order.

When he said that, and told Maria of Sarah's death, her face was drawn in an expression of grief as if it had been her own family lost in Nürnberg. She said something quietly to him in Polish, but before he could ask her what it was, she was telling him to go to sleep.

He leaned back and closed his eyes, and briefly imagined that she had touched his cheek. He didn't open his eyes for fear of dispelling the illusion—or confirming it.

But as he drifted off, he mused that while they looked little alike, perhaps, if she had lived, Sarah might have grown into someone like Maria.

⊕

Josef's sleep was broken by the door to his room bursting inward.

His eyes snapped open to see a hairy, gap-toothed Pole standing in the doorway, backlit by the lanterns in the hallway. The man strode in, followed by the scent of piss and ale, yelling in inarticulate Polish.

Before Josef could form a response, the invader had pulled his sheets off and had grabbed his arm. The smell of alcohol made Josef's eyes water. That, the slurred speech, and the fact that he had broken in an unlocked door told Josef that this man was no representative of his Masovian hosts.

He winced as the man yanked his arm, dragging him half off the bed. It felt as if someone had plunged a glass dagger into his stomach, then broken the blade off.

"Enough!" Josef commanded the drunkard.

But the man continued pulling him off the bed, and the pain was becoming worse. He didn't know what ill intent this man had in mind, but Josef wasn't about to let those drunken plans come to fruition.

The man was facing away from Josef and the bed as he tugged on Josef's right arm, so Josef rolled toward him, unbalancing the man's already forward-leaning posture. Josef helped the man along by reaching down and sweeping his left arm in front of the man's already precariously leaning legs.

The man tumbled face-first onto the floor, losing his grip on Josef as he landed next to the bed. He shook his head and started pushing himself upright, but Josef rolled on top of him. They both gasped—Josef's visitor in drunken shock as the floor came up to strike him again, and Josef in a shiver of agony. It felt as if a demon was clawing his intestines out of his gut.

But that almost happened, didn't it?

The man tried to buck Josef off his back, so Josef slammed all of his weight into the back of the man's neck, as much to keep himself upright as to immobilize his opponent. The pain threatened to make him black out.

"Relax, my friend." Josef spoke quietly, calmly, hoping his tone might calm things even if this man couldn't understand the words. "It is time to rest and contemplate the path that has led us to this unfortunate point."

The man below him uttered an unending stream of Polish that was most certainly obscene. Fortunately, he didn't continue his attempts to dislodge Josef.

It didn't take long before the alarm spread, and soon the doorway was crowded with a selection of Poles ranging from a trio whose clothing marked them as peers of the man underneath Josef to a lordly type with rich robes, a full beard, and a misshapen mouth who, Josef realized, must be the Wojewoda Bolesław himself.

Komtur Heinrich was in the middle of all of them, staring at the scene with rigid disapproval.

Lord Bolesław shouted a few things in Polish, and the man underneath Josef responded in kind, though Josef noticed a distinct change in his diction as he spoke to Bolesław, moderating his volume, speed, and, probably, his vocabulary.

Afterward, Bolesław addressed Josef in German: "You are Brother Josef, are you not?"

"Yes, my lord."

Bolesław sighed and stroked his beard absently with one hand. "You are my guest, and I apologize for this. May I ask if there is anything to this incident you wish to explain? Or is it all as plain as my aged eyes make it out to be?"

"I was in my bed, and this man came in and tried to pull me out."

"Tried?" Bolesław asked. "It appears he was successful."

"Lord, I tripped him, and it seemed prudent to roll off and immobilize him. He appears drunk, and a danger to himself and others."

One of the Poles in the hallway beyond the door started snickering. Bolesław looked pained, pulling his mouth into a grotesque frown. "This is unforgivable behavior. Whatever my people might think of Germans or the Order, you are my guests. I will have this man tied up and lashed to within an inch of his life."

Heinrich asked, "Has this ordeal aggravated your injuries, Josef?"

Josef tried not to wince when he said, "No, Brother Heinrich."

Heinrich turned to Bolesław and said, "The man is drunk; grant him some mercy. My man is unhurt."

"One cannot say the same for my door." Bolesław shook his head and, looking over to the other Poles, said something to the best-dressed of them. After a short conversation back and forth, Bolesław addressed Josef again: "If you would, please let him go back to his master. I've given him leave to discipline this wretch. I wash my hands of it."

Heinrich walked in and helped Josef to his feet as his drunken visitor stumbled out of the room to join his fellows. As his Komtur helped him into bed, Heinrich asked, "Are you being treated well?"

"Yes."

"No one has questioned you about our mission here?"

"No, sir."

"Good. Rest, and gather your strength. Soon the lord here will grant us an audience with a bishop. I suspect that shortly after, we will be able to resume our work." He placed a hand on Josef's arm. "Then we'll need every able man."

"Yes, Brother Heinrich. I'll be ready."

As he turned to go, Josef asked, "Brother Heinrich?"

"Yes?"

"Do you know who that man was? What he wanted of me?"

"He was a stable hand who felt entitled to this particular room. I believe his name was Lukasz."

"Should I have—"

"Don't concern yourself. It is between him and his betters now. It no longer concerns you."

"Thank you, sir."

But it took a long while for Josef to get back to sleep.

VII

Maria left the walls of Gród Narew before sundown, but the sky hid behind a dense cloak of purple-black clouds too thick to hint where the sun might be. The light was gone quickly, and she soon found herself walking through woods blacker than the sky. The trees embraced her as if they were the personification of darkness itself.

She had always had excellent night vision, and usually she didn't need the lantern she carried with her. Tonight, caught underneath a moonless sky, she had to use it just to see where the path might be.

The apprehension she felt was unusual. She had lived around these woods all her life, and the short distance between the fortress and her family's farm was well traveled, the land itself well populated. The presence of men here had long ago chased the more dangerous animals to the fringes of Gród Narew's demesne.

But the Germans had been savaged by some sort of animal.

Maria held her cross. Papa had told her, many times, that it was there to keep the Devil at bay. And this night, the Devil felt very close.

I should have stayed at the fortress, she thought to herself. She either had to stay at Gród Narew, where her work was, or stop prolonging her work there. Familiar or not, the woods at night were too dangerous for her to brave just to avoid the unspoken accusations that weighed upon her at home.

She walked slowly down the dark path, the trees drawing their shadows around themselves. She made her way home accompanied by the sounds of chirping insects and frogs. The sounds were as comforting as the darkness was ominous.

She sighed. However justified, fear was useless. She was on the path, and there was no leaving it now. She tried to force herself to think of something other than the shadows and what might be dwelling within them. So she found herself thinking of Josef, and what it must have been like for him to lose his family in the plague. She wondered about the woman he had lost. Some lady of the court. Tall and shapely, with long blond tresses, and dressed in fine fabrics. A woman who had no need to labor.

Everything Maria was not.

Was it jealousy, she thought suddenly, or did she envy this poor dead woman for once holding a heart she had no hope to touch? Either emotion was sinful, and a further indication of her own unworthiness.

"Why do I . . . " she began to ask herself, leaving the question to hang unfinished in the still night air.

The insects and the chirping frogs had fallen mute. The woods had gone as completely silent as they were dark. She stopped and wrinkled her nose at a sudden foul odor.

Ale?

Something grabbed her from behind and threw her against a tree. Phantom lights danced in front of her eyes as the side of her head slammed against the craggy bark. Her lantern fell to the road and guttered out.

"Hey now, don't you miss me?"

She knew that voice too well. "Lukasz?"

"Why, that warms my heart, it does." He was little more than a shadow next to her.

He pawed at her, and she shoved his hands away, shrinking back from the smell of piss, ale, cheese, and manure. "Don't touch me," she said.

"Oh, you missed me as well. I hear it in your voice." He was close, pressing her against the tree. "Since the Germans came, we've not had a single pleasant chat." His breath was warm, moist, and stank of alcohol and onions.

"Get away from me, you foul beast!"

"Scream what you wish, my love. We are far enough from anyone's ears."

Above, the clouds broke to release the moon from their embrace. The path around them lit up with cold silver light, and she could see Lukasz's face, leering at her with those cold, dead eyes.

He smiled and said, "Also far enough from anyone's eyes. We are free to do as we wish." His hand slipped under her cloak, and she felt his rough, sweaty fingers grope for her breast.

It was too much. She reached back and struck him in the face, as hard as she could. Her closed fist slammed his left cheek with the sound of a two-stone bag of grain dropping onto the kitchen floor. He fell back, taking his vile hand away.

She knew she should run, but she was too shocked at what she had done. Her blow had taken this man almost to his knees. Before she could summon the presence of mind to move, Lukasz backhanded her. She felt the blow across her own cheek as Lukasz screamed, "Bitch!"

As the warmth of blood spread across her own face, she wondered why his blow hadn't landed with nearly the force of hers. Then he slammed her back against the tree with his whole weight. She started to struggle, but the presence of the glittering edge of a knife against the side of her face froze her in place.

"Ungrateful whore," Lukasz spat at her. "You had to be spiteful."

Even in the moonlight, she could see the swelling where she had hit him. It twisted his face, pushing his left eye shut. *Did I break his cheekbone?*

He pulled the knife around in front of her face as the clouds tried to reclaim the moon, plunging the woods into semi-darkness. "Maybe," he whispered into her ear, "if you apologize, I'll only cut you up a little."

She sucked in a breath as she felt his free hand worming its way underneath her chemise. His body was heavy, pressing her into the tree. The bark tugged at her hair, the skin of her face stung where he had struck her, and over everything was the fetid miasma that was Lukasz himself. The vile stench brought her bile up even in the midst of her terror.

Then something rustled in the woods. Something large.

She thought of the fate of the Germans, and her fear redoubled. Lukasz was too occupied with pulling aside her skirts to notice. It wasn't until a shadow darker than the woods rustled on the path behind him that he looked up and said, "Huh?"

Then suddenly, miraculously, the groping hand, the threatening knife, the weight, and the oppressive stench were all gone. Lukasz screamed something unintelligible as his silhouette merged with the shadow that had come out of the woods. Maria heard only a brief sound of struggle; then one shadow tossed the other across the path and into the woods on the opposite side. It landed with a thud amid the sound of breaking branches.

Maria's terror ebbed somewhat when she saw that the shadow that had emerged from the woods had the outline of a man. The stranger moved into the woods after Lukasz. She heard Lukasz curse, and the brief sound of a struggle, followed by a solid thud.

The woods around her slipped into silence again. The only sound was the distant groan and rattle of wind through the trees. Above her, the moon broke free of the clouds, and the path unrolled before her in a curtain of silver light. She reached up and clutched her cross.

"Who is there?" she called out into the darkness.

The woods absorbed her words without comment. She heard nothing—not from Lukasz, and not from the shadowy figure who had torn him off her. An impossible hope crossed her mind that this was Josef come to save her, like the knight had saved the maiden in the ballad.

But she knew Josef was too wounded to walk abroad in Gród Narew, much less follow her into the woods. And the fear started edging its way back into her soul. She called out again, "Who is there?"

She took in a deep breath, and something in the air, some half-familiar scent, fired something in her brain that screamed inside her, *Run!*

But before she could convince her legs to obey, the stranger walked from the woods, onto the path. She looked at him and froze.

He was a man she had never seen before, dressed in a loose linen shirt, the bottom hanging over his mud-stained breeches. His shirt rippled slightly in the breeze, giving glimpses of his chest and abdomen. His face was clean-shaven, and framed by unbound shoulder-length blond hair.

But most arresting were his eyes, which shone blue in moonlight that tried to suck away every other color from the world. They reflected the only imperfection in his face—the fact that his left eye shone a slightly paler blue than the right, matched by a small scar that bisected the eyebrow above, pulling it into an expression of bemusement.

The two tiny flaws only served to make his appearance that much more striking.

He stepped before her, shaking his head and running both

hands through his hair. When he did, the end of his shirt raised up and she saw the handle of Lukasz's dagger sticking out of his belt.

"You saved me," she whispered, again feeling the unaccountable fear welling up. Her mind was still fixated on the rude ballad sung by the knights of the szlachta, where the prize for saving the maid were the favors that had been about to be stolen. Now, however, Josef's role had been usurped by this man, which gave the song a much darker tone.

He paused with his hands in his hair and laughed. Then he lowered his hands, shaking his head, and looked at her with the good humor of someone sharing a joke that held meaning only between two old friends. Unlike Lukasz, his humor fully engaged his eyes—all except the scar above his left eye, which tried to darken the expression toward sarcasm or cruelty.

"Saved you? From that oaf? Please, I did not intend to insult you."

Maria opened her mouth, but no words came out.

He stepped back and looked at her with those strikingly asymmetrical eyes. "I know you could have dealt with him yourself. Blame my impatience."

"T-thank you?" she whispered, unsure of who this man was, what he meant, and why the very air was trying to terrify her with each breath.

He stepped forward and held out his hand. "I've been rude, but I wished to meet you. It has been very long."

Against her better instincts, Maria reached out and placed her hand in his. Looking into his face, listening to him, she could hardly do otherwise. He raised her hand to his lips and kissed it.

The touch of his lips on her skin sent a jolt through her whole body. Everything seemed to freeze at once—her breath, her heart; even the air hung still around her, as if the wind itself had been transfixed by the apparition in front of her. She was thankful for the clouds when they took the moon away again, allowing the shadows to hide the flush upon her cheeks.

Again just a silhouette in the darkness, he lowered her hand.

"Who are you?" she asked, not prepared for the way her voice caught in her throat. *Is this what the maid in the ballad felt? Did she willingly give herself, or was she struck so insensible by her rescuer that she couldn't do otherwise?*

"My name is Darien," he said. "And what is your name?"

"Maria."

"Maria." His voice caressed the word in a way that made her shudder inside.

I cannot stay here. His very presence is seducing me.

She sucked in a breath and forced herself to emerge from her thrall. "Lukasz." She spat the word, and it was an effective antidote to Darien's mesmerizing presence.

"Lukasz?" His voice took on a different tone; Maria didn't know if she was glad or not that his expression was cloaked in shadow now.

"The man who attacked me, he is in service to the szlachta, and he will bring charges against you before the Wojewoda Bolesław."

"Should I care about this?"

"Do not make light of it. Bolesław is the deputy of the Duke himself, and wields that power in his stead. His word could have you face the lash, or worse. He could bond you as a slave to—"

Darien laughed. Like he had laughed before, but something in this laugh felt harder in the moonless dark. Then the moon finally returned through the clouds and she felt as if she might have imagined it—especially as the laugh trailed off, almost as if he was puzzled why she didn't find humor in the possibility of him being condemned.

Her epiphany came in a flash: *Of course. He's outlaw.* What other type of man would lurk in these woods at night but a bandit already on the run from the law of the Duke and his deputy? Of course he was amused. He was probably wanted for crimes far beyond any Lukasz could claim against him.

"Forgive me for presuming to advise you on your affairs," she said.

"After so long," he answered, "I can forgive many sins. And do not worry about your oaf Lukasz. When he wakes, I am certain I can teach him the value of discretion."

"I must go home," she said.

"You must?"

"Yes." She managed to say the word with none of the hesitation she felt. Even so, as she gathered her cold lantern she had the involuntary impulse to speak the lines from the ballad: "Is there anything I can offer to repay your kindness?"

She listened, stunned at the words leaving her own mouth, and her breath caught as she waited for his response. *What do I do if he asks for the same favors given the knight in that ballad?* The thought was terrifying. Why had she said those words?

He reached over and touched her cheek opposite where Lukasz had struck her. He caressed her face as if he knew her invitation for what it was, and the touch was gentle, as if he knew it wasn't her intent.

"All I ask now is your discretion. Say nothing of what happened here. Nothing of me, nothing of your vile oaf Lukasz. If you must go home, go now."

He took his hand away and stepped back. Something in her wanted to reach for him, even as she edged away from the darkness she felt inside him. Again, she spoke against her own will: "How will I find you again?"

"I will find you," he said. "Now go!"

He spoke with such an aura of command that she was out of sight of Darien before she realized she was running.

VIII

Darien stood in the center of the wooded path, still disbelieving. It had been decades since he had entertained even the hope of finding someone else. He had been resigned to being singular, unique.

"Maria," he whispered, savoring the taste of the name in his mouth. He drew in a deep breath and let the remnants of her scent fill his lungs. There was no mistaking it—not her scent, not the taste of her skin.

She had even invited him to do more than taste.

Maria was unquestionably one of his kind. If he had believed in God, he would have thought it providence that had placed her in his path. And, for once, it gave him something more than vengeance to look forward to.

Then he heard a weak groan from the woods.

First things first.

Darien slipped back into the woods and stood above the semiconscious man who had assaulted Maria. He had already forgotten the oaf's name. Not that any name was necessary; he was simply meat that, at the moment, had earned slightly more of Darien's hatred than most men.

The man groaned on the forest floor, not quite recovered from striking the tree whose roots now supported him. A fractured bone protruded from his arm, and the side of his face was swollen and bloody.

Had it only been Darien, he might have left this sack of meat to live or die as it saw fit. If not for his actions, this pathetic man would be beneath Darien's notice. But Darien had told Maria that this man would learn discretion.

He laughed silently at his own joke as he reached down and threw the unconscious man over his shoulder. Almost completely over; he had forgotten how light men were when they wore no armor. He grabbed the man's ankle just in time to keep him from sliding all the way down his back, then pulled as he stood so that his burden was draped properly across his shoulder.

At some point during the process, his burden had awoken and started bellowing at him through a broken jaw, pounding on his back with his good arm. Darien ignored both as he slipped deeper into the woods.

Maria stopped in front of her family's cottage. She had run all the way here after her meeting with Darien. She thought she should be out of breath, but she only felt a little flushed.

Her exhilaration, she told herself, was from the brisk run and the release of her fear upon coming home. She had better sense than to think it had anything to do with Darien. He might have helped her, but he was unquestionably dangerous. More dangerous than her perennial nemesis Lukasz could ever hope to be. Lukasz was young, strong, and armed, and Darien had tossed him aside like a sack of grain, disarming him simply with his bare hands.

He was clearly an outlaw, and the only thing that had saved

her from a fate worse than Lukasz was that outlaw's momentary good graces. Such a liaison belonged safely in a ballad, with knights and maids who needn't worry over consequences beyond the last stanza.

She thanked God that her evening's adventure had spawned no such consequences. Lukasz was spineless in the face of actual power, and she suspected that Darien could buy the wretch's silence with only a few well-chosen words. And even if Lukasz should bring a grievance to the Wojewoda Bolesław, Maria doubted that her name would arise in the complaint.

And even if it did, she would much rather face Lukasz's words than his hands.

The door to the darkened cottage opened. Maria's stepmother stood in the doorway. "Maria?"

"Yes, Mama?" she said quietly, realizing that she had been standing outside for a long time. She looked up; the insects and the frogs had renewed their nighttime singing.

"It is very late."

"I'm sorry, Mama. I had work—"

"Your face." Her stepmother drew a sharp breath and ran to her side, lifting Maria's chin toward the moonlight. "You're hurt."

"It's nothing."

"You're bleeding. We have to wash it, at least. What happened?"

"I—" She almost choked on her words, remembering her promise to Darien nearly too late. "I fell, in the dark." She felt the heat of the lie on her face, and the shame of it nearly brought her to tears. The deception was pointless. Whatever her promise, she was certain that the lie was obvious, drawn across her face for anyone to see.

Especially for the woman who was the only mother she had ever known.

But Maria's stepmother didn't seem to notice the clumsy lie. She kept staring at the bruise where Lukasz had struck her, blinking a couple of times. She stayed like that for a long time, until Maria said, "You said we should wash it?"

Her stepmother broke from her reverie and let go of Maria's chin. "Yes. Come in and relight your lantern. I'll fetch water and some linens."

Maria followed her stepmother into the cottage, thinking how preoccupied she seemed. Then she scolded herself. Whatever her stepmother felt about Maria, she had lost her husband. She had the same right to grieve as Maria did.

In the dark, her stepmother surprised Maria by reaching out and touching her shoulder. Almost as if she knew what Maria had been thinking, she whispered, "I know your father was mistaken. God protects you still."

Maria reached up and touched her cross and wondered if her mother knew about Darien.

The man Darien carried had exhausted his voice after the first mile. He made a token struggle when Darien crossed the river, but after that came only the occasional hoarse plea, which Darien ignored.

Even at the healthy pace that Darien traveled, it was over half an hour carrying his burden back to his current homestead. The cave was hidden on three sides by impenetrably dense woods, the only approach to it a game trail that led up a rise and appeared to dead-end in a solid wall of twisted growth and deadfalls. It wasn't unless one stood on top of the rise itself and looked down the sheer drop that faced the wall of trees that the cave mouth could be seen.

Darien stood at the crest of the rise above the cave and unceremoniously unloaded his burden. The man tumbled out of his arms and down the rise to land screaming in the small clearing in front of the cave mouth.

Darien watched the man struggle below, rolling back and forth while cursing. "Who are you?" the man finally said, comprehensibly. He panted, cradling his broken arm, then struggled to his feet on the uneven footing of dead leaves and gravel. He had to lean against the trunk of a tree, because his left foot now bent at an odd angle. "Who the hell are you? And what do you want?"

Darien took the man's knife and tossed it casually down. It fell with a clatter against a helmet transfixed by a spear of cold moonlight, near where Maria's oaf supported himself. The man looked down at the knife, and at the helmet.

Then he gagged and screamed when he saw the prior owner's head rotting inside it.

"God have mercy! What fiend are you?"

As Darien removed his shirt, the man babbled on, his words increasing in speed and volume as he looked around the clearing, finally seeing the remnants of men, armor, and horses scattered before the mouth of Darien's lair.

Darien didn't say anything to the man. It was more amusing to allow him to come to his own conclusions. As Darien stripped off his belt and removed his breeches, his prey had the presence of mind to channel his panic. He fell to his knees and scrambled toward a sword that had fallen just a few feet away, shoving aside a bloody gauntlet and the partly gnawed skull of a horse.

The man brought the sword up to point in Darien's direction. The point shook, the silvered edge catching fragments of moonlight.

Darien stood naked above his prey and laughed.

"Are you insane? Say something, monster!"

Darien spread his arms and let free the mental chains that held his flesh in check. His bones creaked as they thickened and grew, and he felt his muscles tear and reknit as they spasmed and writhed under skin that darkened and grew a pelt of golden hair.

He had been injured by every weapon known to man, he had broken every bone in his body, he had even felt a silver crossbow bolt pierce his brow, sending bony splinters into his left eye—but no pain matched the feeling of the wolf tearing free from within his flesh. Every nerve fired a welcome agony, a red-hot knife ripping through his body, bringing an ecstatic release in its wake.

He howled and looked down at the cowering man below him. He wrinkled his nose and licked his muzzle with a long, lolling tongue. He crouched on lupine legs, so that his hands, long-clawed and still vaguely human, rested on the edge of the bluff in front of him.

He caught the scent of the man below voiding himself, and his face twisted into a lupine version of a smile.

"Monster," he whispered, too low for his terrified prey to hear. "You call me monster after everything men have taken from me? And for less reason?"

Then he leapt down.

⌖

Maria lay on her bed and stared into the shadows. Below the loft that held her bed, her brothers snored. She was the only one awake in the cottage now, and the night was half over already. In a few hours she would have to get up, draw water for her family, and start the walk down to Gród Narew.

She would have to walk the same path.

It had never concerned her before. She had known these woods all her life. They had never felt threatening to her. But now she had to face them again, and her hands still shook when she thought about what had happened. What had *almost* happened.

She should have told her stepmother, whatever she had promised Darien. Not just because the lie was a sin that weighed on her soul, but because the lie pushed Hanna away. The lie made sure that Maria was alone in her own home.

She held her cross and allowed tears to come.

Who was Darien to ask this of her?

He did save me from Lukasz, she thought, *and asked only for my silence when he could have asked for much more . . .*

It might have been better if he had.

She bit her lip, feeling a flush across her body as she remembered the touch of Darien's lips on her hand, his hand caressing her face. She remembered the look and feel of Josef's chest, and wondered if Darien's would be as strong, as warm . . .

I am not a wicked person.

She couldn't keep herself from imagining his lips on hers, and his hand touching other parts of her body, her hand touching his body. But in her wicked fantasy she was unsure if it was Darien who took her or Josef.

She prayed to God to settle her thoughts; the prayer's answer was long in coming.

But in time, she did sleep.

Interlude

Anno Domini 1331

Twenty-two years ago, when he was a child, Darien hadn't hated anyone at all. His family—his pack—had even adopted human ways in the face of ever-expanding human claims to the dark woods of the Baltic. They lived away from men, but any travelers who had the misfortune to find themselves in the haunted wood where Darien's pack made their home would be well-treated as guests. And, later on, would have a guide to take them back to the normal trade paths.

The village, hidden deep in those woods, had once housed a pagan community that treated Darien's ancestors as gods. But, long ago, the Germans had come and killed those who hadn't converted and carried away those who had. The village had not remained empty for long. The pack of Darien's great-grandfather had decided that it was wise, with human warriors trampling through their lands every season, to add to the camouflage of their human skins.

When the Order came again, they found a Christian village, including a church built upon the ashes of a pagan shrine.

Human gods meant nothing to the pack, so pledging fealty to the Order's was of no consequence. For something over a century, from that generation to Darien's, the village endured.

During his childhood years, Darien knew little of the outside world, other than the fact that there were these creatures called "men" who lived beyond the woods. He was taught, very carefully, that he would wear only a human skin in front of anyone not of the village.

The village was remote enough that, for the first nine years of his life, he saw no one who wasn't of the village. By his tenth year, he had come to doubt the existence of such creatures as men. He'd started to think that he'd been told mere tales, to scare him and keep him from hunting without his parents.

He knew he was old enough to hunt on his own. He had taken down a bull elk all by himself the last moonless night his family had gone hunting. And he had done so in the skin of a full wolf, which was not as hard as he'd thought it would be. Hunting before, he had always taken the halfway skin, which left him hands to grip and tear at his prey, as well as a muzzle to bite the neck. But his parents had told him that to be an adult, he would have to learn to use all the wolf he had within him.

So, despite his reluctance, he'd done so, and the experience had changed him. Everything human became slow, pale, and bland in comparison. Even the power of the halfway skin couldn't compare with the freedom he'd felt when he'd leapt at the animal's neck.

He had become an adult.

Ever since, his bones ached for the change, and his tongue was hungry for the taste of the blood hot from the animal's neck. Even though they were still eating from the carcass he had taken, Darien wanted to take another.

That was why he had slipped away from his parents on a cold spring evening only three days afterward. He had shed his human skin to revel in his fresh, fully lupine form. He didn't understand why his parents were so reluctant to do this more often, or in the light. The freedom he felt was indescribable, the power over every creature in this forest. He could take any creature he wished and taste its lifeblood.

He ran free as evening grew deeper, losing himself in the woods. He ran beyond the limits of his scent without quite realizing it. He was too intent on snapping at stray rabbits, taking the small bodies apart in a deadly snap of fangs and a spray of blood and fur.

The shadows were long, and his muzzle slick with the blood of small animals, before he realized that he was lost. The thought struck him suddenly when he stumbled on an unfamiliar path heavy with strange scents. He stopped with the sudden realization that his disobedience had passed far beyond what his parents might forgive. He had no chance of returning before dark, before he would be missed.

He looked desperately back and forth along the strange path, searching for any sign of familiarity, sucking in the air and hoping for the scent of his mother, his father, anyone from the village.

He would never be taken on a hunt again...

And with the growing terror in his breast, he would accept that as a worthwhile price for finding his way home.

Panic and immaturity kept him from doing what his parents had told him to *always* do if he found himself in unfamiliar territory; he didn't change back. He couldn't. The woods were cold and dangerous, and he couldn't face them clad naked in his weak human form. Fear made him pull himself into the halfway skin, the one he felt safest in while facing whatever terror the forest held.

He was unprepared when the forest finally revealed its terror.

It smelled strange, and stood astride the path ahead of him. Darien stopped, frozen at the sight of the creature. He couldn't make immediate sense of the sight. It was huge, four-legged, and the last rays of sunlight glinted off parts of its body. Something shaped vaguely like a person seemed to grow out of its back.

He had never seen an armored knight before, and it took a moment before his brain recognized that someone was riding on a horse's back—something his people never did. The rider bellowed and pointed an object at Darien. Darien was too confused to recognize the threat as the knight's crossbow fired.

He was saved only by distance and the panic of the rider. The bolt tore past him, grazing his side between his forearm and his shoulder. It stung like nothing he had ever felt before. He took off deep into the woods, where the rider and his beast couldn't follow.

As he ran through the darkening woods, he thought of the stories his parents had told him, about the men who lived beyond the dark woods. There was an especially dangerous type of man—the ones who had killed all the people who had worshipped their ancestors, the ones who had emptied the pagan village and left it abandoned, the ones who were the reason his pack followed the forms of serving Christ. The men of the German Order, whose symbol was the black cross, who ruled all the lands beyond their little village.

As he ran into the night, he tried several times to tell himself that the man on the horse hadn't worn a tabard bearing the black cross of the Order. He had been mistaken. It had been the shadow of a branch, a fold in the fabric, not a black cross.

Anything but a black cross.

The fear grew as he realized that the wound in his side where the crossbow bolt had grazed him was not healing. His fur was slick with his own blood, and it hurt for him to breathe. That wasn't supposed to happen. A cut in the flesh like that should heal in a matter of moments, and even faster when he wore this form.

But the cut from the knight's bolt burned as he bled. His lungs burned as he panted. His eyes burned as he wept.

As fatigue gripped him, he dropped to all fours, letting the energy of the full wolf push him forward. But even the wolf had limits, and he couldn't run forever. Deep in the midnight-black woods, his legs gave out and he curled up under a tree, panting and sobbing, and half-hoping that the knight of the black cross would find him and finish him off, so that he would no longer have to be afraid.

The knight didn't find him, and Darien woke in his naked human form, shivering and tacky with his own blood. He wandered the woods for two days, losing hope until he finally found a familiar scent, and a game trail that he knew. His heart swelled once he was back on familiar ground. He ran along the path as fast as he could in the fading evening light, the branches and briars on the path tearing at his feet and leaving scratches that healed almost as quickly as they were made.

He slowed only as he began smelling other things. Blood. Smoke. Roasting meat.

And a scent that he remembered. A smell he knew belonged to the knight and his horse.

Darien stopped on the path, shaking his head. He tried to deny it, just as he had tried to deny the black cross on the knight's tabard.

Fear rooted him to the spot for what felt like hours. Slowly, inevitably, he pulled his feet free from his paralysis. He stepped slowly at first, moving toward his home as if in a dream. The awful smells wrapped around him, almost choking him, and before he realized it, he was running as if the knight were on his heels, chasing him.

He reached his village before he was ready. Even so, the smells had already told him what he would find.

The fires had died, but the smoke hung over the village like an evil fog, burning his eyes and imperfectly hiding the damage. Every building had burned, leaving nothing more than haphazard piles of broken timbers. The damage was so complete that, once he had taken a few steps into the remains of the village, he could no longer tell whose homes they used to be.

He walked naked through the haze, too stunned to be afraid anymore. He called out, "Mother? Father?" But no one responded.

The smell of horses was almost as rank as the smell of smoke and blood. And when he rounded a smoldering pile of wood that had once been someone's home, he saw one. The animal was sprawled in a muddy track that was a soup of hoofprints, mud, shit, and blood. Its head had been torn nearly free of the rest of it, so that its dead eyes could stare at him over its shoulder.

It could have been the knight's horse. It wore metal plates on its head, and a mail skirt, and draped across it was a torn sheet that, under the mud, soot, and blood, bore the black cross of the Order.

I didn't bring them here.

He kept repeating that to himself, as if thinking something often enough would make it true.

"Mother? Father?" He no longer shouted at the ruins around him. He no longer feared that he wouldn't find his family. Now he feared that he would.

He encountered two other dead horses, left where they had fallen. Darien passed other remnants of battle, stray bits of armor, fragments of a tabard. Human clothing shredded by someone during a change. A severed hand. A broken sword. Crossbow bolts sticking in a tree that had burned into a skeletal hand reaching for the sky.

No bodies.

Not until he reached the church.

Like the rest of the village, the scene was too surreal for him to make immediate sense of it. It was the smell that brought him to his knees, retching into the blood-soaked mud, before he could even acknowledge what it was he saw.

The German Order had taken away their dead and wounded.

Their victims, the inhabitants of Darien's village, had been dragged into the church that their ancestors had built to appease the followers of Christ. Living or dead, everyone had been sealed inside; and then the building had been set afire.

Mixed with the blackened timbers, in what seemed equal numbers, were the bones of everyone Darien had ever known. Some of the flame-blackened skulls were human, some were lupine, and all seemed to stare at him with empty sockets, accusing him.

He shook, on his knees, and said, "I didn't do this."

The sickening smell of his burnt family argued against him.

"I didn't do this!" he scremed at the dead.

But the dead refused to acknowledge him.

For three years, he abandoned his human form. He even abandoned his halfway skin, whose hands were too much a reminder of what he had lost. He became nothing but a large wolf, hiding in the woods the way his ancestors hid in their human forms.

Guilt and despair drove the wolf into an endless hunt. He slept in caves, drank from rivers. He gradually tried to forget things like language, and tools, and clothing.

And thinking.

After three years, the only thing that reminded him of his

early life was the healed wound in his side. It had left a thin scar that tended to ache when the weather became cold. The pain wasn't bad, but the ache always brought tears.

He would have remained in those dark woods for the rest of his life if he hadn't found the dying hart. He was hunting and took the creature without a thought, springing onto its back from the darkness, and twisting its neck in his jaws so it was dead before it fell.

The thought came after it died and struck the forest ground. It had never known that Darien was there, but it had been running in a panic, its pulse under his tongue so rapid that its heart might have burst from the effort. It bled from wounds Darien had had no part in making.

He looked down at the animal's body.

Long sticks pointed up out of the beast's chest, jammed into the creature's lungs, their bases slick with frothy blood. He saw the fletching and pulled the word out of his memory.

Arrows.

Men were here?

He stood over the dead animal, forepaws resting on its side, and felt something shift in his heart. For three years he'd had no focus for his anger beyond himself and his own guilt. For three years he had forced himself not to remember anything beyond his feral existence in the forest. Living far beyond anything that might remind him of what he once had, and what he had lost because of what he had done.

What men had done.

A low growl rumbled in his chest. Standing over his kill, his thoughts a clumsy tumble of half-remembered shame and fury, he felt something slam into his chest. He fell backward, more in surprise than in pain. Looking down, he saw an arrow the length of his foreleg sticking out of the left side of his chest.

Above him, the archer was readying another arrow in his bow.

The man didn't wear the cross or the armor of the knights who had slaughtered Darien's village, but he smelled of man—a scent Darien would never forget.

Almost without thought, his body realigned itself, the spine twisting, muscles rippling, and his forepaws creaking and snapping as they grew into strong, clawed hands. The flesh wrenched itself painfully into its new form, leaving an aching relief in its wake.

He had nearly forgotten his other skin, but his body hadn't. And something within him knew that this was the form in which to fight men.

The second arrow plunged into the ground as he stood upright for the first time in three years, wobbly from the violence the change had wrought to his balance and his center of gravity.

He reached up and pulled the arrow out of his chest. It came free with a tug and a flare of pain, but that was all. Unlike the knight's bolt, this arrow left no lasting scar. The wound was sealed before the third arrow passed completely through his left shoulder. Darien clenched his fist on the arrow he had pulled from his chest, and the thick shaft splintered in half.

He ran toward the archer as a fourth arrow flew by, completely missing him. As he closed on the man, he smelled something else. It was unfamiliar, but it was a smell he would soon learn to savor.

Fear.

He dragged the body to a nearby river so he could wash the blood off the man's clothes. He'd need them, if he was going to walk among men. He licked the blood off his claws and fur, and pulled the archer's corpse into the shallow part of the river. He fumbled with the clothes before he realized that they were designed for human hands.

While the body rested on the riverbed, water washing over it and his legs, Darien tried to pull the old human skin back around himself. For a long time it felt as if he had forgotten how. Perhaps he had never had a form like the dead thing in the water at his feet. Perhaps it was a nightmare. Maybe the wolf thing was all he was.

But as it had with the halfway skin, his body remembered that he had once had a human shape. The change came, like a long-cramped muscle finally relaxing. His flesh poured into the man form suddenly, and with a shuddering relief that caused him to collapse into the river, next to the corpse. Cold water washed over skin that was suddenly naked; his newly flat teeth chattered and his whole body broke into gooseflesh.

He got unsteadily to his feet and stared at his hands, white and hairless, with impotent nails.

As weak as they seemed, it had been hands like this that had destroyed everything he had ever cared about. Hands like these could kill just as easily as tooth and claw.

He bent over the archer's body and clumsily removed its clothes. The river had already diluted the blood, until all that was left were unremarkable stains on the already mottled brown tunic. He tossed the dead man's possessions—belt, tunic, breeches, boots—up onto the shore, until the corpse was as naked as he was. After that, he pushed the body to the deep center of the river to let the current take it where it wished.

Darien watched it go and had the last twinge of doubt about what he would do next. He could return to the woods now...

But somewhere beyond these woods were more men—men who deserved to lose what he had lost. Feel what he had felt. Darien knew, now that the rage in him had awakened, that there would be no release from it except in a tide of human fear.

He dressed himself in a dead man's clothes and started walking toward the world of men.

PART TWO

Anno Domini 1353

IX

After two days' travel, Rycerz Telek Rydz herbu Bojcza and a trio of his best men rode into Warsaw. The city was imposing after their ride through the countryside. It could easily fit a dozen copies of Gród Narew within the embrace of its walls. As he entered the city, he thought that his uncle Bolesław would be relieved that no sign of war was abroad. The people did their business, men ran their shops, and farmers tended their fields. If they chose to glance at the approaching knight bearing the Bojcza standard, it was only with respect and mild curiosity, not the fear that tainted the common man's face in wartime.

Telek was relieved as well. As tense as dealings with the Teutonic State were, the tension was preferable to open conflict. There had been plenty of that over the years, and Telek prayed that the latest treaty with the Polish Kingdom was to spell the end of it.

But it did add an additional level of urgency to his mission. For, if there was war, the presence of German hostages in Gród Narew would be troublesome, but unlikely to cause any great consequences for Masovia as a whole. In peace, however, the Germans became a much more delicate proposition. They needed to move with extreme care lest they give the Order some pretext to resume hostilities.

For today, however, the land was at peace, the stores were full, and Telek's party was greeted by the court of Siemowit III as honored guests. The Duke himself met all of them personally and insisted that they take their supper with him and his court. It was a grand affair, with musicians, and jugglers, and an entire boar roasted for them. But since their presence was unexpected, Telek was left to assume that this was how the Duke took most of his meals.

It wasn't until late evening, when the Duke received him in private, that Telek was able to discuss the reason he was here.

The evening was clear and cool, and the Duke chose to talk to him outside, as they walked along the twilit gardens. "Tell me, my son, how fares your uncle?"

"He does well, my lord. He is, however, troubled by the German Order."

"I fear that will be the case as long as his jaw aches to remind him of the last war."

"I am afraid that this time he has more reason."

The Duke stopped on the path before Telek, folding his arms behind him as he bent to examine a rosebush that was overwhelming the stony remnants of a prior wall. Nothing changed in his demeanor, other than his voice. "Tell me," he said, his voice carrying an edge that hadn't been present before. "What reason would that be?"

"He's received a convent of knights of the German Order at Gród Narew—fresh from battle, given their dead and wounded. He had them disarmed, and they are now being held as our guests."

"Hostages," the Duke said. "What mischief were they up to within my duchy?"

"They refuse to speak of it."

The Duke froze, and turned his head to look at Telek. Given the intensity of the Duke's gaze, Telek was glad not to be the focus of his ire. "They refuse? Knights of the Teutonic Order shed blood upon my lands, retreat to one of my forts, and refuse to inform my deputy of their business here?"

"Yes."

"Should I go to Marienwerder and demand satisfaction from the grand master himself? Must I have an audience with the pope?"

"My lord, their captain has told us that they will speak to a bishop."

"A bishop? Which bishop?"

"They did not specify."

"They did not . . . Am I to understand that they will speak to any bishop provided to them?"

"That is my uncle's understanding."

"I presume, then, that you have come here to fetch one for your uncle?"

"The name my uncle gave me—"

"Bishop Leszek, I would suspect."

"Yes. How did you know?"

The Duke chuckled. "Our bishop served in the wars against the German Order before he entered into the priesthood. He had no love for those troublesome monks, and it would suit your uncle's humor to grant his guests such an unsympathetic ear." He turned to follow the path back to the castle, clapping a hand on Telek's shoulder. "I must ask you to delay your return until I attend to matters here."

Telek paused as the implication sank in. "My lord, you intend to return with us?"

"I have not seen your uncle in an age," he said. "Also, should anything unfortunate happen, it would be best if it had my direct sanction."

⌖

Wojewoda Bolesław walked the short hallway between his private apartments and the guest rooms. The bells were ringing for the last rays of sunset as he stopped in front of the door to one of the most luxurious of the guest quarters. One on a par with his own.

Right now it housed his German guest, Komtur Heinrich of the Teutonic Knights. His tongue unconsciously probed the toothless side of his jaw as he looked down at the letter in his hand. He read it again and wondered at his own surprise.

He sucked in a breath and opened the door.

Brother Heinrich, wearing simple robes, was reading a book set on the desk before him. The German looked up, annoyance flickering briefly across his features. He closed the book as he stood, and the gesture was so casual that only Bolesław's suspicious nature drew his attention to it. It appeared to be an illuminated manuscript that, given the vocation of his guest, anyone would quickly surmise was a book of hours, open to an evening devotional.

Of course, were that the case, there would be no cause to hide it from Bolesław's eyes. Unfortunately, those eyes were too weak with age to interpret a single word, or even the language it was written in.

The illustration, however, had been clear. If the scene he'd glimpsed was in the Bible, it was in no verse that Bolesław was familiar with. An elaborately painted miniature showed a knight holding something at bay with a drawn sword. Bolesław had caught too brief a glimpse of the thing threatening the knight to catch its full form, but it was clearly not human, nor any animal Bolesław knew.

"How might I serve you, my lord?" Heinrich asked.

"I might suggest that you reconsider telling me what brings you to Masovia."

Heinrich sighed. "I hoped I had been clear. Our vows prevent us from—"

Bolesław waved a hand, dismissing the thought. "Yes, yes. You need your bishop." He held up the letter in his hand, which bore seals from his nephew and the Duke. "I came to tell you that a messenger brought us word that your bishop shall be here in a matter of days."

Bolesław hoped for some reaction other than passive acceptance, but Heinrich did not provide it. "That is good news."

"So you say. I might mention that the Duke himself has taken an interest in you and your men."

Again, only infuriating calm showed on Heinrich's face. "I would expect so."

"He will be accompanying my nephew and the bishop back from Warsaw."

"I see."

"Perhaps you will talk to him?"

"With the bishop's leave."

Bolesław laughed. "Well, I am certain that Bishop Leszek will grant you that."

Heinrich frowned slightly, his only concession to emotion. "My lord, you have been nothing less than fair and generous with me and my men. Your tolerance speaks well of you and of Masovia. And I will say as much before God and the pope." He turned around and slammed his fist into the desk with such sudden violence that his book jumped and Bolesław took a step back. "Do *not* think I am being willful! I am quite aware of the implications of our presence here, and this is *not* a matter we take lightly."

"I had no such thoughts, Brother Heinrich."

"We have all made pledges to God and the pope." He looked over his shoulder at Bolesław. "And believe me, that is a much graver matter than you have given credit for."

"As I said, you will have your bishop, Brother Heinrich."

"And, God willing, you will have your explanations." He walked over to the other side of the desk and placed his hand on the book. "Forgive my anger. I find myself preoccupied with the state of my men. Are they well?"

"The injured are recovering. I can have one of my men escort you to see them."

"That would be good."

Bolesław looked at the monk's hand on the book and said, "But I see I was interrupting you. I'll leave you to your devotions now."

"Thank you," Heinrich said. His demeanor was calm, but Bolesław saw his knuckles whiten as his hand pressed the leather cover.

There's something there, Bolesław thought. *Something that might be profitable to know.*

As he left, he thought about his nephew, wishing he were back already. Not only so he would have Bishop Leszek to slice through this knot of Teutonic recalcitrance, but because Rycerz Telek was the only man in his retinue schooled enough to read both German and Latin—the two languages most likely to be found in Brother Heinrich's little tome.

8

Maria hesitated, until the first rays of dawn, to return to Gród Narew. She didn't want to face the path in the darkness so soon after last night. What scared her more than meeting Darien again in the dark was the idea of what she might be persuaded to do—things the night invited that she couldn't even bear to contemplate under the light of the sun.

Avoiding Darien, however, meant she would almost certainly arrive at the fortress as Lukasz was tending to his duties, and facing him again was inconceivable. So she hurried along at a run, not even sparing a breath to sing to herself, racing against the sound of the tower bells—racing as if Lukasz or the Devil himself chased her onward.

But the bells rang out while she was still in the woods, and as she emerged before Gród Narew, she saw the horses being led out to the pasture. Her heart sank as she ran up to the gate, all the time gripping her cross and praying that she would not face Lukasz today.

Today, God favored her. Lukasz did not leap over the stone pasture wall for her. She reached the gate, disbelieving, and looked out over the pasture. *Am I mad, searching for him?*

"Looking for someone?" one of the guards at the gate chuckled.

She turned around and said, "N-no."

The guard peered at her from under a dull conical helmet, and over whiskers as full and wild as a rabid badger. "Looking for the stableboy you talk to, aren't you?"

"No," she snapped, suddenly feeling waves of revulsion that this man might actually think she wanted to talk to Lukasz.

A laugh emerged from somewhere under the bush of his mustache. "That is good, young miss, since you shan't find him."

Maria was about to walk by, but something—a dreadful worry—made her stop and ask, "Why do you say that?"

"Because Master Lukasz was ejected from his household, and I doubt they will accept him back."

"What happened?"

The guard chuckled. "I thought you weren't looking for him?"

Maria sighed. "Sir, would you be kind enough to tell me what happened?"

"Well, since you ask so sweetly, your friend Lukasz partook of much more ale than was wise, and compounded his lack of wisdom by convincing himself of how unjust was the Wojewoda's decision to relocate him to a common room away from his normal quarters by the stables. So, in a haze of drunken inventiveness, he took it upon himself to evict one of our wounded German guests from his old rooms."

"Christ have mercy," Maria whispered. "Did he hurt anyone?"

The guard chuckled more and said, "He should thank Christ *he* wasn't hurt. The German, however badly wounded he was, was more than a match for a drunk stableboy. Tale has it that his master, three stableboys, the German captain, and the Wojewoda Bolesław himself converged on the room to find your Lukasz crying like a little girl, flat on his face, with a wounded monk riding his back as if he were an ass."

Maria shook her head, disbelieving. She was still too close to the memory of Lukasz jumping her in the forest to reconcile that threat with the pathetic clown in the guard's story.

"Bolesław wanted a dozen lashes on the spot, but the German captain pled mercy for the drunkard. The Wojewoda gave the boy's master leave to mete out a punishment."

"And he banished him?"

"I don't know his master's intent, but your Lukasz left last night with the clothes on his back. I'm certain he's not returning."

The more she thought about it, the more sense it made. Lukasz had always been petty and easily offended, and too fond of his own meager status. It was as if all his flaws had conspired to destroy him in one night.

As petty as he was, he had been left with only one outlet for his anger: her. He must have left to run after her straightaway. He knew the path she walked home. She shuddered at what might have happened if he hadn't caught up with her. Would he have come into her house? Threatened her family? Her brothers were strong, but they slept too deeply. She could easily imagine a dagger slitting a sleeping throat or two before enough of alarm was raised to rouse them.

But the events of last night were still such a jumbled mess in her mind that she hadn't spared a thought to wonder which German Lukasz had attempted to evict—not until she saw the broken latch on the door to Josef's room.

Lukasz's room.

"Josef!" she yelled, pulling the door open and almost spilling Josef's breakfast in the process. "Josef!" she repeated, unnecessarily, as he turned to face her, clad only in a long nightshirt, seated at the foot of the bed.

"Are you all right?" she asked, deeply relieved to see him smile weakly in response. The odd realization struck her that, however unknowingly, Josef had punished her nemesis as much as the outlaw Darien had. The thought broadened her smile until she felt the tug of the bruise on her cheek.

"I seem to fare better than I deserve," he said. "From your abrupt entrance, you must have heard of my nighttime visitor."

She looked at him: strong as he was, the injury still weighed upon him. As much as his expression and posture tried to project a hale physique, she saw the lie of it in the beads of sweat on his brow in the cool morning air, and in the lack of color touching his lips. "You shouldn't be sitting up."

"Perhaps not," he sighed. "I thought that when God granted me the strength to resist being waylaid, He might have left me with the power to stand up this morning."

Maria shook her head and set his breakfast down, then helped him back into bed. "You haven't seen how badly you were wounded." She took a clean cloth and wiped the sweat of his exertion from his brow, from his cheek, and from his neck. She lingered a moment with her hand against his face.

"I have felt it."

"Let me look at it, and see what damage you've done to yourself."

His brow furrowed. "My lady, allow me some modesty, please."

His addressing her as "lady" instantly reminded Maria of their relative statuses. Whatever comfort she provided him, that couldn't change. She pulled her hand away, wringing the cloth.

"Sir, did you allow the doctor to see you last night?"

"I was unhurt."

"Do you wish to see him now?"

"I am healing fine."

"You're my responsibility. If you don't wish me to examine your wounds, I will fetch him."

He muttered something quickly in German that Maria couldn't quite understand. Something about God testing him again. Then he said, "Do me the favor of turning your back a moment?"

"As you wish." She turned away from him. "I can fetch the doctor, if that would make you more comfortable."

"I serve the Hospital of St. Mary in Jerusalem. Caring for the sick and wounded is a tenet of my Order. I know doctors and their practices."

"You are afraid of what he might do?"

"No. But I know that such men, once called to assist, find their own vanity ill-served if they do nothing—even if nothing should be the best course of action." He sighed and said, "Turn back around, then, and satisfy yourself that I am in no distress."

She turned, and Josef made a point of staring up at the ceiling and not meeting her eyes. He had drawn the sheets up around his waist to cover his privates, and had pulled his nightshirt up to expose his abdomen.

She stared at him for several long moments. He might not realize it, but she had already seen all that the sheet covered. And, ironically, the concealment only drew her attention, firing her memories of what was hidden. Her cheeks flamed.

"Maria?"

"Yes," she answered, quickly bringing her attention back to the wounds in his abdomen. The linens that bound his wounds were spotted with stains of old blood, but fortunately there were no signs of fresh blood or other discharges.

"These need to be changed, in any event," she told him.

He grunted as she untied the knots and removed the old dressing. She frowned at his stomach. The wound was an ugly, jagged crescent that arced around his navel. The edges were tied shut by coarse stitches, threaded either by his comrades in the Order or by the Wojewoda's doctor.

But, Maria had to admit, as horrid as the wound appeared, it did not display any of the signs she knew to look for. The flesh showed only some flushing next to the black clotted lips of the scar, no white, no red; and nothing seeped from the wound except a few drops of healthy ruby blood where he had stretched too far against his stitches.

Seeing how well he was actually doing was a balm for her soul, as if God had granted a blessing in compensation for the torment of the prior night. She sighed and touched his hand, their relative stations completely forgotten.

"You have not hurt yourself unduly."

"Good."

"God has blessed you with strength." She turned to look at his face. "Please avoid testing the limits of that blessing."

"I can try." He surprised her by squeezing her hand.

She stood still for a moment, then told him, "You need a new dressing on that wound."

She worked quickly, binding the ugly scar with clean linen. As she worked, Josef's sheet shifted slightly and she found herself once more beginning to blush. When she was done, she turned her back again so he could rearrange his sheets and his nightshirt. And so she could hide the burning on her cheeks.

"May I ask, what caused that wound?"

Josef stayed silent behind her.

"Sir?" She couldn't help but look over her shoulder. Josef had already managed to regain his modesty. His expression, however, had gone tense. He glanced at her, then shook his head. "I am not permitted to discuss it."

She turned around. "You can say nothing?"

"No, I have taken vows—" He stopped and stared into her eyes so intently that she reached up to touch her own face. She winced slightly at the touch. "Forgive me, Maria, but you're injured yourself."

She shook her head and turned away. "It's nothing."

She was a lowly servant. No one else at Gród Narew had showed any interest in the small abrasion where Lukasz had struck her. No one had any concern for it. Why would *he* be the one to notice it?

Her heart caught a bit when he asked, "Did some man strike you?"

"No," she said sharply. Too sharply. The false denial hung in the air between them as obvious as the cut on her face.

"Maria, as a member of the Order, it is my duty to protect the innocent—"

"Nothing. It is nothing. I tripped and fell." She brought him his breakfast and added, "I'm sorry, but I have other duties to perform. May I have your leave?"

"Of course. But are you sure—"

"Thank you, sir." She turned and left him before the lie became an unbearable weight.

I'm sorry, Josef, but I've made vows of my own.

God seemed intent on teaching Josef humility. He had worked very hard to conceal the pain he had felt last night, and had used his past as a talisman to keep his thoughts within the bounds of chastity as Maria bent over his half-naked body and tended to his wounds. As she touched him.

But apparently he was not to be permitted to lull himself with such victories. First there had been Maria's direct challenge. He had not expected the question, though he didn't know why. Maria had no reason to know the details of his obligations, or what he was permitted and not permitted to talk about.

Still, it had caught him off guard.

As had the realization that someone had struck her. He had been so preoccupied with his own pains and pandering to his own modesty that he hadn't even noticed the mark on her cheek and the growing shadow under her eye. It had been so unexpected that he hadn't been able to help blurting it out when he had noticed.

She had snapped the denial at him almost as if in retaliation for his own secrets. He had tried to get her to say more, but had only succeeded in driving her away. Now the dark mood that had gripped him as she'd left gave the lie to his pretensions to virtue.

All he knew was that someone had threatened her, and that once he got his strength back, he was going to teach that person some proper manners.

XI

For the next two days Maria forced herself to be brief in her dealings with Josef. He was recovering, and he needed little in the way of assistance other than her changing the dressing on his wound. She told herself that anything beyond that would be less than proper, for more reasons than she cared to count. More than propriety, though, her lie to him weighed upon her, and every moment with him she felt the wound on her cheek and felt the unspoken question in his eyes.

Who did this?

Why hadn't she told him? Why did a promise to some outlaw long gone by now matter so much to her? Why did it matter at all?

In any case, by shortening her visits to the strictly necessary, Maria was able to walk to and from Gród Narew in daylight. That was more of a concern now that she knew that Lukasz had been banished and might be lurking, awaiting some sort of reprise no matter what Darien might have threatened him with.

Then there was Darien himself. Frightening in his own right...

But an outlaw like that wouldn't stay long within the sight of one of the Duke's fortresses. He was likely far away by now, and she would probably never see him again.

So why had she lied to Josef?

The thought struck her as she entered Josef's room with his supper; perhaps it was a fear that Josef would think less of her, knowing that she received the attentions, however unwanted, of someone like Lukasz.

As she stepped through the door, she told herself that Josef was not one to condemn her for something that was none of her own doing. If she was an honest woman who wished to do fairly by him, she should admit her lie and tell him of both Lukasz and Darien.

Josef must have read something in her face, because he asked her, "Did I offend you, my lady?"

"Sir?" It was hard to conceal how much the question flustered her. *I need to tell him.*

"Ever since I asked about your face, you've been distant. Please forgive me if I was too forward in my question."

The words died in her throat. She could not find the strength within her to admit what had happened. Not only because of Lukasz, but because of Darien. And because if Josef would not condemn her for Lukasz's actions, he certainly would for her dishonesty.

She unconsciously touched her still-tender cheek. The eye above it had grown a shadow of a bruise over the last two days, and still he was the only person who'd seen fit to comment upon it.

"Please, there was nothing wrong with your question," she told him, sick at compounding her lie. "It was an honest mistake."

"It was your affair. I have no place trespassing where I wasn't invited."

Her lies twisted into a sour ball in her stomach. She sucked in a breath and tried to put on a glad face she didn't feel. "I bear no ill will for your concern, sir."

He leaned back and stared at the ceiling. "Is there another reason for your silence, then?"

"I—" How could she answer *that*? "I do have other duties, and they must be occupying my mind as well as my time."

"It is selfish of me," Josef said, "but I spend most of my time alone in this room. The solitude wears on me."

"You've seen none of your fellows?"

"My Komtur has come to pray with me." He smiled weakly. "God forgive me, but while he offers me spiritual strength, fellowship is not his strong suit."

She looked down at him and thought that he had not been the selfish one. She had been avoiding him, preoccupied with her own concerns. She had not once bothered to imagine what it must be like for him.

How would she have felt if someone had treated her father like this? At least, unlike her lies, this was something she could address.

She placed her hand on his, and said, "Why don't you tell me about your Komtur?"

⌖

The tensions of her deception drained from her as she encouraged Josef to talk of himself. He needed little prompting, and listening to his stories were enough to push her own recent past out of her mind. He spoke mostly of the trials of a probationary member of the Order, the strong bonds of obedience, poverty, and chastity he'd sworn himself to. There was a bittersweet tone to his speech, as if abandoning earthly things wasn't so much a vocation as a last resort.

When he talked of his service, Maria thought he spoke much like someone trying to convince himself that he was doing the right thing. She wondered how things might be different had he chosen to serve God some other way. Would the two of them be talking like this? Would she be able to hold his hand?

When he turned to his life in Nürnberg, shadows crossed his face that pained her to see. So when he started asking questions about her life, she answered him more fully and truthfully than she expected, leading him away from that dark place, and overcompensating for the one secret she still kept.

She told him of her farm, her family, and of the death of her father. She told him of her brothers, and of her German stepmother. She told him of her work at Gród Narew. She told him that she was a bastard child of her father and some long-departed mistress.

The words were out before she could think of what she'd said. It had so long been a part of her life, and was so publicly known, that it hadn't occurred to her to hide it. She looked at Josef, trying to gauge his reaction.

What he said surprised her.

"Your father must have loved you very much."

"Why do you say that?"

"Few men acknowledge such children, much less take them into their home. Even then, they usually wait until the child can make their own protests."

Maria touched the cross through her chemise. "He was a strict man, but yes, he loved me."

"I wish I could have met him."

Maria didn't know how to respond to that. What she'd told him should have pushed him away. She was a common peasant—a poor, plain, illegitimate woman. Even his Order's tenets of charity wouldn't require him to treat her as anything more than that.

He is hurt and alone. He has no one to talk to. That is all.

Perhaps it was just who he was. Perhaps when he was well and saw a crippled beggar in the street, he would speak to him just as kindly. Perhaps he was just a good man.

But why did thinking that make her feel worse about herself?

"Is there something wrong?" Josef asked.

Again, she had let her emotions leak into her expression. And, again, she had no words to explain them away. "I think Father might have liked to meet you," she said. She reached up and took her cross out from under her chemise. She held it up, the chain still around her neck. "He gave me this when I was a child."

Josef's eyes narrowed. "May I look at that?"

He held out a hand, and Maria shrank back from him as if he had meant to strike her. "No."

"Maria?"

"I-I promised him I would never take this off." She put the cross away.

"You never take it off?"

"It protects me."

"It protects you?" Josef said in a tone that implied some thought beyond that of a man of God contemplating a holy symbol. "It is silver? The chain as well?"

"My father told me that I had to wear it to keep the Devil away."

"And it has?"

She thought of Lukasz and felt her cheek throb. "Yes. It has."

Josef lowered his hand and nodded. "Then keep it with you, always. I suspect your father was a wise man."

She placed her hand over her heart, pressing the cross into her flesh. "I intend to."

⊕

A silver cross?

Josef's thoughts were uneasy as he watched the light fade from the sky outside his window. He kept thinking of the cross around Maria's neck, and what it might mean. It made him nervous about his own lack of a silver weapon, even in the nominal safety of this fortress. The devil he had faced was very specific, worldly, and deadly.

Could a cross and faith alone be protection from something like that? *For a saint, perhaps.*

He felt torn, deeper than his wounds, for not warning her about what was actually out there, even though to do so would be to go against his pledge of obedience to the Order. He should have said something, anything to convince her to avoid the woods, especially at night.

What did the cross mean?

Did the people here have experience with what the Order hunted? Did they know enough to bear silver talismans against it?

He should be relieved that Maria had at least some protection against the demon out there. But then, why was it so troubling to him?

Because of her talk with Josef, Maria left Gród Narew much later than she had intended to. The sun had just left the sky by the time she stepped onto the path into the woods. She walked into the shadows and stopped, barely into the woods, imagining Lukasz lurking, waiting for her.

It made no sense when she thought rationally. If he had meant to harass her further, these paths weren't greatly traveled. He could have just as easily attacked her in the daylight.

It was just, in the daylight, she could *see* that he wasn't there. As the shadows grew, the larger part of the world around her was given over to her imagination, and of late her imagination had been consumed by fancies dark and terrifying.

I cannot stand here forever.

It was not a long walk if she moved quickly, but it would be interminable if she let fear rule her. So she started walking again, at a brisk pace.

The evening air was cold against her skin, chilled just short of drawing fog from her breath. The footing was dry from a week without rain, and the sound of leaves crackling under her feet soon overwhelmed that of the chirping insects around her. Her pace gradually accelerated until, as she passed the point where Lukasz had attacked her, she was running.

When Darien stepped out of the shadows in front of her, she came to a stumbling stop and thought her heart might burst from the shock.

He didn't move, just stood there a dozen paces from her. He was mostly shadowed, but the moon had risen in a cloudless sky, shining its dappled light through the trees. The moonlight caught random bits of him: the curve of his cheek, hair draped across a shoulder, a pale blue eye.

She turned her lantern to face him; it chased away the shadow but made him even more of an apparition, standing out against the dark woods beyond. "Maria," he said, and the sound of his voice nearly made her gasp. "I told you I would find you again."

"You startled me," she said, clutching her cross over her heart. Seeing him now, she realized that she had managed, over the past two days, to dissuade herself from the attraction she felt. The fact that he was here now was more frightening than anything else. When he stepped forward, she stepped back.

"You didn't expect to see me?" he asked. "After what happened? After we finally met?" The puzzlement in his voice was disturbing, because she didn't understand its origin.

"No. I expected you to return to whatever outlaw stronghold you call home . . ."

"You are injured," he said, sounding shocked. He ran to her side before she could react, cupping her chin to raise her face toward his. "How is it your face is so marred?"

She pulled away and turned from him, hiding tears that were half anger and half grief. "You beast, you know exactly why my face is injured! You saw it happen."

"That was two days ago."

"You mock me now! Leave me."

"No, I'm not wrong," he said quietly to himself. Then, to her: "Maria, do you know what you are?"

"*What* I am?" She spun around and faced him. "*What* I am?" She raised her free hand to strike him as she had Lukasz. "You cad!" She swung, but he caught her hand, wrapping his own hand around her fist almost like a gesture of affection.

His eyes narrowed. "Tell me what you are."

"You're scaring me." Her fist vibrated in his grip, the muscles in her arm straining.

"Tell me, how was it that you could nearly drop that oaf Lukasz with an idle blow? How is it that *I* can barely hold your arm in check, yet you don't know what we are?"

"I don't know what you're talking about!"

"What is that around your neck?" He reached out with his other hand and looped a finger around the chain, pulling her cross out from her chemise.

"*Don't touch that!*" Her left hand swung out, and this time Darien was too distracted to block the blow. The lantern smashed against the side of his head, winking out and splashing sharp-smelling oil.

His head snapped back, and he took a backward step, letting go of her other hand.

She darted out of reach, grabbing her cross.

Darien rubbed oil off his now-shadowed face as he looked at her. "Why do you wear that thing? Don't you know what it means?"

"It protects me."

"It *protects* you? Who told you such nonsense? A priest? One of those pathetic German monks?"

"My father."

"Your . . . *father?*"

Maria replaced the cross under her chemise and straightened herself in case Darien came close again.

Instead he shook his head. "You don't just live with them. You were raised by them. They never told you where you came from, or what you are, did they?"

"And what would a stranger, an outlaw like you, know of who or what I am? You think me a whore because of Lukasz?"

Darien laughed, the sound nearly terrifying in its intensity.

"Is my virtue so amusing?" she asked quietly.

He choked off the laugh. "Maria, you have convinced me that you *do* have no idea what it is I am talking about. I've never dreamed of finding you at all, much less so . . . unenlightened."

She started edging toward the side of the path. She was fast; if she slipped by him, she could probably outrun him. "Enlighten me then," she said, trying to keep him focused on the conversation and not on her.

"It's simple. Just remove that trinket."

The suggestion caught her off guard. She shook her head and gave him a curt "No." There was little else he might have asked that could so strongly convince her of his ill intent.

"You never remove it, do you? Your *protection.*" His tone gave the word such contempt that it was as vile in her ears as the worst blasphemy. "What do you think it protects you from?"

You. "The Devil."

"And how many people around you wear such a thing? Your father, perhaps? The cattle that tend to that obnoxious pile of stone and wood on the hillside you walk to every day? Your departed friend Lukasz? Have you ever asked why it was that you alone required such protection?"

Her heart raced. Why? Why not her stepmother, her brothers? Why *did* her father give this to her? "Shut up!" she yelled at him.

"You are special, Maria. You're different from those others, even if you don't know it. That thing protects *them*, not you. They use those silver chains to drag you down."

She ran, dodging around him, and he made no move to stop her.

"You're better than they are," he called after her. "You must know that. Take it off!"

XII

You're better than they are.

The words echoed strangely in Maria's head as she lay on her bed. Her brothers snored below, and the moon shone through cracks in the shutters to cast a pale blue light around the cottage.

Do you know what you are?

"What I am?" she whispered to herself. "What am I?"

She compiled a list: woman, Christian, Pole, servant, daughter, sister, virgin, bastard... Did Darien mean any of those things, or none of them?

And why was the cross so important to him? To Josef, too, it seemed. Was such a thing so unusual?

What would happen if she did take it off?

She felt it under her nightclothes, pressing into her skin. She fingered the small piece of metal, sliding it along the chain that looped around her neck.

She'd seen terrified anger in her father's eyes when he had asked, "Why did you take it off?"

What would happen?

Her heart thudded, accelerating. She had never questioned it, the long habit of wearing this cross. She had never felt it weigh her down.

But she'd never questioned why only she had to wear it.

She pulled the cross out so that it dangled in front of her face. Josef was right. Her father had loved her and wanted her to be safe. The cross protected her.

That thing protects them.

Darien's voice was like a worm in her brain.

You are special.

"I'm not special," she whispered. "There is not one thing special or unique about me."

Then why was she the only one who wore this?

Why did God need help to protect her from the Devil?

She closed the cross in her fist and prayed. The prayer was short, almost violent: "Lord, let me know *why.*"

Her heart thudded in her ears, and sweat plastered her bedclothes to her skin. Her breaths came shallow and hot, and her hand squeezed the cross hard enough for the corners to bite into her palm. She slowly sat up in bed, and for a moment the air felt so still that it seemed even to mute her brothers' snoring.

"God protects me," she whispered. "Not this."

She pulled the chain up over her head quickly, as if afraid that she might change her mind. She sat at the edge of her bed, her head a few fingers' breadths from the rough-hewn rafters supporting the thatch roof.

She froze, waiting for the Devil to come claim her for defying her father. "God," she whispered, "keep your child safe."

The cross dangled from her fingers on its silver chain. Her palm stung where sweat seeped into the cuts she'd made by pressing the cross into her palm. The skin of her neck felt strange without the weight of the cross pulling against her. She held it up in front of her and looked at it. A plain silver cross on a plain silver chain.

She wondered if it had belonged to her mother.

Could that be it? Could this cross tie her to some other family, perhaps nobility? Could Darien have meant that when he'd spoken of her being special, better than everyone else?

When the Devil persisted in his nonappearance, she lay back on her bed, still holding up the cross and staring at it, trying to divine its mysteries.

And she fell asleep before she could replace it around her neck.

Darien ran though the midnight-dark woods, his muzzle pulled back in a snarl of frustration.

She doesn't know.

The first time he had found a potential mate, a potential family, and she was so fully corrupted by her human keepers that she wasn't even aware of what she was. The silver chain around her neck was more limiting than any prison humans might make for his kind.

And more frustrating because it was self-imposed.

He reached the edge of the woods, in sight of the castle where the Germans had retreated. He stood on all fours, panting, tongue lolling. He had run so fast, so intently, that his body had reacted, reducing his hands to forepaws. Right now, should anyone from the fortress walls see him here, they would see only the outline of a wolf. Albeit, a wolf that stood chest-high to a tall man.

He stared up at the hillside and thought of the men inside.

Should I pursue her to the exclusion of my purpose here?

It was the Germans that had brought him here, not Maria. But would revenge have the same meaning if he wasn't alone? He sucked in the night air and could still smell the burnt flesh of his family.

No, the meaning *had* changed. Vengeance could no longer be the soul of his purpose. Now there was another; there was someone for him to protect.

It was no longer a game. He couldn't plan how to toy with them, how to hurt them, how to lead them though unfamiliar territory where they could feel the fear he had once known.

His plans had to change.

Maria panicked when she woke and her cross wasn't around her neck. She sat up in the predawn darkness, remembering her reflections of the night before. She had fallen asleep with it in her hand, but at some point during the night, she had let go of it. After several moments of panicked searching, she finally spotted it, between the bed and the wall.

Her breath caught: the chain had hung up on a peg projecting from the bed frame, and that had kept it from sliding down a crack between the floor of the loft and the wall. It would have been so easy to dislodge it and send it into the hole, where she would never be able to extract it.

She reached for it carefully, thanking God that it hadn't been lost in the crevice. Her fingers brushed the chain, and it came free of the peg instantly. She didn't expect it, and her hand snapped shut.

She caught it before it fell.

She pulled it free and replaced it around her neck. Her meeting with Darien had the hazy aspect of a half-remembered dream, and she wondered why she had been so driven to tempt fate. Even Josef had told her to keep wearing this . . .

And even if the Devil wasn't literally going to pounce on her the moment she removed it, that didn't mean it was wise to lose it. Not to mention the disrespect it would show to her father's spirit.

She sucked in a breath and told herself it was over. She had chores to do.

⌖

By the time she was performing her duties at Gród Narew, the wound on her palm ached badly enough that she had to tie a dressing around it.

It was a constant reminder of a night she was trying to forget. Her frustration must have shown on her face. It seemed every time she caught someone's attention, they looked at her strangely. The first few times, she wiped her face, expecting to find a streak of grease or dirt.

It wasn't until she brought Josef his morning meal that she understood what everyone seemed to be noticing. When she set the bowl down by his bed, he sat up with more vigor than she would have given him credit for. "Maria, your face."

She sighed and pulled a cleaning rag from where she stuffed them inside her surcote. She wiped her face with it and asked, "Have I gotten it now?"

His face had gone pale and, for the briefest moment, she thought she saw an echo of her father's fear in his eyes. "Your bruise."

She froze as she realized that, again, she had unwittingly done something bad. Her hand stopped moving as she felt the fear infecting her. Then, with the rag pressed into her face, she realized something.

Her cheek didn't ache. She didn't feel the tight swelling of flesh under her eye. Her fingers didn't touch the rough pepper of dried blood dusting the wound on her cheek. She lowered the rag and said, as calmly as she could manage, "My bruise?"

"It's gone."

That was what everyone had been staring at. They didn't care to mention it when it suddenly appeared, but if it disappears . . .

Maria shook her head. "It has been days since I fell. It's just been healing."

"You had a shadow as dark as pitch beneath that eye—"

"You exaggerate."

"—and now it is completely gone."

She tried to hide her fear and confusion. "It just healed, that's all. It wasn't as bad as you remember it."

He stared into her face, as if looking for any sign of her injury. His expression frightened her, almost as if he was looking past her, to something else. She was afraid he was looking at the same thing her father had been the night he died.

She couldn't keep her hand from reaching for her face again.

"What happened to your hand?" he asked.

She shook her head and held up her bandaged palm. "I cut it last night, by accident. It isn't worrisome."

His eyes narrowed with a hint of unaccountable suspicion. "May I look at it?"

"It's nothing."

"I allow you to see my scar on a daily basis."

Maria sighed and held out her hand. "The battles I fight are not nearly as epic as yours. I do not think I am in danger from this."

He unwrapped the dressing and looked down into her palm. The two points where the cross had dug in were barely scabbed over. One small wound cut painfully into one of the creases in her palm, and wept watery blood when she forced her hand flat.

He stared at it for a long time. And, strangely, the tension seemed to leak out of him.

"Might I have my hand back?"

"Yes." As he wrapped the dressing back around it, he whispered, "Forgive me," as if apologizing for something much more grave than holding her hand for a moment too long.

When he returned her hand, he asked, "You have lived here, next to this fortress, all your life?"

Even though his character had returned to normal, Maria thought that his question resonated with Darien's speech from last night. Not in its sense, perhaps, but in its tone. As if Josef, as well as Darien, knew something about her past that she did not. She took her bandaged hand away and said, "You know I have. I told you all there is to know about me."

"Did your father ever warn you of anything to beware of, in the woods here?"

Is that the fear you shared with my father?

"In the woods?" she responded, thinking of Darien. Who *was* he? What was it he presumed to know about her? "He lived here all his life as a woodsman and a farmer. Of course he warned me about all kinds of things—wild animals, deadfalls, toxic plants, berries, mushrooms—. Is there something you're concerned about?" She paused, then asked, "Some*one*?"

Josef looked uncomfortable and said, "I am concerned for your safety, Maria. You shouldn't be traveling in the darkness."

"What is it that frightens you? Is it what attacked you?"

"Forgive me. I'm not permitted to speak of it."

"Why?"

"I've told you, I'm sworn to obey my superiors in the Order."

"That isn't what I meant," Maria said. "I meant, if there is some danger out there, why would your Order command you to keep it secret?"

Josef shook his head. For some reason, Maria thought of her father, and how he had never explained the significance of the cross he'd made her wear. Why would Josef's masters explain such things to him if he was already pledged to obey them?

"Forgive me," Maria said. "That was an impertinent question. I should go to my other duties. I will see you this evening."

As she walked though the doorway, Josef said, "Maria?"

She turned around. "Yes?"

"If I haven't told you before, thank you."

She felt her cheeks become warm, which made her uncomfortably aware of the missing wound. "You're welcome," she said and left quickly, without finding out exactly what Josef was thankful for.

⊕

As Josef watched her leave, he felt the clash of his own emotions. Knowing what he did of the demons the Wolfjägers hunted, the quick healing of her face had filled him with wild, panicked speculations, despite the silver cross she wore. But the mundane cuts in her hand gave the lie to his unfair suspicion, as did the fact that she had borne the marks on her face for days. No, his brief mistrust was wrong, and unfair to her. Maria was a good woman, and these things were evil.

What troubled him nearly as much was the fact that he had almost broken his silence. What he had told Maria came close to disobedience in spirit, if not in specifics. And her final question had fired a doubt in him that burned worse than the wound in his belly.

He didn't eat his breakfast. Instead, he got slowly out of bed and began to dress himself. Some servant of Gród Narew had washed and repaired his surcote with the partial black cross of the Order, the lower arm now scarred by stitched repairs and some stains that had faded against the white. They had taken his mail, but there were hose and a shirt for him to wear, along with his belt, complete with empty scabbard and a few tooth marks.

He had to take several breaks as he dressed himself. It wasn't pain. His wound was a constant ache squeezing his stomach, and the level of discomfort didn't vary enough to be noticeable.

No, what occupied his time was the exhaustion. Every movement was tiring, every piece of clothing felt too heavy, and every small task seemed Herculean. But, after a long, laborious effort, he was able to finally go abroad in Gród Narew.

⌖

He found Komtur Heinrich leading a service for his more able-bodied brothers in a small chapel lent by their Polish hosts. He joined the service at the back of the room, feeling comfort in the communal devotion. He had felt too alone lately. It helped him remember that there were others taking this path with him.

It also made him reconsider his doubts. If Heinrich hadn't caught his eye at the end of the service, he might have left with Maria's impertinent questions unasked.

But Heinrich did see him, and called out, "Josef," as his brothers filed out of the room.

Josef walked slowly to the front of the room. Heinrich was not particularly generous with his expressions of emotion, but his lips turned up slightly in as much of a smile as Josef had ever seen the Komtur wear. "Yes, sir?"

"You are walking. I didn't expect a recovery so fast."

"In truth, I am still burdened by this wound. But I wished to talk to you."

"What of?"

"Things best spoken of in private."

"I see. Come with me then." Heinrich led him out of the

chapel, then outside, walking slowly to accommodate Josef's sluggish movements. "You've been confined so long that the open air should do you some good."

They walked through the open courtyards under a blue summer sky that was marred by only a few gray wisps of rain clouds to the west. The sun was warm on Josef's skin, and the air was like a cool drink of water after the confined stench of his sickroom. When Heinrich reached a spot close to the wall and empty of people, he turned and asked, "What is it that troubled you enough to make you leave your bed?"

"The creatures we hunt: are they native solely to the Prussian wilds?"

"What prompts you to ask that question?"

"A servant here, one who lives beyond the walls, in a farm past these woods. Her father gave her a silver cross, in her words, 'to protect her.'"

"You think it means that such beasts reside in these woods."

"It made me consider that."

"I am glad you brought this concern to me. These wolfbreed we fight, you will find legends of their existence as common as wolves themselves. But I caution you not to draw conclusions in haste. The reality is much rarer than the legend. Do not hunt for new paths until our current journey is completed. The beast that wounded you is still abroad."

"That is the other question I wished to ask of you."

"Yes?"

"The beast we hunt could be devastating another village while we remain here, impotent. Right now it may be feasting on innocent flesh."

"That is the nature of fighting evil. No man or group of men can confront it all, everywhere, at once. God only gives us the power to act when and where we can."

"Then why not warn the people? We might not be there, but if the farmer in the village had as much as a silver-clad dagger rather than a scythe—"

Heinrich laid a hand upon Josef's shoulder and said, "It troubles you, our secrecy. It is a fact that the demands of the Order's vows are not easy. Not mentally, not physically, and not spiritually. I find it difficult myself. But there is a reason that might make the burden easer to bear." Heinrich let go of his shoulder and took a few steps away from him to face the outer wall. "Do you know what happened in Strasbourg four years ago?"

"Yes, I do."

"When the pestilence first made itself known, the pope saw what might happen. God saw fit to send the angel of death abroad in the land, and the masses, like the pharaoh's people in Egypt, failed to see it as the hand of God. When Pope Clement spoke and said that those who blamed the Jew were seduced by the lies of the Devil, who listened? The mob in Strasbourg burned thousands, in direct opposition to the Church and the will of God. I heard tell that even some priests and bishops were caught up in the madness." Heinrich turned to look at Josef. "You have a charitable heart, and you believe these are good people, innocent people. But you *must* remember that there are some truths that are too stark. We are all tainted by sin, and when something truly fearsome is presented to a mob weak in faith and spirit, they will not consider. They will *act*."

"Do you imagine that these beasts are as fearful as the pestilence?"

"Random death without warning that can walk among men unseen? Perhaps the Poles here do not have enough Jews around to blame, but unquestionably, if we warned the mass of common people of the threat, we would have dozens of 'wolfbreed' corpses. The man who doesn't shave well, the leper, the man who lives alone on the hill and goes out too often at night, the man who attends Mass less often than his neighbor, the man who once spooked a groom's horse . . ."

"I see."

"Remember, we are to protect men's souls from this beast, as well as their lives."

"Then when do we return to doing so?"

Heinrich glanced over Josef's shoulder. "Go back to your bed and regain your strength. I suspect the man approaching us will lead me to an answer."

XIII

After nearly an hour of searching, Telek found Brother Heinrich talking to one of the members of his Order in a courtyard by the outer wall. He had just arrived with the Duke, the bishop, and their combined entourage, which was probably still sorting itself out in front of the main fortress. The Duke had a score of men with him, and the bishop had ten of his own. Between the two they had brought three wagons of supplies, chests, and clothing.

It would probably be late evening before every horse was stabled and every man quartered.

However, his uncle had made a point of saying that Brother Heinrich needed to be present the moment the bishop was ready to receive him, and the Duke had been no less adamant. As soon as he found Heinrich, he took him back to the great hall, where Siemowit III was to hold court. The crowd was already assembling, and Telek left his charge with a trio of the bishop's men.

With Heinrich in their care, he went off to find his uncle. Instead, his uncle found him, grabbing his arm as he left the great hall and pulling him into a corridor that led toward the kitchens.

"Uncle?"

"I pray your travels were uneventful?" Bolesław said as he led

Telek down the corridor, away from the mass of people gathering to greet the Duke and begin the business of the court.

"Yes," he said. "But why are you heading toward the kitchens?"

"Because, nephew, stealth and subtlety are not your strong suits."

"Pardon me?" They passed by the arch leading to the kitchens, from which came the smells of cookfires, roasting meat, and baking bread as a dozen servants worked at long tables preparing the grand feast that would be the Duke's welcoming meal.

"I have a task for you, and it would be best that our German guests not see you do it." He stopped Telek in front of a narrow spiral staircase. "Forgive me," he said, "but I probably should ask your willingness."

"Whatever you wish of me. You know that, Uncle."

Bolesław slapped him on the back. "No harm in the asking." He pointed up the stairs. "If you go up here, the third door opens across from the first guest chamber. Do try to avoid being seen entering and leaving."

"And what do you want me to do in Brother Heinrich's chambers?"

"Take advantage of your schooling. There is a book there, not a missal or Bible, I think, and I would care to have some idea of its contents."

"You wish me to take it?"

Bolesław shook his head. "Remember, I said *subtlety.* What use is going in without being seen if he knows you were there the moment he looks for his missing tome? No, go in, disturb his rooms as little as possible, and read as much of the book as you can. Court and feast will occupy the Germans for the remainder of the day, should they wish it or not. You should have time to make good sense of the book's contents, if not read the whole of it."

"And if I cannot find this book, or if it is not in a language I understand?"

Bolesław shrugged. "Then slip out and return to the court. If I see you, I'll know what happened, and we shan't speak of it again." He left Telek by the stairs. "I must return before business begins, so get to work."

Telek watched his uncle disappear down the servants' corridor, leaving him alone. He sighed and looked up the stairway. He wondered what suspicion had taken hold of his uncle's fancy this time, or if in the absence of plot and intrigue, his uncle felt the need to provide some. But Telek served at the pleasure of the Wojewoda Bolesław, and should his lord ask him to rifle a monk's library, so be it.

He climbed the stairway and eased open the door across from the German's guest apartments. No one was in evidence along the corridor.

He crept through the door and gave his uncle silent credit for choosing the right time for such skulduggery. Right now, all the nobles would be attending the Duke's court, and all the servants would be busy providing for it and the subsequent feast. The only hole Telek saw in his uncle's plot was the possibility that someone might note his nephew's absence.

Though Telek suspected that any inquiry would have Wojewoda Bolesław's nephew engaged on some mundane task that wouldn't arouse anyone's curiosity.

He slipped into the monk's apartments and shut the door behind him.

⌖

The book was not difficult to locate. It sat on the desk, wrapped in a pearl-white cloth covered by interlocking crosses embroidered with golden thread. He gently unfolded the cloth to reveal a book with a delicately tooled cover. The device of the Teutonic Knights was inset into crawling vines and flowering plants that had been embossed onto the brown leather.

Despite his uncle's suspicions, Telek's initial thought was that this was some sort of devotional book. The first few pages of delicately inked script did not dissuade him. The first few psalms in Vulgate Latin gave the appearance of a book of hours.

He turned the pages with care, not expecting much more.

But a few pages in, he stopped. The text changed from the psalms—the writing was still Vulgate, but in a smaller, more controlled hand. The page itself was different, closely written, with small, angled margins that spoke to being removed from some prior book and rebound into this one. Facing the new text was a miniature painting showing a monk at a scribal bench, wearing robes bearing the black cross of the Order. At the monk's feet, a sword lay wrapped in some sort of animal skin.

The words across from the studious monk read:

These are the observations of Brother Semyon, knight of the Holy Order of the Hospital of St. Mary of the Germans at Jerusalem, written by order of His Holiness, Pope Gregory IX, this year of Our Lord one thousand two hundred and thirty one, and with the intent of illuminating the nature of those creatures discovered a decade past, within the pagan wilds of Burzenland, south of the Carpathian Mountains.

Telek arched an eyebrow as he worked his way through the Latin text. He found it somewhat harder because the words were not familiar biblical verses, and because the writing was so cramped.

But it was clear that he was not looking at a typical book of hours. He was reading a copy of a report from the Teutonic Order to the pope over a hundred years ago, before the Germans had pacified half the pagan wild that was now the Monastic State to the north. As usual, his uncle's instincts had proved sound.

He turned the page and sucked in a breath at a monstrous illustration. A demon with a massive snarling wolf's head faced him. It stood upright on a wolf's legs, ending in massive splayed paws, and it was covered in shaggy brown fur. Its arms were long and ended in clawed, half-human hands, one of which held a severed human leg, which it gnawed upon. It stood in front of a dark cave piled high with human bones.

These beasts, which I have called wolfbreed to distinguish from the natural wolf, parts of whose aspect they borrow, have several unique attributes that separate them from other worldly creatures. It is important to first establish from what sphere of God's creation they arise. While fearsome they may be, it is clear from several points that they are of earthly matter. Primarily this is shown by the mortality of these beasts. They are birthed, they age, and they die to have their flesh decay as any other worldly being, man or beast.

Likewise, it can be shown that, despite the appearance of human-seeming aspects to their nature, these beasts are not humans possessed, as some might argue. Rites of exorcism show no power over them or their changes; nor has there been discovered any of these beasts that were not birthed to be what they were by any mother that was other than what they were.

Telek stared at the passage. He had heard travelers' tales of any manner of strange men and beasts. Men with mouths in their stomachs or skin black as coal; horses with horns growing from their noses. Giants. Dwarfs . . . He had even heard, on occasion, stories of men who could become beasts at will.

Of course, most such tales were told by some wit who had heard tell of the tale from someone who had heard the tale told by someone who might have once met someone who had known someone who had actually seen such a thing. Of things that moved in the world, Telek trusted his own eyes and ears more than any story. He had known too many drunkards in his life.

But the character of this tale was different, and not only because it was written in the book of a warrior monk who should have little interest in these travelers' tales. There was something to Brother Semyon's words—an absence of anything that might be called passion or awe at the telling. For all the vitality of Brother Semyon's words, he might have just as well been describing the proper aspects of cheese making.

Telek skipped to the next page, and the illustration there was even more disturbing: the same scene, the same skull-strewn cave. Only instead of a brown-furred monster, a naked man stood in a similar posture, still holding a severed human leg. The blood on the man's chin was angry scarlet against his pale white skin.

> *We now proceed with the confident knowledge that these creatures are a natural-born part of God's creation. They are a beast like any other, but one that can at will disguise itself as a man. Also, like any beast, they are deadly to man when wild and untrained.*

Telek wondered, now, exactly what had attacked the Germans. The dead and wounded had borne marks of tooth and claw from some monstrous animal. Was the wolfbreed of Brother Semyon's words the same beast that the Order had faced, and had they fought such a thing in Masovia?

The phrase "wild and untrained" hung uncomfortably in his mind.

So we now turn to cataloging the unique aspects of this creature, those that differentiate it from both wolf and man.

In first, it is marked by extraordinary strength and endurance in all forms it presents. Even when appearing as an unarmed human child, a beast such as this can overpower a fully armored human warrior. They can outrun any lesser prey, and their ability to leap exceeds that of all other animals I have studied.

These animals also heal extremely quickly from any cutting, crushing, or burning wounds. Simple cuts in the flesh seal themselves in seconds. Crushing wounds and damage from fire take only slightly longer. Such a beast may lose a limb and find it grown back in a fraction of an hour.

Of course, the main distinguishing feature of the wolfbreed, and the source of their utility, is their ability to change their outward form as they will between that of a man and that of a wolflike thing with the posture and mobility of a man. As the latter has no twin in nature, we may consider this form their natural state.

"'And the source of their utility'?" Telek repeated the Vulgate, uncertain if he understood the meaning. *Utility for what?* The passage had an additional note in a hand different from Brother Semyon's. It was hard to decipher, as the writing was not from one trained as a scribe, and it was German rather than Vulgate. When Telek translated the words as best he could, it read something like: *Brother Gregor reports that those of Semyon's wolfbreed he has seen can also take on the aspect of a true wolf to hide themselves in the wilds . . .*

He turned the pages, scanning the text as fast as he could

while still managing to form sense out of it. Brother Semyon expounded upon the "wolfbreed" at length and exhaustively, writing in such detail that Telek had to assume that the monk had direct personal knowledge of these things.

Some passages were written as if Semyon himself had carried out the tests—battering the creatures' legs to see how quickly and perfectly the bones would knit back together. And when he spoke of cutting flesh, it was with uncomfortably close attention to the effect upon male circumcision and a virgin's maidenhead.

The illustrations, likewise, became more bloody and graphic as he progressed—especially when he came upon the itemization of these creatures' weaknesses. When Brother Semyon wrote, "*The preternatural healing of these beasts does have precise limits. Any damage that destroys the brain or heart, or severs its connection to the body, shall be mortal to these creatures,*" the miniature facing it showed a decapitated wolf thing, its bloody lupine head resting in its lap. Next to it, and more disturbing, was a naked woman's body with a hole carved between the breasts.

Other limits were enumerated with similarly grotesque illustrations. The wolfbreed required air, so they were susceptible to drowning. They could also be burned to death if held within a large enough fire, as the fire would burn the flesh faster than they might heal. But the most important limit was their vulnerability to silver.

Not only could silver chains bind these creatures, but contact with the metal would halt their changes as well as limit their healing prowess to that of a normal creature. And wounds inflicted upon them by a silvered blade wouldn't heal much faster than like wounds inflicted on any other creature.

The text left Telek with little question about what had attacked these Germans. Even without the wounds that had come from some large predatory animal, they had the weapons of silver.

A treasure of the metal strapped to the sides of men who had ostensibly taken a vow of poverty.

Telek cursed at the arrogance of it all. How could an honest Christian man chase something like this into someone else's lands, then refuse to speak of it?

What were they hiding?

⌖

It was late evening when Telek slipped from Heinrich's apartments. Since he was only the length of a corridor from his uncle's private rooms, he went there to remain unobserved and wait for the Wojewoda Bolesław. He propped himself in a chair, folded his hands together, and fell into a weak, troubled sleep.

His uncle came in sometime after nightfall and woke him from fitful dreams of devil-wolves.

"So my nephew has spent the evening lazing about rather than entertaining my guests?" There was humor in his voice, but it was colored by something darker.

Telek stretched until his joints popped. "Dear Uncle, I did not wish to appear before your guests and complicate whatever explanation you had given for my absence."

"Good instincts you have, my boy." Bolesław walked around to a chair facing Telek's and dropped into it with a grunt. He shook his head and pointed at his nephew with the folded piece of parchment he carried. "So did you learn anything useful, or did you use this only as an opportunity to nap through the Duke's court?"

Telek leaned forward and nodded. "I learned what they are hunting."

"Ah." His uncle smiled wider than usual, showing the gaps in his scarred jawline. "Tell me, and we can see how closely your knowledge aligns with the tales our guest deigned to tell the bishop."

"This is a bit extraordinary."

"Go on. After this night, I expect no less."

"Well, from what I read, there is a century-old group within the Order that calls itself the Wolfjägers . . ."

Telek told his uncle about Brother Semyon's wolfbreed creatures, repeating their strengths and weaknesses as he had read them. Once he had given a full accounting of what the creatures were, his uncle grunted and glanced at the parchment in his hand.

"You have presented much more detail on what it is they hunt." He handed the parchment to Telek, who immediately noticed the papal seal next to a signature.

"Brother Heinrich was kind enough to lend me his letter of authority, once the bishop encouraged him to," Bolesław explained.

Telek scanned the letter. It gave the Wolfjägers of the German Order papal authority to travel without let or hindrance through all Christian lands in their pursuit of agents of the Devil. Telek lowered the parchment and said, "Agents of the Devil? Isn't that a somewhat vague premise on which to invade Masovia?"

"I think Brother Heinrich recognized that, which is why, I suspect, our guest hesitated in producing this letter. Apparently they are pledged to secrecy on the exact nature of these demonic forces but are permitted to discuss such with high officers of the Church." He leaned over and took the parchment. "Of course, after his audience with Bishop Leszek, I asked as much. But now the bishop shows a similar reluctance to deal with the details of the matter. A 'wolflike demon abroad in the land' was as close to a description as I was given."

"I see. And is the Duke satisfied with this?"

"I left the bishop in conference with the Duke, who has the final say, of course."

"Of course."

"I suspect he may allow the Order's men some freedom, in deference to the diplomatic delicacy of the issue. However, my long experience with the Order inclines me toward suspicion." Telek's uncle looked thoughtful for a moment. "I must admit, your tale seems to belie that. It is indeed some great evil that they are searching for." Bolesław's gray brows wrestled above his nose as his eyes narrowed. "But your face tells me that there is more to this."

"Uncle, I base my suspicions on a single hasty reading of a single book. But I believe that the Order may in fact be chasing a demon of their own creation."

Bolesław snorted. "Are you saying these men of God are in league with Satan? I have no love for these troublesome monks, but even I don't easily see them as practicing diabolism."

"That is not what I am suggesting."

"You just informed me that these monks created this wolf-demon they're hunting."

"Much in the same way the Duchy of Masovia is responsible for creating the Teutonic State that so annoys us."

Telek's uncle leaned back and looked at him silently for a moment. Telek could almost see all the permutations of his suggestion playing out on his uncle's face, until he said, "You mean something inadvertently unleashed?"

"An attempt to use something that they were unable to control," Telek said. "The text betrayed knowledge that by necessity must have been gleaned from contact with many of these creatures. There is talk of how these things could be trained, Uncle. Like a dog or a warhorse."

"They would corrupt themselves by using demonic forces?"

"According to the Brother Semyon who authored this treatise, these beings are not demonic, any more so than any other worldly beast. And, if the words are to be believed, his interpretations had the favor of the pope."

Bolesław held up his parchment. "The pope doesn't seem to hold so anymore."

"There's a gap in the book between the notes of Brother Semyon and those of another scribe who did not name himself. Afterward, there is no reference to Brother Semyon, or to what he did to acquire his knowledge of the wolfbreed. However, the other scribe's observations do contradict Brother Semyon's original interpretation. In the last third of the book, the wolfbreed are clearly portrayed as the work of Satan."

"So perhaps Semyon was mistaken."

"When you hear this change of heart, that is your first conclusion?"

Bolesław sighed. "No, it is not. I may hesitate to see the German Order meddling in the black arts, but I have little trouble believing that they would throw a diabolism shroud over an embarrassing mistake."

"What shall we do?"

Bolesław laughed. "Leadership, my nephew, is in part knowing when to do nothing."

"We should inform the Duke."

"Why? I may serve my liege, but this knowledge—aside from the debatable means of its acquisition—will gain him little. These are his lands, and the Order will wish not to provoke him more than they have already. He has all the power he needs, papal letter or not."

"But why keep it secret?"

"Because the Order is also on my land, and there may come a time when we want slightly more than the threat of the Duke's hand behind us."

XIV

After serving her duties at the feast for the Duke, Maria came late to Josef's room. As soon as she entered, she saw that his clothing had been moved, then tossed casually aside. Josef lay in his bed, flushed and sweating.

"You got out of bed."

Josef turned his head, as if he had just noticed her arrival. "I needed to talk to my Komtur. I went walking for a bit."

"You aren't healed enough for that." She ran to his bedside, setting down the supper tray she had brought him from the feast. She pulled aside the bedding and the nightshirt to see his wound. Josef made only a token protest, grabbing her wrist but putting little force behind it.

"I am fine," he said. "It was just tiring."

She took off the dressing and said, "I am surprised you haven't pulled this open again." She didn't want to admit it, but he was healing much better than she had expected. The scar was red, but unbroken and free of discharge.

"See?" he said. He leaned back and stared out at the window as she replaced his dressing with a clean one.

"You need to take more care," she told him, placing a hand on his chest. She could feel his heart under her fingers, strong but too fast. She bent over to look into his face. "I don't want you to hurt yourself."

"It's late," he said, placing his hand on hers. "You're very late today."

She flushed at the contact. "The Duke's visit has kept everyone busy."

"I missed your company."

He squeezed her hand, and she felt her heart race ahead of his. Suddenly his skin felt very warm, and she didn't think it was from fever or exertion.

Then he let go and said, "But you must go. Now."

She drew back, his words feeling like a slap on her face. "What?"

He sat up, even though the pain it caused him was visible. "Please, go now. Go home before the sun sets. Don't face these woods after nightfall, I beg of you. And please don't ask me why."

She saw pain and fear in his eyes and said, "You're scaring me."

"Good."

"Josef?"

"Please, now. There is nothing more important for you to attend to here."

The intensity of his words, and of his look, pushed her away. "As you wish," she said, backing out of the room.

She left wondering if, somehow, he knew about Darien.

Even so, there was little chance of her leaving before nightfall. The feasting had still been ongoing when she had brought Josef his meal. She couldn't go until the revelers themselves had decided that the evening had concluded. So when she left Gród Narew, the sun had long since set.

Once she had no work to occupy her, her thoughts drifted to

her face. On her way out, she stepped through one of the display halls where the devices of many allied clans hung on the walls: the threefold cross of Bojcza, the double-headed arrow of Bogorya, the cross-studded horseshoe of Dabrowa, the split-tailed cross of Kostrowiec.

What stopped her wasn't the collection of arcane glyphs of the many clans allied with Wojewoda Bolesław but the weapons on display between the painted shields and banners. The blades had been polished before being set to peacetime rest in this hallway, and she could observe her reflection in the flat of an axe blade.

Her face was clearly unmarked.

It made no sense to her. Yesterday her eye had been inflamed, her cheek livid with the bruise from Lukasz's blow. Josef had been right to wonder. But perhaps she had been mistaken about the severity of her bruise, because it was clearly healed now.

It took an effort of will not to rub her cheek, drawing even more attention to her sudden healing, as she left the fortress.

Outside, the night was starless and without a moon. Dense clouds glowed a dull silver, giving the landscape an unearthly aspect beyond her lantern's reach. She walked to the edge of the woods, thinking of Josef. His warnings frightened her, but some other part of her welcomed his concern. She had spent so long being burdensome, irrelevant, beneath notice, that just an interest in her welfare from someone without any obligation to care was comforting.

If only . . .

But even though she could still feel Josef's heartbeat beneath her fingertips, she didn't finish the thought, because there was nowhere good it might lead.

When a man finally took her, it would not be someone young or handsome or noble. Her marriage would be to an old widower looking for someone to care for his children or his household. The best she might hope for would be some measure of kindness.

She walked home on the path, her mood darker than the woods around her. Was that her life? Was that all she could look forward to? A reward in Heaven? And what would she have before then?

Perhaps she should follow Josef's example and join a holy order.

With her downcast mood, it wasn't surprising when Darien chose to reveal himself.

Why are you haunting me? she thought when she saw his lithe, muscular form stride out of the woods in front of her. She stopped walking and they stood facing each other, just a few steps beyond arm's reach. For several moments, the only sound came from the wind rustling through the treetops.

The woods always turn silent around him.

"So you took it off, didn't you?" he said finally.

She caught her breath, then placed her hand over her heart, holding the cross, and shook her head. "No, I didn't." *I'm still wearing it. It's still protecting me.*

"Lies do not become you," he said. "The marks on your face are gone."

She touched the side of her face where Lukasz had struck her.

"Do you understand yet?" he asked.

"Understand? You talk in riddles that don't make sense! How could I possibly understand?"

He took a step forward, his smile sharply underlit by her lantern's flame. "I told you, Maria. That chain around your neck keeps you imprisoned. You remove it, even momentarily, and you become much more than you think you are."

"What do you mean? Why is my bruise gone?"

"It is gone because you chose, however briefly, to be who you really are. It means that you need only cast off your chains and you can become as free as I. It means we're fated, sweet Maria."

He reached up and gently touched her cheek. The feeling of his skin against hers sent a jolt through her body. He looked down at her and said, "I have been looking for you for a long, long time."

She sucked in a breath and whispered, "Are you the Devil?" She wondered if, right now, she cared what the answer was.

Darien laughed and shook his head. "I have nothing to do with God or the Devil, or anything so common from the world of men."

His hand slid back, caressing the nape of her neck and sending shudders down the length of her body. She breathed in his scent and felt the muscles in her legs melt like wax in the sun. His face was now so close that his breath danced across her lips as he spoke. "You must know how much better you are than the rest of them. You're stronger, faster. You can endure so much more than they can, even with their chains on you. You must know how beautiful you are."

You lie, she thought. *But they're such lovely lies.*

He brought his other hand around her back, pulling her gently toward him. She let go of the cross and touched his chest. His shirt was loose and open down the front, and her hand slid in to touch skin. She felt downy hair, and a warmth that almost burned. She felt him breathe.

Then she remembered Josef's skin under her hand, the feeling of Josef taking breath. And something in her felt as if this was a betrayal.

But before she could push herself away, Darien's lips touched hers.

The feeling made her forget every reservation she'd had. It didn't matter who he was, or where he came from, if he could make her feel like *this.* For a brief, ecstatic moment, she tasted him, almost became a part of him. She lost herself in the smell, the touch, the *need.*

Then he let her go and took a few steps backward, chuckling to himself. Maria's pulse raced, and her breath caught in her throat. *Why did he stop . . .*

"No." She saw something dangling from Darien's hand, and her own hand went to her neck. "Give it back!" She stepped forward and grabbed for her cross, but Darien skipped backward like a child teasing a hungry cat.

"You heartless cur, you are nothing more than a thief!"

Darien backed away again, dodging her grabs. "Oh, I am not a thief. I will gladly give this back to you."

"Then please return it." Maria held out her hand, surprised at the coldness in her voice and the tone of command she found there.

Darien shook his head. "This is my game. If you want this back, you'll have to catch me." Then he turned and ran down the path ahead of her.

Maria ran after him, her pulse thudding in her ears. In her gut churned a mixture of embarrassment, self-loathing, and growing anger. How cruel and thoughtless could one man be, coming to her just when she was aching for someone to care for her, then making a game of the most precious thing she owned?

He knew what it meant to her. How could he do something like this?

The anger throbbed in time to her pulse, pushing her legs to move faster. She barely noticed when the lantern's flame guttered out. Darien reached a straight part of the path, and he was little more than a blurred shadow against the silver-lit darkness.

"Stop!" she yelled at the retreating shadow. Darien refused to listen, diving into the woods with an infuriating grace.

She was not going to allow him to get away with this. She couldn't. He was *not* going to steal her father's cross.

Her lungs worked like a bellows as she turned to follow him into the woods. She grabbed the trunk of a downed tree and leapt over it without caring about dropping the lantern, or the rip torn in her surcote. She focused all her attention on the fleeing form of Darien, barely a shadow within a shadow ahead of her. But even though she couldn't quite see him, she still heard him running through the woods, crunching dead leaves and branches, tearing through the underbrush.

Even more than that, she *smelled* him. The intoxicating, earthy maleness that had turned her insides to water hung in the air, marking his trail more clearly than any sounds or any footprints.

She pushed herself, racing after him until it hurt. Past the point where it hurt. Not only her muscles but her skin and bone burned, as if she were running through hellfire after him. The pain throbbed through her core until it became something else—a pulsing release that pushed her forward, her body shuddering in rage, her attention focused completely on the object of that rage.

For a time, it was as if the thinking part of her mind had shut down, ceding all authority to the ecstatic wrath within her. She felt the seams give way on her clothes, but her only reaction was to cast her skirts aside because they encumbered her legs.

His scent grew sharper, closer, and she snarled without thinking how inhuman the sound seemed.

She was catching up to him, closing the distance as her stride lengthened. Her tongue lolled out of her mouth, and she started grabbing the ground ahead of her with clawed hands, pulling herself more quickly through the forest.

Then he was in front of her.

She screamed, "Darien!," her voice half a growl as she leapt at him. He tried to dodge, but she wasn't about to let him get away. She swung her arm at him as she passed by him. Her hand connected with his back, and he tumbled to the ground with the force of the blow.

She felt her claws bite flesh, and suddenly the air was filled with the scent of blood.

Claws.

Blood.

She slammed into the ground, rolling across the forest floor. The focus of her rage crumbled.

Claws.

Blood.

Maria swallowed as she pushed herself up out of the dead leaves and undergrowth. She panted, shaking her head, trying to deny the things she felt. The things she saw. Her hands weren't her hands. They were the hands of some demon—clawed, black-furred, twice as large as her hands should be.

And even though the hands didn't belong to her, they moved when she flexed them.

"No," she whispered, tears of fear and rage blurring her vision. When she spoke, her tongue felt a mouth too long, teeth too sharp, lips too thin. Her entire body felt as if it were on the verge of explosion, every muscle vibrating with the effort of remaining still.

He is the Devil, she thought, *and he has taken me.*

"You win."

She spun her head around, muzzle snapping at the sound of his voice. She saw him clearly in the silver-gray light, holding her cross in front of him.

"You can have it back, if you still want it."

She roared at him and jumped. "*What did you do to me?*" This time, he managed to dodge aside with a speed he hadn't shown before.

"I set you free," he called to her. "I set you free, and you are magnificent!"

She spun around, but she didn't see him. "Don't hide from me!"

His scent was all around her now, and so was the sound of rustling underbrush. He moved faster than even her demon senses could follow. It was as if he was on all sides of her at once.

She kept turning, trying to discern where he was in the shadows around her.

"I won't hide from you, Maria." The voice came from behind her, and she spun to face it. "But I don't wish to face you in anger." Behind her again, farther away.

She turned, screaming something that was half words, half a lupine howl: "*Face me!*"

"Return to the woods with a calm heart, and I will show you things you've never imagined." His voice was far away now.

"A calm heart? *Are you mad?*" She struck out at a shadow. It wasn't Darien, but she attacked it anyway. When the haze of anger faded, she found herself in front of a young tree, its trunk the thickness of her thigh, splintered and bleeding sap.

Maria, do you know what you are?

"Darien!" she screamed into the night.

He didn't answer.

She stared down at her hands.

Splinters and bark stuck to black fur on the backs, and when she turned them over, her fingers and palms had pads like a dog's or a wolf's. She licked her lips unconsciously and felt her nose at the end of a long, pointed muzzle. She raised her hands to her face.

It isn't true. This is some sort of nightmare.

She turned away from the tree and tried to take a step, but now that the rage had leaked away, she suddenly became aware of the changes in her legs. She tangled herself up in them and toppled over.

She curled into a ball on the forest floor, crying.

"What am I?" she sobbed.

But no one answered.

XV

After a time, praying to God to return her body, Maria began to itch. She rubbed her arms and realized that her fingers touched naked skin. She sat upright, hugging herself, realizing that her prayers had been answered. The skin she inhabited was suddenly her own again. Like the change before, she had been too absorbed in emotion to remember exactly when it had happened.

A dream, she thought. It had all been some nightmarish fantasy.

But when she looked behind her, the wounded tree still bled sap from its splintered trunk. And bark and splinters were caught under her fingernails.

She was also sitting naked on the forest floor.

"This was no dream," she whispered, flexing her now-human fingers.

She stood, brushing leaves and branches from her skin. A few paces away, the cross lay where Darien had dropped it. *If you still want it,* he had said.

She picked it up.

Was this all that had been keeping that nightmare from happening? The wolf thing she had become, was *that* the Devil her father had been warning her of? Was *she* the Devil?

That thing protects them, not you. Darien's words echoed, unwanted, in her skull.

Her hands shook as she placed the cross around her neck. She stood in the forest, naked and alone, staring up at the small sliver of glowing cloud visible through the shadowed trees.

"What do I do?" The words were barely a whisper, but her whole body shook with the anguish of the question. "God, please help me. What do I *do*?"

Somewhere, far away in the forest, she imagined she heard Darien laughing.

For a long time she resisted going home, afraid that the beast within her might hurt her family. But where else could she go?

After a while, she decided to trust in the cross. Removing it had been what had called forth the demon. If she obeyed her father and kept it on, her family should be safe…

"Forgive me, Papa."

She followed her trail back to the path, finding her damaged, mud-stained clothes. She barely remembered shedding them in her fury.

I have never been so angry. Not even at Lukasz…

But what would she have done to stop Lukasz if it weren't for the cross she wore? Even without it, she had landed a blow that had broken his cheekbone. What if that hand had been massive, furred, and clawed? What if she had done to Lukasz what she had done to that tree?

I could have been that angry at him. If Darien hadn't stopped him.

She walked home, her mind tumbling over itself, asking questions she didn't have answers to. Who was Darien? How did he know what lived inside her? Why did he find such glee in drawing it out, tormenting her with it? Why was she cursed with this thing?

What do I do?

She stumbled though the gate and pushed open the door to the cabin.

"Maria, my child, what happened?"

Her stepmother ran to her out of the darkness and grabbed her shoulders. "Where have you been? What happened to your clothes?" She looked into Maria's eyes with a familiar intensity. Even in the dim, overcast night, Maria could see the same fear and terror in her stepmother's eyes that she had seen in her father's before he died.

"Did you take it off?" her stepmother asked.

Something sank in her heart as she suddenly realized why her father had screamed the same question at her. The Germans had been torn apart by some vicious animal, and that news had reached him before she had returned from the fortress. He had heard the descriptions of what had happened to the Germans and he had thought *she* had done it.

"Maria." Her stepmother shook her shoulders, trying to get her attention. "Your cross. You still wear it?"

Maria blinked up at her stepmother and nodded. It wasn't quite a lie, but she could barely bring herself to speak. She pulled aside her immodestly torn chemise to show the cross resting over her heart.

"Thank God," her stepmother whispered. She pulled Maria into a hug and rocked her back and forth. "Thank God, you're safe."

Do you know what you embrace?

"Please, child, tell me what happened."

"A man, in the woods. He . . . " She sucked in a breath and

buried her face in her stepmother's shoulder. "He frightened me," she whispered. "I saw him, and he frightened me. I ran. I ran for a long time."

"Oh, my baby. You're safe home now." Her stepmother paused a moment and asked, "Did he harm you?"

"No." *Not in the way you mean.* "I was lost, and I didn't see him again."

"You're safe at home now," her stepmother whispered. "Nothing will happen to you here."

As Maria cried into her stepmother's shoulder, she began to realize that her stepmother didn't blame her for her husband's death, or care that she was her husband's bastard.

But maybe she should.

⌖

A *calm heart.*

Darien thought of the words he had spoken, and what he had asked of her. He knew more than ever that she was his, that their meeting was fate. More than fate—it was something as self-evident as the coming dawn.

It didn't mean that things would be effortless, however.

In the years he had hunted the creature man and sought revenge on the Order itself, he had never come across another of his kind. Not living, in any event. When she'd chased him through the woods, he had not even seen her embrace the wolf in her rage. When she had jumped upon him, he'd been ill-prepared to feel her claws dig through his back. Though it had been glancing, he'd felt a rib give way under the blow.

That had ended the game. He couldn't hang on to her trinket as splinters of bone pierced his lung. He gave up the cross and scrambled away from a creature that was awe-inspiring in its raw fury.

Even in his pain, he circled around, just so he could look upon her. Long-limbed, lithe, and muscular, wrapped in a pelt of pure midnight, her face long and narrow; and in her muzzle, her teeth glistened like stars as she snarled at him.

She *was* magnificent. And it was all he could do to keep from running to her, even if the result would be more clawed flesh and broken bones.

But it wasn't the time. It was clear that these human wretches had raised her as one of them. Bound her. Crippled her. There was no telling what lies she had been fed about herself, or her kind. He needed to take care with her, no matter his own excitement or his own desires.

In the end, he wanted her to come to him.

But still, he followed her.

And in the morning, when she left her cottage, Darien was in the woods, watching. He watched as a man accompanied her, bearing an axe. He tensed his haunches, preparing to tear the throat from this man, but then he heard them speak, and heard her call him her brother.

So he didn't attack. And when they walked along the path toward the fortress, he followed—a giant wolf padding silently through the woods next to them.

⌖

There was no question now that her eldest brother, Władysław, would escort Maria to the fortress and fetch her back. Even though she wanted to object, there was no way she could. A man had approached her in the woods, after all. It was clear that she needed the protection, and she could not explain her fear for her brother without explaining what had happened.

And even if she could have convinced her stepmother that

Władysław was best off working on the farm, he knew that his half sister had come home weeping and with her clothes torn. She had seen the look in his hazel eyes and knew that even if he did not leave the cottage with her, he would follow.

So she accepted his unwanted company as they walked from her father's farm, she in her hastily mended surcote and borrowed chemise, he in his leather breeches and linen shirt, with an axe slung over his shoulder.

Władysław was two years her senior, the inheritor of her father's household. He had not spoken very much since their father had died, and it had been longer since she had seen him smile. While Maria and her stepmother had tended to her father during his illness, Władysław had been the one to care for the farm.

Walking silently next to him, Maria saw for the first time how that responsibility weighed on him. She saw the wear in his face and felt a wave of guilt for not thinking of the responsibility he must feel: for his mother, for his brothers, and for her.

Władysław caught her looking at him, and she turned away.

After a time, he asked, "Did he abuse you?"

"No," Maria said, shuddering a bit inside. Did he know what she was? Her father must have, and her stepmother; they had put this cross around her neck. But had they told Maria's brothers? She looked at Władysław for any sign of the horrifying fear she had seen in her father's eyes and, to a lesser extent, her stepmother's. "No. No one has raped me."

Władysław visibly winced at her language, and she wondered at it briefly; that was what he had asked about, after all. Then he shook his head and said, "Promise me, if anyone ever—" His voice caught and he looked away from her. "Promise you will tell me."

"Nothing happened to me." The lie was out before she even

knew she was lying. How could she say nothing had happened? What had happened was worse than any rape. She hadn't lost her virginity, she had lost . . . *everything.* Everything that made her herself.

"Promise."

How could she not? "I promise."

After a few moments of silence, he added, "I have been thinking, since Father died, of what our family should do, and how I should handle what we have."

"Oh?"

"You aren't to be serving at the fortress anymore." He hefted his axe. "You will stay with the farm and help."

Maria sucked in a breath. She didn't know what to do. "Władysław, I work there because the taxes—"

"The burden is not that great, and it will be easily borne with another set of hands to bear it. You belong with your family, until you make one of your own."

Maria shook her head, wondering how she could be touched, terrified, and angry all at once. The prospect was terrifying. How could she risk her family, knowing what she was? With something inhuman inside her?

And, on a very basic level, Władysław infuriated her. Here was her big brother, with barely a wisp of hair on his face, acting like the head of the household and presuming to solve problems he had no knowledge about.

She would end her service at Gród Narew, and that was that. As if she had no say in the matter, or as if she were nothing more than a horse, some dumb beast led to plow wherever Master wanted. All to save her from . . . what? For all the terror she had endured, the attention of someone like Lukasz was beneath notice as a possible worry.

Lukasz should be frightened of *her.*

And there was Josef. The last thing she wanted was to abandon him. Even if her caring for him, and how she felt, would be doubly impossible with this thing living within her. She owed him more than to simply vanish without a word. She had commitments, she had duties, and she would not renounce them to save her brother from some phantom worry.

She found the strength within herself to speak, slowly and deliberately: "Władysław, I will continue to work at Gród Narew."

"No, Maria. It is too dangerous."

She whipped around, her fury barely contained. She felt something within her body and thought that, if not for the cross on her neck, they would both be in true danger. "You are not my father!"

Władysław took a step back at her outburst. "Maria!" he snapped, putting a force into his words that didn't reach his eyes. "This is my family now. Don't defy my wishes!"

"Your wishes? *Your wishes?* Did you even consider *my* wishes?"

"As a member of this family—"

"*Stop it!*" She shook her head violently, the anger intense and horrifying. The anger fed off the fear, and the fear fed off the anger, spiraling away from her so that she wasn't even clear what had sparked it.

"Maria?" Now she saw the fear in his eyes—eyes that looked so much like her father's. He reached out for her.

Did he know?

Did it matter?

"No." She backed away from him. "You should stay away from me."

"Maria, what's the matter?"

"*Stay away from me!*" she screamed, and in her panic she imagined a hint of a growl in her voice. She turned and ran, as fast as she could, away from him.

"Wait! Maria!" She heard him call after her, then heard him begin to run himself. He couldn't catch her, though; she had always been faster.

⊕

Darien saw them argue and, again, almost attacked the axe-wielding man. But he had already heard enough to know that the death of this Władysław would not make it easier for Maria to come to him.

Although it would be satisfying to taste the blood spilling from that arrogant neck, Maria saw the man as family, however impossible that actually was. Darien knew too well what the loss of family could do to the spirit, and the hatred it could nurture. He would never touch Maria's "family," if only to avoid igniting such hatred directed at him.

But she had turned on the man, so perhaps she was already shedding this human family.

If so, so much the better.

Darien wove through the woods and followed her, leaving the axe-wielding Władysław alone on the path behind them.

⊕

She reached the end of the forest before the morning bells rang. She looked up the hillside, to the walls of Gród Narew, as if staring at an apparition out of a nightmare.

What was she doing here? What was she doing anywhere? A monster lived inside her, a raging beast, and now that it had been loosed once, she felt it pushing against her skin every time she breathed.

"Stop it!"

She surprised herself by speaking.

"Stop it," she told herself again. Directing her anger at herself, at the spiraling loss of control, seemed to shock her renegade emotions into a moment of clarity. She took deep breaths and reined in the fear.

She didn't know what had happened to her; she didn't know what Darien had done. But she knew that right now, at this moment, she was herself. She knew that, for all the rage she had felt, she hadn't lost control. She didn't even know if what she had experienced was real. She might have suffered from some waking nightmare. Perhaps Darien had bewitched her.

There was no reason not to live her life as she always had, if she wore her cross and took care for her anger.

But there was another reason to go up to Gród Narew. Josef had seen something. He and the men with him had been attacked by something. And her father had thought that something might have been her.

She needed to know exactly what that was.

XVI

"What attacked you, Josef?"

Josef opened his eyes groggily. He used to wake for dawn prayers, but during his convalescence he had allowed sloth to overtake him. Maria's voice woke him, and he was alarmed at how late in the morning he must have slept. He blinked and looked up at her. Her face was radiant in the rosy light from the window.

"What attacked you, Josef?"

When she repeated herself, the sense of the words finally penetrated his sleep-addled mind. "Maria, I am not permitted to speak of—"

She leaned over him and said, in a low voice, "I am not asking what is permitted."

Something had changed in her manner—enough that he imagined that her appearance had changed slightly, too. Her skin almost glowed, even as her eyes bore down upon him. "What happened?"

"I need to know what you chased into the woods here. What did you bring with you?"

"Why are you asking me these questions?" He pushed himself

upright and realized that the sky outside was lit only with the first rays of dawn.

"*Why?*" He saw her ball her fists, and her arms seemed to vibrate. "Why did you tell me to avoid these woods at night?"

"Did something—"

"Happen?" she whispered.

Josef looked at her and felt fear grow in his heart. Obedience was a weight upon him, and he was being forced to ignore the danger to Maria—to everyone at this fortress. They had chased this thing here. Could they not take *any* responsibility?

"It is not my place to reveal my Order's secrets," he said, more to himself than to her.

"Is it anything like a wolf?" she snapped.

Josef froze, staring at her.

She knew.

Maria stared into his face and whispered, "But not a wolf, is it? Something horrible, something so angry . . . "

Her breath caught, and her eyes glistened. Her shoulders shook, and Josef reached up and put a hand on her arm. "How did you—"

"Don't touch me!" she shouted, knocking his hand away. She ran out of the room before Josef could respond.

He didn't know what shamed him more, the fact that he had placed the Order's rule between himself and Maria's safety or the fact that he was considering placing Maria ahead of his vows to the Order. *I am an imperfect servant.*

In his heart, he knew what was right. He pushed himself out of bed.

It was clear now that the creature they hunted was still present, closer to this place than they might have imagined. He needed to tell Komtur Heinrich, and they needed to act before the demon left another village in ruins, before Maria was hurt.

But as he moved, driven by fear for her, he remembered the

bruise on her face and how it had disappeared. That quiet, ugly voice told him that there were other ways to know what they hunted.

He forced the thought away.

⌖

Outside the chapel, Komtur Heinrich said, "We know that the legends of these beasts are manifold."

Josef pulled in a shallow breath; deep breaths ignited fiery pains in his gut. "Sir, forgive me, but this servant seemed to speak from direct experience."

"I see. What details did this person provide to you? Was there anything that could be of help in our search?"

Josef shook his head. "I thought just the confirmation that it was still in the woods was worth bringing to your attention."

"Yes, Brother Josef, but we need details to act. Generalities do not provide usable strategy."

Josef bowed his head. It felt as if his heart were melting and oozing through the wound in his belly. "Forgive me, sir."

"You do not require forgiveness," Heinrich said, "but perhaps more of an investigative nature. You asked no questions?"

"I was concerned that too intent an interest would betray our purpose here."

"I am glad you've taken our prior discussion to heart and err toward caution."

Josef found himself unaccountably angry at his master. He tried to tell himself that it was the pain of his wound doing ill things to his mood, but in his heart he also knew that he had begun to doubt the reasoning behind their secrecy. It was clear that Maria knew something of what they hunted. How could telling her of the Order's work be wrong? Wouldn't the knowledge that there were servants of God here to root out the monster reassure more than alarm? If the beast began rending flesh in their midst, would their silence do anything to keep the peace, or to keep the innocent from being hunted?

He gritted his teeth and forced out something appropriately humble.

Heinrich placed his hand on Josef's shoulder and said, "Do not fret for our task. The Duke has heard our petition and has seen our writ from the pope."

"He knows, then?"

"Only what he needs to know: that we hunt a murderous servant of the Devil."

"But not what it is?"

"He is sending out a group of Poles, along with Brother Reinhart, to search for evidence of our cause."

"Are they armed with silver? Do they know that this thing can walk abroad like a man?"

"Don't concern yourself. Reinhart shall see the Duke's men safely through. They merely need to find a scene of this creature's bloodlust; he will not lead unprepared men to face the thing themselves."

"But—"

"I said not to concern yourself," Heinrich snapped. "Mind your words, Brother Josef, and do not presume to instruct your superiors."

"Yes, sir," he said, and the words were like ashes in his mouth.

⊕

Brother Reinhart marched through the woods accompanied by a half dozen Poles from Duke Siemowit III's personal guard. They were led by the Duke's deputy, Wojewoda Bolesław himself.

In the Duke's wisdom, he had decided that his men would take their survey of the area on foot. Reinhart had the uncharitable suspicion that this was to avoid returning a mount to one of his German "guests."

Though, he had to admit to himself, such a search through the woods was done more easily on two feet than on four. It was also because Komtur Heinrich's men had been mounted in close woods such as these that the creature's attack, the last time they had last faced it, had been so costly.

Maneuverability alone, however, was not so much a comfort with the Order's weapons still stored within Gród Narew. The Duke hadn't permitted Reinhart so much as a knife. He had been sent out with this troop of obnoxiously loud Poles to tramp through the woods barely better than a prisoner. He questioned the utility of including him in the party at all. If the monster had left evidence of its passage here, it would be quite obvious even to the boorish Bolesław, who tromped ahead, shouting commands to the Polish guard with broad and unsubtle gestures that lowered Reinhart's already low opinion of Slavic nobility.

And the large, heavily bearded Bolesław was probably as fine an example of the szlachta as anyone might find.

At least the man could speak passable German, even if he shouted orders in the cacophonous tongue of the Poles. Reinhart found their language even more unpleasant in the ear than the few words of Old Prussian he had heard, spoken by the handful of unrepentant pagans who haunted the woods within the Order's domain.

Ahead of them, Bolesław raised a hand and shouted to his men. As one, six men in mail and heavy boots ceased moving and talking, and the woods around them grew suddenly silent. Reinhart felt his own breath catch in his throat. They had found something.

"Shall our monk come forward and examine this?" Bolesław waved Reinhart forward. "You are interested in unnatural deaths?"

Reinhart flexed his hands, wishing for the pommel of a sword.

He said a silent prayer as he walked up next to Bolesław to see what the man had found. The monster they hunted was not subtle, but Reinhart had not expected to come across sign of its passage so soon after leaving the fortress.

"So, Brother Reinhart, tell me if this is the work of satanic forces."

Reinhart looked down at Bolesław's feet, where the corpse of a mange-ridden hare lay half-buried in leaves and pine needles. Crusts of mucus covered its nose and mouth, and scavengers had already taken the eyes, leaving an empty socket to stare up at Reinhart.

"This is not a joke," Reinhart said. The wrath he felt now could not be kept out of his voice, and it was only with God's grace that he prevented himself from closing Bolesław's obnoxious mouth with his fist. "What we hunt is deadly, and evil."

"As you have said, but perhaps you might be more forthcoming about what signs you seek?" Bolesław kicked the hare's corpse, lifting it off a writhing bed of maggots to flop over onto the tip of Reinhart's boot. "Are you sure this is not the handiwork of our quarry?"

The other Poles laughed, but there was a deadly serious glint in Bolesław's eyes.

"You will know its work when you find it," Reinhart said. He kicked the dead hare off his boot and turned to the Poles. "And when you do, you will not laugh."

"I do not—" Bolesław was interrupted by a shout from one of his men. Reinhart turned to look at the commotion. One of the Poles held up an empty boot.

⌖

The trail grew more obvious as they followed: broken branches, bloody bits of torn clothing. As soon as it was clear to Reinhart that they had found the trail of their quarry, he asked Bolesław to order the party's return so that Reinhart's brothers could rearm and come out to finish the thing.

"For a boot and a few rags? My Duke would require something more substantial, Brother Reinhart."

It was only a couple miles deeper into the woods that Reinhart saw Bolesław regret those words.

They followed a game trail into a dense thicket, then up to a rise that appeared to end in a twisted mass of undergrowth and deadfalls. They might have turned back if not for one man who saw something in the undergrowth. The Pole ran up and retrieved a dirty brown object.

He lifted it to reveal a severed human head as ill-used by scavengers and as maggot-ridden as the hare Bolesław had kicked upon Reinhart's boot. The grotesque sight was met with a number of gasps, and the whole character of the expedition changed.

Bolesław took a step forward and stared at the dead, eyeless face. "Lukasz," he whispered.

"Do we have substance enough for your Duke?" Reinhart asked. "If we return now, we can—"

He was interrupted by another Pole, who had taken a position at the highest point on the rise. He was shouting something as he looked down, crossing himself, then making gestures Reinhart thought were purely pagan.

Bolesław turned and charged up the rise with more speed than Reinhart would have credited him for. As Reinhart followed, he saw the color leach from the massive Pole's face so quickly that, when he reached his side, the large man had taken on the aspect of a wraith.

Reinhart looked down and shuddered.

"Jesus wept."

He prayed as he gazed into the bowl-like ravine before a cave mouth. The ground was black with tarlike mud, covered with flies and the prints of a massive wolf. Scattered evenly around the small clearing were the remains of men, horses, and animals less identifiable. No body had been left intact, and some of the men still wore bits of armor.

Reinhart saw the Devil's hand. The dead had been taken here, placed here, carefully arranged so the fiend could revel in its handiwork.

"You are right," Bolesław told him. "We must return and arm your fellows—" Bolesław was interrupted by a wolf's howl. And when the woods swallowed the last echo, the only sound left was that of Reinhart's breathing and the creak of the other men's armor.

Without any prompting, Bolesław pulled his sword from its scabbard, and Reinhart saw the glint of silver on its edge.

"God help us," Reinhart said. "It is here."

⌖

Darien followed the men from the fortress, silently and beyond their sight, breathing in the scent of eight men. One scent was familiar, even if he hadn't seen the black cross on his surcote.

Darien allowed the men to walk far from the paths and the walls of the fortress. They marched, loud and unconcerned, into Darien's domain. If the loud ones had been alone, he might have ignored them. But in their midst was a member of the Order, and Darien could not turn away from the opportunity to reduce the Order's ranks. He recognized where they were when one of the men found a boot that had once graced the foot of the oaf who had attacked Maria. The men followed Darien's trail, picking up cast-off rags, until they found themselves at the edge of Darien's lair.

When they stopped, he padded to just within sight of them.

Three looked down upon his cave, and another held the head of Maria's oafish attacker up by the hair.

Now was the time, while they were distracted and had no weapons in hand.

He sat on his haunches and concentrated. His forelegs creaked as they lengthened, and his forepaws became clawed hands. His back and chest broadened, his shoulders twisting painfully, bringing forth a howl.

The howl reduced his element of surprise, but it brought him the smell of fear, which was worth more. He dove into their midst as the men scrambled to draw their swords. He landed on the back of the rearmost, slamming him to the ground as he clamped his jaws around the back of his neck.

The words were barely out of Reinhart's mouth when yells of alarm rose from the Poles. He turned around to see a massive golden-furred monster taking down one of Bolesław's men. He saw slavering jaws crush the man's neck and shake his head like a rag doll's, independent of the body.

The monster straddled the corpse on doglike legs, balanced on huge splayed paws that dug claws into the forest floor. Its forearms were long and ended in clawed imitations of human hands. When it raised its massive wolf's head, its muzzle was stained with gore and its lips were pulled back into something between a snarl and a demonic grin. One pale blue eye seemed to stare directly into Reinhart's soul.

The two Poles near the fallen man drew their swords and raised them against the creature.

Reinhart yelled at them: "The head! Sever the head or pierce the brain!" Next to him, Bolesław shouted in his own language as he stepped between the creature and Reinhart, holding one of the Order's silvered swords.

Bolesław's words must have been a reprise of Reinhart's instruction, because both swords came down toward the wolf's head. But the creature moved blindingly fast. One forearm rose to deflect the flat of one incoming blade, and as the other blade swung toward its throat, the beast snapped at it, catching the blade in its jaws and tearing the sword out of its wielder's hands with a shake of its head.

The other swordsman tried again, but the beast leapt on him as he raised his sword, slamming him into a tree. That man's sword went flying, along with part of his arm. A third man ignored the admonishment to attack the thing's head and drove a plain steel sword into the creature's side as it eviscerated its victim against the tree.

In response, the beast whipped its head around. It still had a sword clenched in its jaws, and the point of it pierced its attacker's face. The man fell at the beast's feet as it turned to face the three armed Poles converging on it.

Reinhart ran to the first fallen man, who had not had the time to draw his weapon. He had to roll the body to get the sword out. As he struggled to free the weapon from the dead man's belt, he heard screams, and growls, and the sound of rending flesh. His heart thudded in his throat as he finally pulled the sword free.

Not silver, but through the palate into the brain . . .

He whipped around to face the monster.

But it wasn't there.

The headless corpse of Wojewoda Bolesław, lord of Gród Narew, had fallen across his disemboweled countryman, his leather-gauntleted hand still clutching the pommel of a now-broken sword. The other half of Bolesław's silver sword was embedded in the heart of a tree. Of his head, Reinhart saw no sign.

Two other attackers lay on either side of the tree, throats torn open in awful symmetry as they stared sightlessly up at the sky.

Reinhart spun around, looking for the beast, but the closeness of the trees limited his visibility even in broad daylight. He backed toward a tree to gain some cover behind himself. Something rustled to his right, and he spun to face in that direction, keeping the tree at his back. He thought he saw a shadow move between the trees.

Then he heard a scream.

The last man, Reinhart thought. The man who had swung his sword into the beast's mouth only to be disarmed. That man had fled into the woods.

Not far enough, or quick enough. His scream was cut short with a horribly liquid sound, followed by a soft crunch.

Reinhart tightened his grip on the sword in his hand. He wanted to pursue this fiend, do his best to finish it, even as poorly armed as he was, but discipline made him hold his ground. Running—either after this thing or away from it—would be suicide. The creature was faster and could attack from any angle. If he showed his back, even in pursuit, he would suffer the same fate as the Poles.

"Face me, demon!" he yelled at the woods.

Even without a silvered weapon, it was still possible to kill it, if he could strike before it inflicted a mortal blow. He prayed for the strength to do what was required of him.

A morning breeze carried the sound of a soft growl from the surrounding woods, wrapped in the nauseating scent of blood. He edged around the tree, stepping over the outflung arm of a corpse, carefully minding his footing as he stared at the trees for any hint of motion, any signal of attack.

It would rush him, he decided. It would wait for a break in his attention and rely on its speed and strength to overwhelm him before he could bring a blow to bear. Expecting that, he braced his sword in both hands. He could use the creature's momentum to pierce its skull.

"Do you fear God's judgment?" he called. "Face me!"

Something low spoke from the woods, a growling sepulchral voice that could have belonged to Satan himself: "Why would I concern myself with your God?"

A creaking growl filled the air, coming from just beyond the trees in front of Reinhart. It was as if the woods were hungry.

"Show yourself," he called, willing his voice not to tremble.

"Speak more," it said. "Yell, scream, call on your God. Let me hear it."

A bead of sweat dripped out from under Reinhart's helmet, stinging his eyes.

"You may mask your fear from other men, knight, but to me you reek of it. I taste your terror in the air around you, and it tastes as sweet as your flesh."

"I am ready for you, Devil."

"I am no devil," the trees whispered at him. "And you are far from ready."

Something exploded out of the underbrush at him, and Reinhart swung his sword, aiming head-high. As he had hoped, the momentum carried the onrushing body onto his sword, impaling it through its open jaw and through the back of its skull.

But it wasn't the wolf whose deadweight pulled his sword arm down. It was the Pole who had tried to run, his face torn away so that only a blood-soaked skull looked up at Reinhart. He put his boot on the corpse's chest to pull his sword free.

A gold-furred shadow leapt over the corpse as Reinhart pulled. He felt its breath against his cheek, followed by a wrenching pain in his neck that sent the world away into a blood-soaked darkness.

XVII

"Do not concern yourself," Josef muttered to himself as he limped through Gród Narew. "Do not concern yourself."

The thoughts he had for Komtur Heinrich were not those of a probationary member of the German Order. They had more in common with the black thoughts that had filled his head when he had seen Nürnberg decimated around him. But this was worse: this pestilence had a snarling face and could be seen coming.

In his mind he kept picturing innocents falling victim to the gold-furred demon, the life torn free of their bodies while Heinrich played diplomatic games with the Masovian nobility. He saw body upon body, and above them all his Komtur's unmoved face. Obedience before all.

Worse, perhaps, was the unease he felt about Maria. Everything about her drew feelings from him he thought had died with Sarah—her quiet strength, her voice, the gentle touch of her hand, the curve of her lower lip... At some point his thoughts had abandoned their pretense of propriety and he had accepted that he cared for her much more than Komtur Heinrich would find proper.

So, as his thoughts descended their dark spiral, the victims of the demon's attack most often bore Maria's face.

Though, at their darkest points, his thoughts also cast Maria into other roles. The suspicions raised by her healing face and her silver cross refused to go away.

Why do I keep thinking this? She bore the wound on her face for days before it healed. She was right; it had simply appeared worse than it was.

But the silver on her neck would impede such healing.

The thoughts were insane. There was no logic to them. What he hunted would not bind itself so.

So why does she lie about the source of the wound?

Yet if some man had struck her, how many women would admit such to a near stranger?

Whatever his suspicions, they were outweighed by his sense of the woman he had seen during her visits. The woman who'd lifted his heart, and showed him a gentle strength that seemed to bear much more than she was able to show. And he knew that she needed help. He felt, somehow, that she was more at risk from Komtur Heinrich's demon than he was.

His gut tied itself into painful knots, and only partly because of the wound in his belly. But until he entered the great hall where the members of the szlachta took their meals, he was only guilty of sinful thoughts.

He stood in the doorway and looked at the Poles eating and talking and singing. To Josef, the sight bordered on unreal when compared to the Order's tradition of taking meals silently as scriptures were read.

He stared at the chattering mass of Slavic nobility and began to have second thoughts. Who was he to place his fears and concerns above those of the Church and the Order?

He clutched at his stomach with his fist and turned to leave, but a man placed a hand on his shoulder, stopping him. "Are you looking for someone?" the man asked in comprehensible German. "You've wandered far from your brothers."

Josef turned to face a man taller than he was and twice as broad. For an instant he thought he faced the lord of Gród Narew, Wojewoda Bolesław himself. But this man was younger than that and had a beard darker and more closly trimmed.

"I apologize for intruding."

"No need. You are guests of our house." Somehow he managed to say it with no trace of irony. "Perhaps there is something you need?"

Josef straightened. There was a reason he was here. "I wished to ask if my weapons might be returned to me."

The man smiled. "Your master has talked to the Duke of this, I am sure. The Order's weapons will be—"

"I talk only of my own," Josef said.

"You are a member of the Order."

"But I speak for myself."

"Do you?" The man led him out of the hall and down a long corridor. As they walked, the man said, "I am curious why you might think anyone would return *your* weapons, in particular."

"Perhaps Komtur Heinrich has not said everything about what it is we hunt in your lands."

The man stopped and turned to face him, a questioning expression on his face. "Who are you, Brother?"

"Josef."

"I am Telek. You sleep in my uncle's bed." He placed a hand on Josef's shoulder and said, with a dire earnestness, "Do you know what you are offering to do?"

"Yes."

Telek squeezed Josef's shoulder and said, "Then perhaps some accommodation can be reached."

He led Josef to a series of storerooms deep in the stronghold. No one challenged Telek's presence, or asked about the pale German who accompanied him. He stopped Josef before a large door, banded with iron, and said, "Should anyone care to ask, say I dragged you down here to identify some inscriptions upon these weapons."

"Do you not have men who read German?"

Telek muttered something in Polish that may have been a curse. "It's a pretext, of course. It would be suspicious for us to be alone without some claim that I attempted to gain information from you. Better for you if I requested your presence with a transparent ploy."

"I see."

"I hope you do. Otherwise you would be a very short-lived spy."

Josef's gut clenched, trying to deny the truth of what Telek said. But was there any other word for it, whatever his motivations? He was betraying the Order. He tried to tell himself he wasn't being traitorous; Heinrich himself had said that the Poles would work with them on this. If they were allies, could it be traitorous to inform them of exactly what they faced?

Telek opened the door, the thick slab of oak swinging past Josef on creaking hinges. The interior was dark, dotted with fragments of light—reflections from the lantern in the hallway. Telek retrieved a lantern and led Josef inside.

The room smelled of oiled steel and dry wood. Every wall was crowded with wooden racks holding as many implements of death as Josef could imagine. In the middle of the room sat several large wooden chests, a sheet of canvas draped across the top of them. On the canvas rested the Order's weapons. The reflections from their blades had a different, softer character than those of the blades racked against the walls. Josef looked over the small arsenal of swords, daggers, and crossbows.

Telek picked up a dagger and held it up before him, the inscriptions bold in the reflection of the lamplight. "Ornate weapons for an Order that has taken vows of poverty."

"They are necessary."

"Then perhaps you can explain why."

⊕

Telek stood and quietly listened to the German, and gradually he realized that, for whatever reason, this Josef was genuine. At first he'd thought this man was some feint by Heinrich, to get some weapons out of the stores; or perhaps Heinrich suspected Telek's visit to his quarters and wanted to confirm it.

But this man went beyond anything Telek had expected. Not only did he confirm the nature of the beast the Order hunted, but he conveyed an urgency that Heinrich's tome could not. Telek listened to the man and asked the questions he would have if he had not known much of this beforehand.

One thing he noted: there were gaps in Josef's knowledge. He couldn't answer some questions Telek asked that would be apparent to anyone who had read Heinrich's tome. He never mentioned the name Semyon, and he didn't know how long these creatures had been hunted by the Order. To Josef, these things were demonic and always had been.

He gave Telek a few new elements, though. A description of the beast: the golden fur, the ruthlessness. It was quite a different sense hearing about such a thing from a man who had seen it than reading a sterile description on the page. Hearing about how this beast had savaged a heavily armed and mounted contingent of the Order, armed precisely against such a creature . . .

Telek began to fear for his uncle and the men with him, armed only with the silver sword that Bolesław had taken from this room. *We should have armed them all,* Telek thought, cursing the impulse that had made his uncle keep their knowledge from the Duke and the Duke's men.

When Josef had finished his confession, Telek set the dagger down and said, "Take what you need."

Josef picked up a cleaning rag and wrapped one of the silver daggers inside it, so that he had a nondescript bundle that could have been anything. Telek was relieved that the man had chosen something he could carry away without raising questions.

A wounded man is not going to go on a solo hunt for this thing with only a silver dagger.

"Tell me, Josef: Why is it that you need that now? Do you not think that your captain will convince the Duke to allow you to resume pursuit of this thing?"

"I—I need to protect myself," he said. It was the only obvious lie he had spoken, but Telek decided that it was worth more to retain an ally in the Order than it was to ferret out that bit of information.

⌖

Telek left Josef with an assurance that they could "continue to help each other." The massive Pole was obviously troubled by Josef's tale; though what sane man wouldn't be?

Josef shambled back to his sickbed, weighed down by the dagger in his hand. He wondered if the silver in the weapon was more or less than thirty pieces' worth.

She needs something with which to defend herself, Josef thought.

But, if he was honest, she needed to not be here. The dagger was little more than a gesture—as Telek had said, a pretext. The Poles needed to know what they faced and what its weaknesses were. It was too great a monster to be taken down by Heinrich's men alone. The dagger was an excuse not only to tell Bolesław's nephew but to tell Maria.

She would not be safe until she knew what was out there, and he could not in good conscience keep the Order's secrets. He would give her the dagger when she came with his evening meal, and he would tell her everything. If she left at daylight and then kept to the farm where she lived, he would be able to count her safe.

He had come to care for her more than any woman since Sarah. And, in the end, he would do for Maria what he had been unable to do for Sarah. Even if she could never be his—it was wrong for a member of the Order to think otherwise—just knowing that she lived was reward enough.

Even so, his pledge of chastity had begun to chafe as much as his pledge of obedience. Had he only turned away from worldly things because he had seen the world turn away from him?

He fell into his bed, aching from the exertion, unable to undress himself for the pain in his belly. He checked his dressing briefly but saw no blood seeping from the bandages, even though it felt as though there should be.

As he closed his eyes and waited for Maria to come, he thought of Sarah and the awful time in Nürnberg. He remembered entering the house of Sarah's parents, dark and smelling of death. Her family and the servants had long since fled to the countryside. He remembered the goats that had wandered in from the fields to take up residence in the kitchen. He remembered her body, left in her bedchamber, where she had died. It sickened him that he remembered the smell in that room better than he remembered her face. Every time he tried to picture her smile, or hear her laugh, it was now Maria's face he pictured, Maria's voice he heard.

And it was Maria he kept seeing dead in her bedchamber.

And his grotesque imagination made it all the worse when Maria didn't come with his evening meal.

XVIII

Maria walked out of Gród Narew wondering if she could ever repair the damage she had done after she had spoken so insolently to her brother. Could she go home after that, after what she knew dwelled within her?

She held her cross and looked out over the woods, watching the evening shadows grow to engulf them. She had left without bringing Josef his meal, but she didn't want to face his questions—spoken and unspoken.

She believed that she knew the answers, and they frightened her.

I can return, she thought. *I can pretend nothing has happened.*

The events of the previous evening had already taken on the hazy aspect of a nightmare. The fury that had burned in her then had flickered out, leaving only ashes behind.

Dusk was coming soon, and her brother would be approaching the walls. She watched the sky and thought of what a disaster it might be if Darien met them in the woods. She remembered how he had overpowered Lukasz; she did not want anything similar to happen to her brother.

Her hand tightened on the cross as she thought of the other reason she had left early and alone.

She turned and walked around Gród Narew, to the northern side. The side without any gates or paths, just hilly pasture ending in a wall of unbroken forest. She walked across the pasture, away from the fortress, from her brother, from Darien. She climbed over the low stone fence marking the pasture and walked north, through the trees.

Her heart raced and her face flushed as she pushed inside the shadowed wood. Within a hundred paces she was truly alone. She hugged herself against the first prickings of fear.

I am not a wicked person, she thought, even as her breath shuddered and her flesh tingled with the anticipation of...

"I need to know," she whispered.

Had it been some uncontrolled fantasy? Or was it her?

She took off her shoes and placed them neatly by a tree. She took off her belt, her surcote, her chemise, and carefully placed her clothes so they would not be soiled. For nearly half a minute she stood wearing nothing but her father's cross. The wind was chilly against her exposed skin, and her arms drifted unconsciously to cover herself, even though the only eyes watching belonged to birds and insects.

She shivered, and only partly because of the cold.

It took a long time for her to muster the courage to remove the cross. When she finally lifted the chain off her neck, she did so very slowly. She held it in her hands and kissed it before placing it upon her folded clothes.

"God help me," she whispered.

She took a step back and stood before the tree where her clothes lay. She felt wicked, blasphemous, evil. Not for her nakedness but for what she felt inside herself. What she *wanted.*

She told herself that she didn't want this thing inside her. She wanted it to be a dream, some bewitchment that had addled her memory or twisted what she'd seen and felt and heard. Even some form of insanity would be less threatening to her soul; a madwoman was blameless in the eyes of Church and God.

She opened her arms to the woods around her.

"Is it me?" she whispered to the evening sky.

Even possession by some sort of demon—that would be beyond her volition; she could ask succor of the Church. They would help her to exorcise the evil within her.

"Is it me?" she repeated, more loudly, looking upward toward God.

She shouldn't want this thing. She shouldn't want to feel that bestial strength.

She shouldn't.

But she did.

"*Is it me?*" she screamed.

And what God refused to answer, her body did. Pain cracked her like a whip, twisting her voice into a breathless scream. The sudden flare of pain seemed to radiate beyond her, resonating through the woods, causing insects to go silent and birds to cascade upward in an apocalyptic flutter of wings.

This time, without the focus of rage, she felt every bone in her body come alive, twisting and growing, pulling writhing muscles and tendons in a throbbing dance under her flesh. She fell to her knees and pulled in a shuddering breath. The sensation rapidly passed beyond mere pain. Every fiber of her body screamed to her of its existence; every nerve an eye staring into the sun.

She watched her hands as they lengthened, the flesh darkening and sprouting a pelt of midnight-black fur, claws growing to dig agonized grooves into the dirt. She tried to scream, and her mouth and nose fell down toward the ground, pushed by a growing muzzle. Each tooth twisted and sharpened as her legs bent and reshaped themselves.

Her body twisted itself in an ever-increasing spiral of agony.

And then it released her.

When the release came, it was a shuddering climax through the core of her body—an ecstatic inverse of all she had just endured, all at once. It dropped her shaking to the ground, moaning. Lesser shocks jerked through her body five or six times before she could move without trembling.

When the ordeal was over, she lay panting on the sweet-smelling pine needles coating the forest floor. For several moments she couldn't think clearly of anything except what she had just felt—something that was simultaneously the best and the worst thing she had ever endured.

"It *is* me," she whispered, surprised that she could still speak.

The character of the woods had changed with her. The smell of the pine-needle mulch was sharper, deeper, filled with traces of things she could almost taste. Even the air felt different, the breeze now pulling against a fur pelt rather than her naked skin. The colors of the evening seemed deeper and of a different character.

She pushed herself into a crouch and realized that the woods were silent around her. She rested on her haunches and ran her newly strange hands across her face. The rough pads of her fingers traced a narrow muzzle and a fringe of fur around her neck. She touched a cold nose, and ears that projected above her head.

She shuddered, realizing that this was no dream. She had called this thing forth from inside her. She didn't move for the longest time, waiting for the will of this creature to overcome her, to feel the overwhelming rage she had felt the last time it had come.

She licked her lips, her broad, thin tongue tracing teeth made for rending flesh. She stretched her unnatural hands until the joints creaked and her claws ached in the tips of her fingers. But the will of this creature did not come to bewitch her mind.

It began to sink in that this *was* her: her bones, her flesh, her skin, her fur, her teeth, her claws...

Her will. Her mind. Her anger.

Her soul.

She reached over to her folded clothes and picked up the cross. She half-expected it to burn her or to forcefully evict the monster that had taken over her body. Lightning should strike, she thought, or a fissure open in the earth.

But nothing dramatic happened when she touched the cross, or when she lifted it up.

The metal appeared blood-red in the evening light as she held it before her face. She whispered a prayer to God, begging for forgiveness, and strength, and understanding. God did not rebuke her for such words coming from an unnatural mouth, but He didn't answer her, either.

"I want to be myself again," she whispered.

She tried to will herself back into the woman she had been, will the beast inside herself.

But nothing happened.

Her heart began racing. What if she had done something wrong, broken some rule? What if she was forever confined to this bestial form?

No. Please God, no . . .

She concentrated, tensed her muscles, tried to reenvision the ecstatic anguish of the transformation, but nothing happened. Something about her new body made it easer for her emotions to cascade, grow in intensity, and she could feel the fear and rage bearing down upon her like a panicked warhorse.

"Stop it!" she growled at herself.

It made no sense that she couldn't change back. She had done it the first time without even thinking about it, and if she couldn't now there must be a reason. She didn't need to panic; she needed to think.

A calm heart, Darien had said.

Thinking of him made the anger begin to rise again. It was

Darien who had brought this upon her, telling her to remove her cross.

She looked down at the cross, still dangling from her clawed, black-furred hand.

Was this really what kept this monster from claiming me?

Yet could the cross also keep the monster from leaving? That made no sense. If a cross kept a beast at bay, shouldn't it also drive it out? Shouldn't it force her back to her natural body?

"Is it the cross?" she asked.

It is silver? Josef had asked her. *The chain as well?*

They use those silver chains to drag you down, Darien had said.

Silver was supposed to have power over unnatural things. Could it be that it wasn't God that had kept this beast slumbering within her but the metal this cross was made of? Perhaps it didn't suppress the beast, only its ability to change.

"My ability to change," she whispered.

She gently replaced her father's cross on top of her clothes and looked at it resting there. Then she pulled her hand away and sucked in a breath, trying to will the beast back into herself.

This time her body responded with a shuddering force. She fell backward, toppling off her wolf legs. It felt as if her whole body had melted and was draining through a hole inside herself. There was pain, but not the orgasmic agony of the beast. Instead she felt the empty ache of a long-cramped muscle finally relaxing.

She sprawled, naked and sweating, on a bed of pine needles.

She brought a hand up to touch her face, and her lips were human. Her fingers traced the outline of her jaw, and she felt the same face that she had worn all her life. She got unsteadily to her feet and looked down at herself, and saw the same breasts, the same stomach, the same thighs, knees, and feet.

There was no sign of the creature.

Not on her body, anyway. Next to her feet, pressed deep into the forest floor, was a single pair of footprints where the creature had—where *she* had—crouched on her haunches. The prints were those of the splayed rear paws of a gigantic dog or wolf. Only the pair, without any prints coming or going.

She bent and traced the pawprints with her fingers. If she needed to confirm that she was not mad, that what she had seen and felt existed outside her own head, here was proof, embedded in the forest floor.

She dug her fingers into the damp earth and buried the pawprints—filling them in, tamping them down, erasing any evidence of their presence.

By the time she had brushed her skin off and replaced her clothing, the sounds of birds and insects had returned. Apparently they were satisfied that the creature had gone.

⌖

She left the forest, uncertain about exactly where she was going. She ended up by the walls of Gród Narew because that was the closest place she knew to go. She walked around to the southern gate and stared out at the path back toward her family.

How could she return? Not only after running from her brother, but going home to face her stepmother. How could she, knowing what secrets her stepmother had kept from her? They had hung this cross around her neck without giving her the vaguest inkling as to *why*. She shuddered when she thought what might have happened if Lukasz had ripped the cross from her neck.

The first time she had been rage without a thought. If Darien had been just a little slower—

No, I did *strike him.*

She had been so tied up in what had happened to her, she hadn't spared much thought to what she had *done*. Now that she had brought the creature forth herself, she knew it hadn't been a vision or a nightmare. And if that transformation had been real, she had to assume that her blow to Darien's back had been just as real.

She closed her eyes and pictured it: her leap at him, her clawed hand striking, slamming into his back, claws digging deep into the muscle. She had felt his flesh tear under her fingers. She had seen him slam into the ground with the force of the blow. She could have killed him.

"Maria?"

She whipped around, eyes wide, half-expecting Darien to be looming behind her.

"Josef?" The unexpected name escaped her lips before she fully realized who was standing there, his face drawn and pale, his body listing slightly to the right as he pressed his fist against his stomach just above his belt.

All her thoughts fell apart. She ran to his side and took hold of his shoulder to support him. "Josef, you should not be out of bed."

"I am fine. The wounds are healing."

He was not fine. He was strong, but she could feel the tension in his shoulders, and she could hear the catch of pain in his breath however much he tried to hide it. She imagined that she could even smell the agony that possessed him.

Please don't hurt yourself, Josef. I am losing everything else. Don't let me lose you, too . . .

But it was already sinking in: *she* was what the Order was hunting.

Her heart ached as she realized that this might be the last she'd ever see of him. Knowing what she was, she would have to leave here. Unfallen tears blurred her vision as she forced her voice to be as firm and cheerful as she could manage. "Your wounds won't stay healed if you go wandering about like this. Come, let me take you back to your room."

"No." He pulled from under her supporting arm and faced her, taking her hand in his. "You need to go home, before all the light of day is lost."

She looked him in the face, wanting to ask him what he knew of what she was. Instead, she whispered, "Is there anything in these woods at night that isn't there in the daytime?"

"It likes the dark," he replied, turning his gaze away from the gate, toward the woods. "It is there now, but given the chance it prefers surprise, slaughtering its victims with no warning at all."

"Josef, you said you couldn't—"

"Listen!" he snapped. "I'm defying everything I've trained to be to tell you this. It hunts in the dark, traps its victims in confined spaces. It can come to you looking like a human, but it is not. Do not trust any strangers you might see. Most important, only silver can truly wound it."

Like a blow it struck her: her healing bruise, and the wounds that still itched in her palm. It *was* her.

"W-why are you telling me now?" Did he know about her slipping into the woods? Did he know that she was the monster of which he spoke?

"I was frightened for you. You didn't come this evening, and I thought my silence had driven you away. I was afraid that I had lost my chance to protect you."

He pressed something into her hand. She looked down and saw a silver dagger. It had been hidden against his stomach, beneath his fist.

"What is—"

"Shh. Take it. It is the only protection I can offer while we are kept by the Duke. But once he satisfies himself of the legitimacy of our hunt, we shall finish this thing."

"This thing," she whispered. *Me,* she thought.

"I know you must have suspected its presence, seen something of it, for you to talk of wolves. So, perhaps, I may be forgiven my disobedience. I would rather have that hang upon my conscience than anything happening to you."

Then he bent and kissed her forehead, and the touch of lips on her skin fired a panic of impossible emotions—a tumult that might have called forth the wolf from within her if the silver on her breast had not kept it dormant. Instead, it left her with a shuddering weakness that made her stumble backward as he turned to reenter the fortress.

She turned to face the road home before the guards could catch sight of the weapon in her hand, or Josef could see the tears on her cheeks.

"Thank you," she whispered.

XIX

Władysław had been sitting on a log at the edge of the woods, waiting for her.

She stopped when he saw him.

He stood, bending to pick up his axe.

"You came back," she said.

"You're my sister."

She ran to him, tears welling up in her eyes, and threw her arms around him. "I'm sorry."

He patted her back. "I forgive you." He coughed and added, "Now let me go, so I can breathe."

She released her embrace and said, "I thought . . ."

Władysław laughed. "It'd take more than a little yelling for me to stay angry at you. But who was the man with you at the gate?"

Maria froze, uncertain about how to respond. When she saw the true inquiry in her brother's eyes, she turned away to hide her flush.

"Josef," she said. "His name is Josef."

"What trinket did he give you that was so shiny?"

"He gave me a dagger, to protect myself. Like you, he is overly concerned."

"Such interest must be flattering," he said, but there was a kernel of hard suspicion in the statement. It felt worse because she knew, for her part, that it might be merited.

She tried to answer the unspoken question. "Josef's taking holy orders. He was wounded and I've been tending to him—"

"You mean he's one of the Germans?"

"—and I think he meant to repay my service," Maria finished, ignoring Władysław's increasing alarm.

"Maria, do I need to remind you—"

"No, you do not," she snapped.

There had been a point in her life when her brother's concern for her chastity might have made her collapse in shame or embarrassment. Today, after what she had seen of herself in the woods, his alarm about Josef's attentions was less than trivial, and she had to strain to keep her frustration from igniting into true anger at someone far from deserving it.

He opened his mouth, but when she looked into his face something in her expression kept him from pursuing the topic. They walked a few more moments in silence; then he finally asked, "May I see it?"

Maria handed him the hilt of the dagger, and Władysław held it up before him. The polished surface glinted in the evening light. Now she could see the scrollwork and the German script engraved on the sides. It seemed more an item of jewelry than a weapon.

Władysław grunted, obviously gripped by his own frustration. "And this toy is supposed to protect you from what, exactly?"

The same Devil as the cross around my neck.

Maria couldn't bring herself to speak. She couldn't repeat Josef's words—not after having learned that she was what the Germans hunted. She also couldn't give voice to yet another lie.

"Maria?"

"Władysław," she said finally, "did you know my mother?"

"What do you mean? Mother is—" He paused for a moment, and all the tension drained out of him. The frustration in his face turned to melancholy as he said quietly, "Oh."

Maria loved him dearly for that moment of confusion.

"Do you know anything of her?" she asked.

"I'm sorry, but I was two years old."

"Father never spoke of her?"

"Not to me." He handed the dagger back to her. "I'm sorry."

Maria nodded and took the dagger. When she did, he reached out and touched her hand. "Please, if you speak to Mother about this, be kind with her. Anything that happened was not her doing."

"I promise." She looked across at her brother, who stared steadfastly down the path ahead. The evening dusk had faded into night, and his face was cloaked in shadows that made it hard to read his expression. "Is there something you're not saying?"

"I truly know nothing about your mother..."

"But you know something about me?"

Władysław was silent for a long time before he said, "I might have been five, and you were just three, when you first put that cross around your neck. Do you remember what happened?"

Maria shook her head. "I thought I always had this." She reached up and touched the chain around her neck.

He craned his neck and echoed her gesture with his free hand, tracing the ghost of a scar on his neck. "It wasn't really your fault. For some reason I thought that yanking your hair was great fun."

"I did that?"

"Only after I made you burst into tears." He lowered his hand. "I don't remember much of anything after you stopped crying. But you certainly put me in my place."

Maria's heart thundered in her chest. Ever since Darien had loosed this thing in her, her greatest fear was that she might strike out at her family. It had never occurred to her that she might have already done so. "I *hurt* you?"

"Nothing serious. Cuts and bruises, a black eye, a bite on my neck."

"God have mercy."

"Please, don't be upset. It was sixteen years ago."

His reassurances did nothing to calm her. If she had changed, bitten his neck, she could have killed him.

"He gave me the cross after that, didn't he?"

"It was Mother, actually." He stopped and sighed. "I was feverish, bedridden, and they thought I was asleep. I never told them otherwise. For a while I thought I'd dreamed it..."

"Dreamed what?"

Władysław was silent for a long time, and his silence allowed her dread to grow unchecked. Something small and still told her that she didn't want to know what her brother might have dreamed.

"What?" she asked.

"I shouldn't—"

She grabbed his arm, stopping him, and pulled him around to face her. "*Tell me!*"

"Father wanted to get rid of you," Władysław said finally.

Maria dropped his arm and backed away as his words came spilling out.

"Mother and Father argued. They screamed. He was horrified about what had happened. He kept saying that if I died, it would be his fault for bringing you into the house. Mother finally convinced him not to abandon you in the woods. She left that night, making him pledge that he would keep us both safe. She was gone for two months. When she came back, she had your cross with her."

He paused, probably expecting her to argue, to yell again, to insist that Father would have done no such thing to her, say no such thing. Yesterday, she might have.

"She brought this cross?"

"Yes. I don't know how or where she found it. I never asked about the night she left. I don't think Mother or Father knew what I had heard."

"You never told me."

"If he was alive now, I still wouldn't." He shook his head. "What purpose does this story serve? Father spent the rest of his life trying to earn forgiveness for that night."

And his last day on earth, he believed it was all for nothing.

She probably should have felt anger at her father, for ever considering abandoning her to die in the woods. She couldn't. She understood what her father feared, even if her brother didn't. She could see how, in his telling or in his memory, he had considerably lightened the injury she had given him. He didn't remember the attack itself, and the wounds she had given him had sent him to bed with infection.

What kind of horror was it to face the fact that one of your children had almost killed the other? How much heavier the guilt when the violence came from a bastard child you'd brought into the house?

Maria could barely conceive of what he must have gone through.

"Thank you for telling me this." She started walking down the darkened path again.

"You are going to talk to Mother about this," he said.

"Wouldn't you?"

"Please remember," Władysław said, "that anything she did, anything she's kept from you, was all done because she loves you as her own."

"I know," Maria whispered, holding the cross to her heart.

⊕

Her stepmother met them at the gate, the worry in her face obvious. "Władysław, you left hours ago. Does it take so long to bring your sister home?"

"It isn't his fault," Maria said. "I was late leaving, and I made him stop and talk."

Hanna kept talking to Władysław. "After last night, why would you let her—"

"I said it wasn't his fault!" Maria snapped.

Maria's stepmother looked at her, and even her brother seemed a bit shocked at her outburst.

"Don't raise your voice to me," her stepmother said. Even as she spoke, Maria could see a hint of fear in her eyes. She could almost smell it in the air around her.

Had that fear always been there?

"We need to talk about my mother," Maria said.

"I am your mother."

Maria saw Hanna's eyes search her face for something. "You know what I want to talk about."

"You . . ." Hanna turned to Władysław and said, "Please go into the house. I need to talk to your sister."

"Remember what I said," Władysław told her as he walked toward the cottage. He left Maria and her stepmother outside, under the night sky. Around them, leaves rustled in the breeze, and somewhere an owl hooted.

"Maria," her stepmother said, "there are reasons we never talk about your mother, some things we're best off not knowing."

"What if I know those things already?" Maria reached into her chemise and lifted the cross's chain up from around her neck.

"What are you doing?" Hanna reached out a hand to stop her, grabbing her wrist. Even though Maria knew she could easily break the grasp, she just ducked her head down out of the encircling chain.

"What if I know why I should wear this?"

"Please, put it back on. You don't know—"

"You're afraid I'm going to hurt someone, like I hurt Władysław?" Maria saw the panic growing in her stepmother's eyes, and she wanted to reassure her that she hadn't hurt anyone—but it would have been a lie. She had hurt Lukasz, had broken his cheekbone, and she had hurt Darien, clawing through his back. The fear was real, and it was justified.

She dropped the cross back around her neck and told her stepmother, "I walked out into the woods today and took it off."

"No, please tell me you didn't—"

"What am I?" Maria asked her stepmother. "What am I, and where did I come from to be your daughter? Why would you take something like me under your roof?"

"You are my daughter," her stepmother said.

"I'm not of your blood. I've known at least that much all my life. After what I became in the woods, I wonder if I bear any of your husband's, either."

Her stepmother slapped her face, the impact ringing through the woods around her. Maria's cheek stung with the impact. "Do not say that! You are Karl's daughter—*never* doubt that, or him. He was a flawed man, but to him you were the one thing that granted him some grace." Her stepmother sniffed, and Maria realized she was crying.

Quietly, Maria said, "Do I not deserve to know?"

"Yes, you do. But we didn't want to lose you."

"Even after what happened to Władysław?"

"You were barely a child. How could we hold you responsible?"

"Please, Mother, tell me where I came from."

Interlude

Anno Domini 1333

Her name was Lucina, but she didn't remember who had named her. She lived in the deepest woods east of Gród Narew, mostly ignorant of the humans dwelling there. The people who lived on the fringes of these woods—especially those whose families had spent generations in its shadow—knew of her and her kind. Lucina's ancestors haunted the tales that had been spoken of in hushed tones ever since the land had become Christian.

However, it had been a long time since Lucina had had family. And a long time since her kind had haunted these woods in any numbers. She was alone, and the old folks' tales about wolves clothed in human skin had become less urgent, less of a deterrent for hungry men who needed to stock their families' larders.

Lucina would watch these men as they made their pitiful attempts at hunting. Sometimes she would watch with the eyes of a wolf, sometimes with the eyes of a raven-haired maiden. She would watch them come into her wood and, more often than not, return empty-handed.

She watched not out of any malice but out of curiosity and a deep loneliness. She was the last of her kind in these woods and, she thought, perhaps the last of her kind anywhere. These men who came to find game, they all had a home to go to.

Home was as alien a concept to Lucina as having to trap her prey or shoot it with an arrow.

Each winter, her despair grew deeper. She would always be alone, and she envied these human women who sent their men out to parade in front of her. Why? What could these frail human women give that she could not? She was stronger then they were, faster, and a better hunter than these poor men...

It was not long before she decided that there was no reason she couldn't have what they had. Once she resolved this, Lucina studied these men with a new eye, looking for someone she could love, and who could love her back. She watched how they moved, how they hunted, and how they carried their kill.

And only days into the winter, when the snow barely dusted the needle floor of her woods, she saw the man who would become her mate. This man had broad shoulders and seemed to stand above all the others who braved her forest. He also had a masculine scent that made Lucina lick her lips in anticipation.

This was the man who would free her from her solitude.

⌖

When Karl met her, a light snow was falling. Lucina stood in a clearing, white dusting a red cloak she had stolen from a cottage close to the woods. She smiled at him from under the hood—smelling him, watching him.

She stood between him and a dead hart. The freshly killed animal lay sprawled in the snow, slowly leaking blood from the wound Lucina had torn in its neck.

"What is this?" he asked. "Who are you, and why are you alone in the woods?"

"My name is Lucina," she said, her voice hoarse from so long without speech. "These woods are where I live."

"It is dangerous. The animal that killed that deer may still be about."

She walked up to him and placed a hand on his chest. When the cloak parted, it became obvious that it was the only thing she wore. His breath caught, and in his scent Lucina could tell that he did not dislike what he saw. She leaned forward and whispered, lips brushing his ear, "The kill is mine." He didn't move, didn't speak, as her hand found its way under his shirt. "Do you wish some of it?"

"That is your kill?"

"I smelled it, tracked it, and tore its lifeblood free with my teeth." She licked his ear, tasting his sweat, smelling the first hint of fear.

"What are you?" he asked.

"You know," she said. "These are my woods." She caressed him, running her hand down the side of his chest. "Do you want a share of my kill?"

"What are you asking?"

"A leg perhaps? The meat would feed several mouths."

"You would give that to me?"

She brought her face around in front of his, their lips a finger's breadth apart. "In return for something."

"What?"

Her hand traveled lower, into his breeches.

"Respite from my loneliness," she said, before she kissed him.

It may have been fear, or shock, or the thought of a hungry family, or simply the heat of Lucina's skin so close to his own. It may have been the fact that her loneliness was manifest in every word she spoke. It may have just been the fact that Karl was a man, and men are weak.

Whatever the reason, any or all, Karl did not pull away from Lucina when he could have. He tasted her mouth, and let her place his hand on her naked bosom. Her cloak fell away and she led him down to the snow-covered earth and buried him under the weight of her solitude.

He came to her many times that winter, and each time her heart grew fuller at his presence. To him, she was a secret vice, a spirit that lived in another world, one of trees and bloody carcasses and lovemaking in the snow. To her, he was a reason to live, a joy, a lover and a husband in what sense she could understand the term. They spoke little—he walking in his dream, she drinking in obsession beyond words.

There was no doubt in Lucina's growing heart that the next time Karl came to embrace her, he would tell her that he would stay. It was that hope that carried her through the depth of winter. And it was that hope that slowly died in the spring.

As the snow melted and the ground softened, the men who braved these woods stayed upon their plots of land to till the soil and grow the harvest that would keep them and their people through the next winter. There was no one to explain this to Lucina; for all her watching of the men in the forest, for all her listening to their language, she didn't understand. All she knew was that as the first buds grew, her Karl did not return to her.

Many times she stood, in her red cloak, next to some beast she had taken. She attacked larger and larger prey, as if Karl might be enticed back—bucks, a bull elk, a mountain cat, a bear.

As the months passed, her heart shrank, and her belly grew.

And as summer became verdant, and Karl's seed grew large within her, her heart grew black and cold. She had been cast aside in worse isolation than the loneliness she had thought to escape. As gravid as she was, she found it impossible to change, to run as a wolf does. Hunting became difficult, and she grew gaunt.

When she gave birth, it was with blood and screams and the rending of flesh. However, she survived, as she could bear far more injury and insult than any human woman. Three children she had, all girls. And as she licked the blood off Karl's daughters, she decided that Karl would *have* to come help care for them. And that meant she had to take away any reasons he had for staying away.

She found Karl's farm in the midst of a horrible storm at the end of harvest season. Ice fell like needles from a sky boiling and black as ink. The wind howled and bit with a force that felt as if it could tear flesh from bone.

Her howls were louder than the storm, louder than the thunder. Karl heard her cries as he huddled with his family around the fire in their cottage. At first he didn't want to admit to himself that he knew what made those terrible, terrifying sounds.

But he knew.

Even though he had never seen his dreamlike winter lover in other than her human guise, he knew. Just as he knew that his trysts were no dream, and the wood where they had happened no fairyland.

He had bought more than meat, and at a much dearer price.

Karl took an axe and told his wife to protect their young son, to bar the door and the shutters and let no one in before morning—not even him. Then he left the cottage to face the beast that cried for him in the storm.

She stood in front of the cottage, waiting for him. She was naked, but no longer human. Lips that had borne his kisses were curled in the lupine snarl of a feral she-wolf. The hands that had caressed him were now dark-furred and long-fingered, ending in hooked claws. The legs that had straddled his body were now the crooked legs of a wolf.

He didn't want to know her. He wanted this apparition to be something new and strange to him. But he looked into her eyes, and he knew whom he faced, and what.

"You left me." Her voice, always rough from lack of use, came out of her lupine throat as little more than a growl.

"I had to tend the harvest." The words were empty in Karl's mouth. She had come to him, true. She had been the one to place her lips on his—but he had never pulled away. He had never said that he had a family, a wife, a son. He had pretended, because the situation was unreal, that it wasn't real. That because she wasn't human, it didn't matter.

And the horror he felt was more for what he had done than for the monster standing in front of him. She panted, steam rising from her muzzle as lightning carved highlights from black ice-matted fur.

"You left me alone, with child." She growled and took a step toward him. His axe dangled impotently from his hands and he shook his head, trying to deny the truth of the allegation.

"I didn't know," he said finally, as knives made of falling ice scoured the tears from his cheeks.

"I birthed your whelps, alone in a cave, and swaddled them in the skin of a bear I had killed... *for you.*" She stood before him, barely taller than he and starvation-thin, but still seemed to loom over him. He felt her breath on his face as she growled.

"I didn't know," he said again, as if those were the only words he knew anymore.

"You will care for our children."

As she stared into his face, he saw the head of a starved she-wolf, ice matting her fur into spikes, muzzle wrinkled into a snarl.

But the eyes were hers, and in them he saw the pain, the loneliness.

"Yes," he said.

The creature before him froze, as if she couldn't quite understand the word. Her muzzle lost its snarl as she pulled back from him. "You will come back with me. To your daughters."

"I will go with you," Karl said. He thought of his wife and child, barricaded in the cottage. He couldn't leave them to the anger of this beast. Better that the she-wolf received what she wanted, what he'd implicitly promised her.

"You will come back? With me?" The voice softened in her inhuman mouth, and her eyes shone from more than melted ice. In a flash of lightning, Karl thought he saw one side of her mouth pull up in a melancholy smile. "Our children are beautiful."

"Take me to them," he said, all the time thinking of his wife and son, in the cabin.

And, in a moment of fear and weakness, he glanced back. He knew it was a mistake as soon as he turned his head, because he could hear Lucina growl.

"Liar."

He turned back. "No, I—"

She backhanded him in the chest—a blow that knocked him rolling into the icy mud of the path.

"*Liar!*" she shrieked at him, jaws snapping at air. When the lightning lit her face, he saw nothing but fury.

He raised a hand, hoping to pull back the thread of hope he had seen in her eyes a moment ago. "No, I will—"

She pounced on him, knocking him down, pressing his shoulders to the ground with her massive clawed hands. "You will tire of me, like you did before. You will come back with me, but you will leave. Like you always have. You will *always* come back here."

"No, not this time."

In another flash of lightning, he saw her lupine mouth smiling again, but this time it was the rictus grin of death staring down at him, dripping saliva that burned a cheek that was frozen from the icy needles of the storm. She bent down so her muzzle was next to his ear, lips brushing him as they had the first time they met. "No," she whispered. "Not this time."

She leapt off him, growling words that had lost their meaning in her fury. To his horror, she ran to his cottage.

His wife. His son.

The sudden threat drove all thought of his own guilt away. The woman Lucina had been was wiped from his mind as he saw this atavistic shadow bearing down on his family. As she attacked the door, slamming herself against the splintering wood, he pulled his axe out of the mud and ran after her.

Strong as she was, she had been weakened by her troubled childbirth and months of hunger. Were she the same Lucina that had greeted Karl in the woods, naked under her red cloak, the door would have given way with a single blow. But now she splintered one board at a time, reaching in with a furred arm to cast aside the bar sealing the door.

Karl came upon her as her shoulder pressed against the hole she had smashed between the planks of the door. She turned her head to see him, and as the axe came down on her neck, he saw resignation in her eyes.

The first blow was grave—an awful wound tearing through her neck, spilling her life out over frozen black fur. Had she run then, she might have survived, healed from even such a massive insult. But she didn't run. Instead, she used all her strength to say two words to Karl through her damaged throat—words that came in a froth of blood.

"Our children."

The second blow landed before Lucina's weakened body could

begin to seal the damage from the first. The third took Lucina's life. The fourth was just the formality that completely removed her head from her body.

Karl left his wife and son, and his dead lover, to find his daughters. He slogged through the ice storm, deep into the dark woods, to the clearing where he had made his trysts with the wolf. As he searched he raged and cried—cursed himself, and Lucina, and God. As he stumbled in the dark, he selfishly hoped for the peace death would bring him.

Then he heard an infant's cry.

He found them in a shallow hollow in a hillside, wrapped in the raw hide of a bear that smelled foul with decay. For two infants, it was already too late. Their bodies were blue and cold. But the last child was pink and healthy, and screamed as the ice bit her skin.

He brought all three home, the tiny corpses slung across his back in their rotting bearskin. His one living daughter he carried tightly inside his shirt, so that she would have his body for warmth. When he reached home, the storm had broken, and a cold dawn had begun chasing clouds from the sky.

PART THREE

Anno Domini 1353

XX

Maria stayed silent throughout the story. Her heart ached for Lucina, and she could see her fate written even as Hanna described Lucina's first meeting with Karl. Maria's mother had been doomed from the start, and it was all the more heartbreaking because Lucina didn't even understand why.

Her stepmother wiped her cheeks and said, "We had lost a daughter, less than a month before. She would have been barely older than you. You took her place at my breast. I know where you came from, what gave birth to you. But you were my husband's child, and you became mine."

"I had sisters," Maria whispered.

Her stepmother gave her a long look and said, "Come with me."

She led Maria along the stone fence marking the edge of the field, to a trail into the woods. The trail ended in a clearing marked on opposite sides by two piles of stone, one somewhat smaller than the other. The rocks were weedshot and reflected bone-white in the moonlight.

"This is where we placed them to rest." She pointed to the larger of the piles and said, "Lucina is here."

Maria walked up to the rocky pile and tried to picture what

Lucina had looked like, what her voice might have sounded like, what she might have told her about what she was.

And as she did, she felt twin stabs of shame. The first came from not having spared the time to think about her mother before now, before she'd had cause to question what she was. But worse than that was the shame of having doubted her stepmother. The woman who'd raised her had shown her more grace, more loving forgiveness, than Maria had thought the human heart was capable of.

She knelt by Lucina's cairn and said, "Thank you."

"You're right. You deserve to know your own history, whatever it is."

Maria turned to face her stepmother. "Thank you for being my mother."

"How could I do anything else?"

"When I hurt Władysław, you could have let my father take me away."

"I—" Her stepmother sucked in a breath and turned her face away. Maria realized that Władysław had told the truth when he'd said that their parents never knew he had overheard them.

"And you gave me this." She touched her cross.

"It was to keep you safe. We weren't trying to imprison you. We didn't want . . . " Her shoulders shook as she wept, and Maria stood to place an arm around her.

"You didn't want me to end as she did," Maria said, holding her still. "I understand it now."

Her stepmother hugged her, and Maria realized that sometime in the last few years, she had grown taller than her.

"Don't hate your father," Hanna sobbed into Maria's shoulder. "He made mistakes, bad ones. But he loved his family, and *all* his children."

"I know."

"Please, whatever happens, always remember that you have a family, and that we love you."

"I know," she whispered quietly, as her own tears came.

She returned to her own bed, with her stepmother and her brothers. And for the first time since her father had died, it felt like home to her. Yet through some evil sleight of hand, the feeling made her situation all the worse. Could she hang on to this, knowing what she did about herself? Knowing that the Order hunted her kind?

Curled up on her bed, in the loft above her brothers, she lay without sleep. Her nerves strung themselves tight beneath her skin, her muscles tense with unexpended energy. She felt as if she could jump out of bed and run into the woods, and keep running and running, away from all of this.

She ran her fingers over the dagger she had set next to the bed, the inscription rough and cold against her skin.

Josef...

What about Josef? She could explain things to her mother. All children leave home in the end, and she was no different in that respect. But could she explain things to Josef so that *he* understood?

Why had he given her this? Why had he kissed her so tenderly? Why did he incite the evil hope that there could be something more between them?

He belonged to the Order, and she was the demon they hunted. By all sane measure, he was her enemy—and a deadly one. So why did she care what happened to him?

And, as far as he knew, she was a lowborn bastard servant. Why should *he* care what happened to *her*?

I'm defying everything I've trained to be to tell you this.

She thought of him saying that, and her heart ached. He had no idea he was trying to aid the very thing he fought. Should he do anything else to help her, he might lose everything. She couldn't let him sacrifice himself for a lie.

If she truly cared for him, she had to tell him what she was.

⌖

By the time she left, it was after dawn. When Władysław chose to escort her, she didn't object. They walked for several minutes in silence, as birds sang under a cold, overcast sky. After a long time, Maria stopped and said, "I am sorry I hurt you."

"What?"

"When we were children."

"Oh, it wasn't serious—"

Maria placed a hand on his shoulder. "No, Władysław, it was. I love that you care enough for me to pretend, even to yourself, but I might have killed you."

Władysław chuckled uneasily. "You were only three years old."

Maria looked at him and said, "Would it be so remarkable for a three-year-old wolf to kill a five-year-old child?"

"What are you talking about?"

"Mother explained things to me."

"You're not making sense."

Maria squeezed his shoulder. "Just remember, whatever happens to me, I love you and I'll never do anything to hurt you or our family."

"I know that—"

"I swear it, Władysław," she said. "I swear on the graves of both my parents that I would give my own life before that happened."

He stared into her eyes and asked, "What did Mother say to you?"

"She said I take after Father's mistress."

Then she told him what she was.

Władysław, of course, didn't believe her. "Do not make such jokes, not on our father's grave."

"Here," she said, and handed him the silver dagger.

"What is this?"

"You are the head of the household; you need to protect our home. There may come a time when you need this. I don't think I will."

They reached the edge of the woods and stepped into the shadow of Gród Narew. He still seemed half angry, half confused. "Why do you spin such a tale? And give me this?"

"Tell Mother that I am doing what I can to keep our family safe."

And she left before he could ask her more questions.

⌖

When she came with Josef's meal, he was dressed and standing by the window, staring out over the stables. She set down his breakfast and said, "You are looking well."

He nodded, his expression grave. "I am healing, and I wish to be able-bodied when we ride forth again. You should stop coming here, even in daylight."

"Josef—"

"The Wojewoda Bolesław led a band of men out yesterday, looking for signs of the beast. The Duke has sent more men to search for them. They haven't yet returned." He looked at her, and the concern she saw there made her want to weep. "I need to know you're safe."

"What do you know of these beasts you hunt?"

Josef frowned, as if her words confused him for a moment.

"You know what kills them. You know they can look like men."

"Yes."

"Have you ever spoken to one?"

"What?"

"If they become human, then they can talk, explain themselves . . ."

"Don't speak such nonsense."

"Nonsense?"

"These are demonic monsters that have no conception of—"

"This is not nonsense!"

Josef's expression froze.

"How is it you know that these creatures are demonic?" Maria asked, "What makes them so much more horrid than any wolf in these woods?"

"Have you not seen what it has done? To me, my brothers? You haven't seen the ones it has killed—"

"Worse than men have done?"

He opened his mouth to answer her, but a shadow played across his expression.

"What you hunt, Josef—is it because of what it has done, or because of what it is?"

Josef grabbed her shoulders and shook her. "What do you mean by this? Why do you speak of such things?"

She looked at the growing terror in his face and felt her heart sink. "I pray to the same God you do," she said. "Doesn't Christ offer forgiveness to all who follow him?"

He stopped, as if she had struck him.

"Is it what this creature has done, or what it is?"

He let her go. "It is different. This thing is not human."

"But it walks abroad in human skin."

"Maria, you don't understand—"

"Is there such a difference between a wolf who becomes a man and a man who becomes a wolf? Does a man lose his soul because of such a thing?"

Josef shook his head and said, "Such things have no souls."

Maria had to restrain the impulse to strike him. Instead, she backed away from him. "So you know God's mind on this?"

"It is a demon, a spawn from the fiery pit—"

"And you beat upon it with swords? Where are your priests, your rites of exorcism?"

"I shouldn't have told you. You don't underst—"

He was interrupted by calls from outside. "Make way! Make way!"

Josef turned toward the window and looked out. He took a step back and muttered something in Latin, his face draining of color.

Maria stepped to the side so she could see past him. She opened her mouth, but no words came out. She reached up and clutched her cross so hard her hand hurt.

Past the stables, she could see the inner wall and the main entry gate. Rolling through the gate were a pair of wagons drawn by shaggy plow horses. In the carts she saw indistinct lumps covered by rust-spotted canvas. But the spots weren't rust. Even at this distance, the scent of blood stabbed through the earthy smell of the horses below them.

She saw Bolesław's nephew, Telek, run out to the lead cart and jump on board with an urgency that belied his girth. He reached down and cast aside one end of the canvas to view what was beneath.

Bolesław, she thought. *It is Bolesław himself.*

Even at this distance, she could see the expression freeze on Telek's face. Her own breath seized as she watched him stare down at his uncle's body. Time stopped as neither she nor Telek moved.

The men who had gathered the bodies had been respectful enough to place the lord's head back in proximity to his body, but there was no hiding the fact that there was no connection between the two anymore. There was only an awful dark hollow where Bolesław's throat should have been.

A hush had fallen across everyone in the courtyard. Even the horses fell silent enough that Maria could hear Telek speak. The words came quietly, almost as if he were conversing with his uncle: "This shall not stand."

"Reinhart," Josef muttered. He whipped around toward her. "There! Do you see? This is the work of the Devil himself. Can it be anything else?"

Maria backed up, unable to find the anger that had been driving her just a few moments ago.

"Eight men. Eight men . . ." His legs wobbled slightly, and he pressed his fist into the bridge of his nose. "I should have been able to kill it."

"Kill it?"

"If only I had more strength—"

"Josef? What did you do?"

"I stabbed it in the eye with a crossbow bolt," he said. "A mortal wound to any other creature, but for this—"

She was suddenly aware of an awful knowledge she had been harboring, unwilling to articulate, even to herself.

"Which eye?" Maria demanded, though she didn't want to know.

"What?"

"Left or right?"

"Are you mad? What point is there to—"

She grabbed his shirt. *"Left or right?"*

"Left, but—"

She ran out of the room, leaving him with his question. Only one word filled her thoughts.

Darien.

XXI

Maria ran into the woods, abandoning Gród Narew. No one paid her any mind; the entire population had become an impromptu funerary procession. She pushed through crowds that pressed into the streets to follow Bolesław's body to the main stronghold, led by Telek.

Wojewoda Telek.

The world was disintegrating around her, but none of it mattered anymore. What mattered was what she was, and what Darien was. She ran off the path and into the trees.

"*Darien!*" she called out, frightening birds into flight above her. She screamed, her fear and anger pressing against the cross hanging over her heart. She felt the beast clawing against its confines within her.

"*Darien!*" She thought of the dismembered men being wheeled into Gród Narew, and of the horrible wound that Josef himself had suffered. How could she think that the thing he'd faced was anything but the Devil himself?

"*Darien!*" She ran through the woods, ducking under dappled shadows, searching for some sign of him.

"Maria?" The voice was low, calm, and behind her. She stopped running and turned around to see Darien walking out from behind a tree. His golden hair spilled to his shoulders, and he stared at her with eyes of piercing blue, the scarred eye paler than the other. "I asked for a calm heart."

"You ask too much, after what you've done. What kind of monster are you?"

He smiled at her. "What kind of monster are you?"

"You slaughtered eight people—"

"And what would they have done to me?" He walked up to her, and Maria felt her pulse race as he touched her cheek. "What do you think they'd do to you if they knew what was hiding behind that cross you wear?"

She covered her cross with her hand and stepped away from his touch. "Do not touch that again."

"Do you love your chains so much?"

"You're evil."

Darien's laugh echoed through the woods around them. "By whose account?"

"I've seen what you've done."

"Have you seen what they've done?" he countered. "How many of our kind they have slaughtered in sacrifice to their own bloodthirsty God?"

She shook her head and said, "Do not blaspheme."

"Maria." He stepped forward and cradled her chin. "Do not blind yourself to what they are. Am I the first of us you have seen? Have you asked yourself why?"

Maria remembered the tale of her mother, how she was alone of her kind.

"I had a family," he said. "Mother, father, uncles, sisters, brothers, cousins. Then one day the Order came and slaughtered every last one of my kin. They herded them into a church and set it to fire."

Maria felt her breath catch.

"I have been alone for more than twenty years, hunted by them. Hunting them. I never thought I would find you."

Maria looked up into his face and wondered how her mother's fate might have been different if she had found one of her own to share her life with. Her heart pounded against the cross on her chest, and her breath felt so hot it burned her nose. She stared at the outline of his face, framed by a halo of backlit golden hair.

He lowered his head and she felt his lips touch hers. But she backed away from the contact, and he didn't resist her movement.

"No," she said.

"No?" Darien's scar-bisected eyebrow gave a sharper edge to the word than found a way into his voice. "Is that why you came into the woods? Why you called to me? To say no?"

"I need to know what I am," she said. "What you are."

"We are the same, my dear Maria."

She stood for a long time as her tongue slowly dried in her mouth. A bead of sweat rolled down her back, firing tiny tremors along her spine. She was suddenly very much aware of the smells of the woods around her—the sharp scent of the pine, the rich smells of the earth, and the almost intoxicating scent of Darien in front of her. She licked her lips and said, "Show me."

"Show you?"

"Show me what it is we are."

"Are you ready for this?" He took a step back and held out his hand. "We are not like them, Maria."

She reached out and took his hand, "Show me. I'm ready to know."

"Remember that." He clasped her hand and led her through the sun-dappled woods until they came to a sunlit clearing. The grass here was high, and naked trunks pointed gray fingers at the sky, testifying to a long-ago fire. "This seems a good place," he said.

He let go of her hand and took a few steps away before pulling his shirt off over his head. His back was turned mostly toward her, and she saw the ripples of muscle under pale bronze skin, marred only by a white scar along his side.

"What are you doing?" she said, when she caught herself staring.

He folded his shirt and placed it on the log of a fallen tree. He turned to her. "I do not wish to damage my clothes." He reached down and pulled the boots off his feet and sighed. He flexed his toes and curled them into the grass. "What purpose do they serve?"

He bent down to remove his breeches and Maria forced herself to turn away, feeling the flesh burn on her face and her pulse throbbing in the back of her throat.

"You said you were ready for this."

Maria nodded, not trusting herself to speak.

"Then face me."

She turned to look at him and couldn't breathe. He stood naked before her in the clearing, brazen and unashamed, and without even a shadow for modesty's sake. She found herself staring at his manhood, which even dormant was the size of both her fists, one on top of the other.

"You want to see what I am?" he asked.

She raised her gaze to his face and said, "Yes."

Darien took a deep breath and spread his arms. He clenched his fists and his jaw, and every muscle in his body pulled tight. Tiny shudders crawled across his flesh—trembles that were echoed in her stomach. Even as he froze, unmoving, his muscles took on a life of their own, writhing under his naked flesh.

As his skin rippled, its surface darkened, softening with a downy golden pelt that grew and roughened while she watched. The movement under his flesh became more violent, and more directed, as the flesh appeared to pull bones after it. His arms lengthened, and his fists spread open as his fingers did likewise, sprouting curved claws at their tips.

Maria heard a groan; she didn't know if it was Darien's voice or his body that had made the sound.

He tilted his head as his tensed jaw muscles pulled the bones of his face forward, a lupine muzzle pushing out from within, and his golden hair coarsened and spread itself to become a furry ruff around his neck. His shoulders broadened, his chest swelled, and his hips twisted to accommodate the wolflike legs that supported him. And between those legs, his member was an engorged fleshy red that began to subside only as he let loose a triumphant howl.

Maria stepped back from the thing Darien had become.

The giant wolf's head tilted as he licked the length of his muzzle. His eyes were still the same—the left one paler than the other, marked by a white slash in the golden fur of his face.

He crouched, so his face was the same height as her own.

"Do I frighten you?"

Maria opened her mouth, but speech was beyond her. She just nodded.

"Why?"

"Why?" Maria repeated. She stared at the muscles rippling under Darien's fur, at the way his muzzle wrinkled in a near grin, revealing sharp canine teeth. "Why shouldn't I be frightened?"

"Can you not protect yourself?"

She thought briefly of the silver dagger she had left with her brother, but that wasn't what Darien meant.

"You know we're of a kind." His nose wrinkled. "The smell of the wolf is so rich upon you. Join me. Let me show you."

"You want me to . . ."

"You wish to see? To know?" He reached out. Maria was surprised by his touch, but she didn't pull away as a claw traced the curve of her arm. "You cannot by pretending that this is all you are."

Maria hugged herself.

What was she?

Woman, Christian, Pole, servant, daughter, sister, virgin, bastard . . .

Wolf?

She bit her lip and pulled off her surcote. Under Darien's gaze, she pulled off her shoes, her chemise, everything. She stood before him, naked, skin burning with embarrassment, but forcing herself to leave her arms at her sides, as brazen as he had been.

He reached out a clawed finger, brushing shudderingly across her breast, to tap on her chest, next to her cross.

"You still wear that."

He didn't try to remove it, and she stood there while the wolf touched the naked flesh between her breasts. She could no longer admonish herself, protest that she was not wicked.

She reached up and removed the cross, then let it slip through her fingers to fall on the ground next to her clothes.

She closed her eyes and breathed deep his scent, which was earthy, strong, and male and hinted at every forbidden thought she had ever had. It filled her with a shudder that refused to stop. She bit her lip hard enough that blood trailed across her tongue and dripped down her throat. Her flesh moved and flowed around her, tearing and reknitting, stretching her skin in a cascade of agony where the only fixed point within her was her heart trying to hammer its way out of her body.

Every pulse of her spasming heart sent bolts of agony along her arms, her legs, every muscle in her body. With her eyes closed, she felt as if every part of her body was bursting open, to spill her life on the ground.

And mixed in with the incredible pain was the throb of something deeper; something in the core of her that writhed with pleasure at every twist of a knotted muscle, every thrust of malleable bone; a thing that moaned on the brink of ecstasy as her skin pulled against itself to the breaking point and beyond.

I am wicked, came her single coherent thought. *I want this!*

When the pain stopped, her climax slammed her like a blow. She howled, the lupine wail vibrato from the waves crashing within her body. She fell to her knees, but did not topple over. She opened her eyes while the aftershocks still shook her body. She heard a growl and realized it was her.

She was nearly overwhelmed by different sensations, as every part of her body reminded her that she was no longer what she had been. The points of her teeth rubbed against her lolling tongue as she panted. A light breeze tickled the fur on her back. In her crouch, her backside, muscular and narrow, rested on heels far more pointed and knobby than those of a human foot. The balls of her feet, now great splayed paws, dug clawed toes into the cool earth.

Power filled every joint and muscle—an intoxicating energy that made her feel that she could leap beyond the tops of the dead gray trees that surrounded them. She felt as if she could leap to embrace the sun itself.

Her muzzle wrinkled as she breathed in the now-overwhelming scent around her. It was as if her nose had been packed with linen that had suddenly been removed. She could pick out the scent of moss, the different types of grass, the woody scent of a hundred slowly decaying trees, the vapors from an unseen nearby marsh, and over all she smelled *him.*

Darien faced her, staring at her as if her transformation had racked him as much as it had her. "Are you still frightened?"

She licked her muzzle, feeling her new canine lips and the cool leather of her nose. "Of course I am," she said. She stood, slightly unsteady on her new legs, turning to let the breeze caress her new black-furred body. She took a deep breath and added, "But that doesn't matter, does it?"

He stepped around to face her, moving with a lithe grace that showed none of the clumsiness she felt balancing on a pair of oversized wolf paws. As he moved, she saw that he had a tail, and seeing it move made her aware that she now had her own. She felt it twitch, and the feel of the base of it brushing against her backside was perhaps the strangest sensation she had experienced yet. Just thinking of it made it swing faster, caressing the backs of her thighs.

"You are beautiful," he growled at her, his voice lowering in tone so much that she doubted the human Maria would have understood him.

"I am a monster," she said. The words came out as low as his, and it seemed that it was someone else talking—*something* else talking. As much as fear gripped her, for the moment she couldn't find shame in the statement. She repeated, more to herself than to him, "I am a monster."

The words held more revelation than horror.

He reached out and touched her cheek, stroking the side of her face. "You want to see what we are?"

"Yes."

"Then follow me."

Darien turned and ran, becoming little more than a golden shadow disappearing into the woods.

XXII

Maria hesitated for only a moment before running after him. She was clumsy and uncertain of her own strength. Her first leap carried her nearly ten paces over a deadfall, slamming her shoulder into a tree. But the pain was nothing compared to her transformation, and she rolled and was back chasing his scent before she realized she had fallen.

He ran so fast.

The faster she went, the more her body pushed her forward, wanting to use her arms to grab the ground before her. It was awkward, and she could barely keep up with the golden shadow rushing ahead of her. In glimpses, she saw him through the trees and realized why he was so fast.

He ran on four legs now, completely a wolf—a massive gold-furred creature running though the woods, tongue lolling.

The sight shook her for a moment. She'd been half-prepared for the monster she was, but to become fully an animal? It didn't seem possible.

She was losing him in the forest.

Could she do that? Did she want to so completely change?

I want to know what I am . . .

She focused on the golden wolf ahead of her as she reached for the ground beneath her. She leaned into her arms as if they were forelegs, holding her head up as if she was meant to run this way. She pulled against some form of internal resistance, a barrier within her between what she was and what she was becoming. But she forced herself through it, pushing her new self through her skin as if she was giving birth to herself.

The internal resistance gave way with a shuddering wrench. Another transformation rippled through her body, tearing spasms of pain and ecstasy—and she threw herself into it unreservedly.

But she never stopped running.

Even without looking at herself, she knew that she was now fully a wolf. Black-furred, smaller than Darien perhaps . . .

But now she was faster.

And she caught up with him.

She could see—in his panting, his strides, the scent of his exertion—that if he had been holding back for her sake, he was no longer. She was catching up, and on four legs she had lost all trace of clumsiness.

He darted around trees, leaping over fallen logs, plowing through underbrush, sending twigs and leaves flying. And she chased after him, on his heels, close enough that she tasted the dirt he kicked up as he ran. Close enough that she could have snapped and grabbed his tail. She let out a low growl—one that let him know she was right behind him.

He had been holding back, a little. He sprang forward, throwing a clod of dirt that exploded against her face. She licked the aromatic mulch off the fur of her cheek and realized that a wolf could smile. She bounded after him, barely winded, and saw her chance as he scrambled down a nearly treeless hillside that sloped down to a shallow brook.

She crested it right after him, but he was already halfway down. Without hesitation, she leapt from the crest of the hill. For the brief moment she was airborne, she had the time to think, *What am I doing?* Then she tackled him, sending them both tumbling down the hillside.

One of them yipped in surprise as they hit the water. Maybe both of them. For a moment, she had him pinned below her, her forepaws resting on his chest as he lay on his side in the shallow water. For a moment she saw him—wet, golden, beautiful. She felt a rush of incredible power as he looked up at her.

Then his lips curled back in a savage snarl as he snapped at her neck. He bit only air, but he jerked his body upright, throwing her off him. She yipped and sputtered as his paw came down on her back, slamming her face into the water. He might have said something in his growling wolf's voice, but she couldn't hear it for her own growling, and the water rushing through her ears.

She fought two instincts. Maria the woman, the servant, the bastard—she knew that she had somehow overstepped her bounds, that she needed to accept the consequences. Maria the wolf, the monster—that one knew that, right now, the human rules didn't apply.

She didn't *have* to submit.

She let loose with her own waterlogged snarl and pushed up from the riverbed against his weight. He might be stronger than her, and outweigh her by half, but she felt that the strength of this lupine body could lift two of him.

And she felt his mouth clamp onto the back of her neck, forcing her down.

No!

She dug into the mud of the creek bed, pulling herself and Darien forward, toward deeper water. He pushed her head down, into the water, but she pulled it back up again. She tried to shake him off, but his grip was painful and tenacious.

She pulled them both into the deepest part of the creek, chest-high on her, and when he shoved her head down, she allowed it to be submerged. She folded her legs and dove, dragging his head down with her. She could feel him gag, but he held on.

She held her breath, and wondered how long he could hold his.

Her lungs burned for air. The old Maria inside her screamed for her to surface. The new Maria knew it was a test of wills between them. His jaws tightened on her neck, and she felt the points of his teeth digging through the thick fur of her neck. He tried to shake and pull her up, but his movements were slow and halting underwater.

The rush of water filled her ears, accompanied only by the thudding of her heart. The core of her body ached for air, but it was still less painful than becoming what she was had been. Darien struggled above her while she forced herself to be still.

A calm heart, she thought, feeling a canine smile on her lips.

Magnificent.

That was the word that filled Darien's mind. It had been decades since he had seen his own kind outside a reflection. He watched her transform from the weak human form into something sleek, black, and incredibly alluring. He stared at her as she racked herself in the heat of the change, and he nearly climaxed in sympathy. When she was finished, crouching on the forest floor before him, his world consisted only of her and the scent of her excitement.

He'd never thought such a creature would ever be his.

Fear still cloaked her, but now it mixed with other smells, some of which he couldn't identify. Soon he would show his mate the joy of what she was. "Follow me," he told her.

He led her on a race though the woods. At first unhurried, she was clumsy in her body, slamming into trees, almost falling with each turn. But he heard her closing and glanced back to see that she had dropped to all fours and had, like him, become completely wolf.

Smaller than him, she still made a fearsome sight. Midnight-black fur, long of limb and body, a narrow wolf head like a snarling arrow. She moved faster than anything Darien had ever seen. He pushed himself to run faster, digging his paws into the earth and thrusting himself forward over the crest of a hill.

Halfway down the other side, she slammed into him. He tumbled down into a brook that ran by the foot of the hill. He fell onto his side, and for a moment the simple shock of her standing above him, holding him down, paralyzed him. For a moment he was overwhelmed by memories of childhood—of adults or siblings holding him down until he admitted who was in charge.

But he was no longer a child, and she was *not* in charge here.

He snapped and threw her off him. She was his mate. That was the *point*. That was the only possible reason for them coming together. And that meant that she had to submit to *him*.

He slammed her down into the water under him, his paws on her back, snarling that he was to be obeyed. But she didn't listen. She bucked him off her.

This wasn't what was supposed to happen. Darien's conscious mind became a confused tumble of anger, embarrassment, and uncertainty. But while he couldn't think, instinct still allowed him to act.

He bit the back of her neck.

She snarled as if he was trying to hurt her, then dragged him deeper into the creek. He tightened his hold on her neck. She had no choice but to concede to him; he was larger, stronger, and there was nothing she could do to break the grip of his jaws on her neck.

But she didn't yield, and he didn't know what to do. He tried to push her head down, but she would struggle up, growling, pulling deeper into the water. He'd already bitten down as hard as he dared without crushing her neck.

The wolf within him grew furious at her defiance, while the man in him pleaded silently with her to give in. He knew she wanted this, wanted him, so why was she refusing him now?

Her head slid under the water, and the wolf felt a brief surge of triumph as the man felt the first hint of alarm.

She won't be able to breathe—

Then his thought was cut short as she dragged him under with her.

Water rushed into his nose, leaking into his mouth. He tried to pull her back up, but his legs didn't have enough purchase in the soft creek bed. His paws just sank into the mud, turning the water cloudy and blinding him. She was deadweight in his mouth, dragging him down. He pulled, her submission becoming secondary to his need to breathe.

He let go, thrusting his head up out of the water to suck in gasping lungfuls of air. She exploded to the surface before him in a cascade of water and mud. She whipped around to face him, her black, mud-streaked face contorted in a feral snarl. It took a conscious effort of will not to back away from the challenge.

His anger rose, and he felt his own lips curl. He quickly tamped down his anger as he realized: *She doesn't know.*

The she-wolf in front of him had been raised by men. She might be his kind, the first he had seen in more than twenty years, but she didn't realize that she *needed* to submit to him.

And, of course, she would. They hadn't even mated yet.

"What kind of game are you playing?" She spoke through the snarl, the words barely words.

Game?

"Do not hold me down," he responded in kind, deciding that there had been enough correction for that already.

She sniffed, turned, and leapt onto the shore, shaking the

water from her fur. She turned her head toward him and cocked it, silently asking, "What now?"

Without the water, he could jump and pin her down, make her submit, force her to mate. Once that happened, there would be no question whose pack this was...

But he held back, because he had smelled her excitement and knew that she would willingly give him what he wanted if he was patient.

She was still watching him with her head cocked, and he jumped onto the shore in front of her and answered her unspoken query.

"We hunt," he said, and shook the water from his fur.

The two of them, the black wolf and the golden one, ran through the woods. No more words passed between them; the instincts of their bodies were enough to communicate. As one they caught the scent of a young bull elk, and they pursued, though not quite as urgently as she had followed him.

The elk, young and healthy, was large enough to deter most predators. But the pair that stalked him were not like any other predators, and in some part of its brain it must have known that, because as soon as it became aware of their presence, it ran off at a speed that seemed impossible for a beast its size.

They followed it through the woods. It ran at a pace driven by sheer terror, but they loped along, barely winded. The elk never had a chance. It finally cornered itself between a deadfall and a steep hillside.

Maria stopped in front of it as it turned around, the human part of her completely forgetting to be afraid as the terrified beast spun wildly, kicking out, looking for an escape. She watched in fascination, bordering on awe, that she could inspire such a reaction.

As she stared, Darien leapt from behind her, burying his teeth in its throat. The elk bellowed—a long tragic groan as it shook frantically, trying to dislodge the gold-furred demon chewing its neck. It jerked its massive head to the side, slamming Darien into a tree. Darien fell to the ground, his back twisted and one foreleg broken so badly that the bone pierced the flesh.

She stared at him, open-mouthed. She needed to get him away. Those wounds...

He barked at her, and inarticulate as it was, it drew her attention back to the rampaging elk. It reared, blood flowing down its chest, frothing from the wound in its neck, and she barely had time to dodge before its forelegs came crashing down where she had just been.

It had stopped being a game.

Anger came easy. She looked at the bellowing creature spinning around and felt a cold fury envelop her. She growled and leapt, not at the neck as the elk thrashed and reared, but at the rear legs. Her jaws seized on its left hind leg as it reared at her, biting down above the joint so hard that she felt the bone splinter in her mouth. The beast screamed and fell forward. She moved in the opposite direction, then spun around to see it thrashing on the ground with three legs.

Most of the fourth leg dangled from her mouth.

As she stood there, realizing the enormity of what she had just done, Darien moved to the front of the thrashing beast, bent down, and finished tearing out its throat. He showed no sign of a broken back or a fractured leg.

He lifted his bloodstained muzzle from the elk's throat, then lowered his face into the soft underside of the dead beast. Watching him attack the elk, Maria realized how hungry she was. The changes and the running had left her with a burning emptiness, and the blood from the leg in her mouth tasted like the sweetest wine.

She lowered herself to the ground and set the elk's leg down in front of her. Something of the human within her rebelled at the thought of raw, unskinned meat. To the wolf, however, the freshness of it had a scent more appetizing than any cookfire.

While Darien buried his head in the guts of the elk's carcass, Maria held her leg down with her forepaws and tore strips of flesh off the bone. She ate slowly, savoring the taste, the sensation of the raw flesh sliding down her throat, the feeling of quenching the fire in her belly.

She finished eating before he did. The leg of the beast was more than she needed. When she was done, she rested her muzzle on her forepaws. Her body was content, allowing her to think.

I am a wolf...

What did this mean to the old Maria? Was that person gone? Had she ever existed? The feeling of power Darien had shown her was intoxicating—and terrifying. At the moment, with her belly full, she could easily imagine running deep into the woods, far past where her mother had lived, wrapping herself in this wolf skin and never coming back.

The thought was alluring, but something in her balked at it. What about her family, her brothers, her *real* mother: the woman who had raised her? They deserved more than to mourn her disappearance.

And what about Josef?

She shook her head, as if some river water were still trapped in her ears. Why had she thought about Josef? Him, of all people? For all she might care for him, want to be with him, what she was now was, to Josef, a soulless beast at best, and a demon at worst. He was part of the Order that hunted Darien, had killed his family...

Did Darien know, showing her this, that he was doing to her what the Order had done to him? Taking away her family, everything she had ever cared about?

That's unfair. My family, even Josef, will live without me.

Wouldn't they?

She looked at the beautiful, brutal animal eviscerating the carcass in front of her. Darien had just slaughtered eight men. She had no doubt of the truth of his statements; they certainly would have killed him, given the chance. But the hunt for him would be redoubled now. Maria could not imagine Telek leaving his uncle's death unavenged, and could not imagine the Duke abiding the loss of his chosen deputy. Even without the Order's presence, all of Gród Narew would now be arrayed against Darien.

And Josef? She remembered him vowing to "finish this thing." This *thing. Her.* Whatever she felt or thought she felt, whatever Josef might feel—she was the monster he hunted. There was no way around it, no way to fix it. She wasn't human, and there was no place for her with Josef, or her family, no matter what she pretended to be.

All she had now was Darien.

And if Josef and the Order had their will, she wouldn't even have that.

What can I do?

Perhaps if she talked to Josef, maybe she could convince him to lead the Order away from here, to look for their wolves somewhere else. Leave these woods safe for Darien.

For her.

Darien lifted a shaggy, bloodstained head from the carcass of the elk and looked at her. She stood, stretching, as he watched. For a moment he seemed angry, as if he was upset that she had finished eating first. However, there was something else in his eyes, and in his scent.

When he leapt over the carcass, she knew it was his turn to chase her.

XXIII

She turned tail and ran as if she mocked him. It infuriated him. It had been his hunt, his kill. She'd had no right to eat from his kill before he was sated. It was as much an affront as—no, it was worse than—holding him to the ground. He remembered the times when, still a child, he'd taken part in the hunt, and how badly he'd been beaten when he ran to taste before his elders. Even when his parents took only a token bite of flesh, they were always *first*. Others ate only when *they* gave approval.

Not only had his mate, his bitch, tasted flesh first, tearing her dinner from the beast while it still lived, but she'd finished *before* him. The brazenness of the act infuriated him. He wanted to punish her. He wanted to make her submit to him.

He wanted her.

So he chased after her lithe form—a black-furred shadow weaving through the woods. He chased her as if he chased life itself. Her scent trailed behind her, mixed with the odor of creek water and elk blood, and it set his brain on fire.

It swirled within him as he ran, stirring up a stew of emotions and instincts: anger, the need to dominate, the need to possess, the need to mate. The lust for her consumed him, igniting every nerve in his body. He chased her, and when she glanced back, his excitement was turgid and unmistakable.

She barked something back at him—not words, just an animal sound, a sharp, playful bark that was almost an invitation. Then she flicked her tail at him and bounded off into the woods.

She invited him.

He scrambled after her, his body desire personified.

He caught up with her only because she had stopped within the clearing where they'd started. She stood, stretching, the sun shining on glossy black fur. She held her head up, nose in the wind, mouth slightly open, eyes closed. Her tail moved, and he saw a flash of moist color in the fur. That, combined with the smell of her sex, was more invitation than any bark.

She ran from him, leading him through the woods. She panted, intoxicated by the speed, the power, all the sensations running though this body of hers. Half in despair, the human Maria had stepped aside in favor of something unthinking, wild, free.

When she looked back at Darien's excitement, she saw his erection without embarrassment or shame, but with something akin to satisfaction. She yipped at him to hurry up as she ran back the way they had come.

She stopped in the clearing where the remains of the old burnt trees clawed gray fingers up at the sky. She heard him approaching, crashing through the woods like an old pagan god come for his maiden sacrifice.

In the stillness, as he approached, the human Maria regained some of herself—enough to ask herself if this was what she wanted. Did she want to give her virginity, here, now, without so much as a promise of betrothal? The doubt was strange in her head, dissonant with the animal she had become, the animal she had been reveling in.

But she wasn't an animal.

And she wasn't human either…

She looked at the sky and opened her mouth to ask silently of God, *What am I?* And of herself, *What am I becoming?*

She smelled his scent before he emerged from the woods at the edge of the clearing. She tensed, expecting to be trampled. But, instead, she felt him brush up against her side, and felt him lick the blood off her muzzle. She turned her head at the surprisingly gentle gesture, and he climbed upon her back.

She gasped as she felt the size of him pushing aside her tail, brushing the tip against her maidenhead. Again she felt his jaws clamp down on her neck, but she barely noticed as he thrust inside her. She spasmed and her forelegs collapsed as he filled her with the same agonizing pleasure she had felt when she had changed. She screamed at the sky—screamed for the pain, for the pleasure, for what she felt filling her body.

She howled until her voice was little more than a hoarse, exhausted groan.

⌖

Above her, the sky darkened toward evening. Maria lay on her back in the grass, with Darien's head resting on her stomach. As she stroked the fur on his neck, she realized that sometime after Darien had spent himself, she had shrunk back into her human skin. She looked at his muzzle against her naked belly and realized how massive a wolf he made. His jaws could easily snap someone her size in half.

Her hand was tiny against his skull, and she realized that she had allowed this beast to mate with her. She had torn the leg off an elk and had eaten it. She rubbed her face and found that there were still traces of dried elk blood on her. The whole day was some horrible nightmare—more horrible because of how attracted she was to it. To what she was.

At least she hadn't fallen into the trap Lucina had, trying for a human husband when she wasn't human. Darien might be a killer, but he had reason. If she could get the Order to go away, to hunt other lands for their wolves, they could have Lucina's woods for their own. There would be an endless supply of game to feed them and their children.

I just have to give up everything...

She needed to do what she could about that, while she had time. She also needed to say good-bye to her family, tell her mother that she had found one of her own to be with. She glanced up at the darkening sky and sighed. She slipped out from under his head and stood up. Darien opened one groggy eye at her and half-growled, "You're mine now."

She crouched before him and said, "I know."

Shouldn't I be happier?

He made a contented grumble and closed his eye again.

"You sleep," she said. "I'll be back."

I have nowhere else to go.

She walked over to where they had left their clothes. She stared at hers for a long time. This morning she had been consumed with embarrassment just watching Darien disrobe. Now her own clothes seemed alien to her, so divorced from her experience that for a moment she couldn't clearly envision their purpose.

She bit her lip and shook, hugging herself.

It would be so easy to let it all slip away—everything she was, the person she had been. But even if it had been a lie, it was who she was. She didn't *want* to lose that.

But what choice did she have when such an animal lived inside her?

She dressed hurriedly, afraid that she would lose the will to go back and do right by her human family. They deserved better than to be abandoned without a word of explanation. But all the while, she had to wipe tears and blood off her face.

When she glanced back at Darien, his golden fur had become red-tinged in the evening light.

What else did she have?

She came within sight of her cottage just as the sky faded from red to purple. She had spent the walk back rehearsing what she would say to her family, how she would explain shedding her human identity to be with someone who was the same as her.

She just wished she could stop crying.

She didn't understand what she felt. It made no sense. Darien had to be right that it was fate, some special providence by God that had brought her to him. How else would she ever have found another like her? How else could she avoid her mother's fate?

But why did it weigh on her heart as if something tragic had happened? She was mourning the loss of things she had never had in the first place. Crying over the loss of her old life made no more sense than crying over not being raised in one of the families of the szlachta, or not being born a man, or being too tall.

She was what she was. What was done was done. Pray as she might, neither would ever change.

She thanked God that she hadn't broken down like this in front of Darien. Wolf he might be, but she had known men like him. Men who demanded submission, but who also despised weakness. Her doubt, her tears would enrage him, and he was volatile enough without any encouragement.

And why did that make her think of Lukasz?

"What did you do to him, Darien?" she whispered to herself as she reached the open front gate. Her thoughts were prepared to descend a very dark path when her brother's voice called to her.

"Maria!" She looked up to the doorway and saw Władysław running toward her. He scooped her up and hugged her. "We were so frightened for you, with this beast roaming the woods."

"I'm fine." She patted her brother's back and looked up at the doorway to the cottage. Her stepmother stood there, and next to her—

"No," she whispered. "Why is *he* here?"

Josef took a few steps forward, still slowed by his injury. Władysław let her go and said, "He came to me while I waited to escort you home. He told me that you had left when the victims were brought in. We've been searching for you."

She turned to Josef and spoke in German: "The Order is confined to Gród Narew."

"Not anymore," Josef replied. "The Wojewoda's death and his nephew's pleas were enough to convince the Duke to allow Brother Heinrich's Wolfjägers to search the countryside fully armed, as long as they are accompanied by Telek's men or the Duke's own officers."

Maria backed up a step and glanced nervously from her mother to Josef. Her family had kept her safe for so long. They wouldn't now turn her over to the Germans, would they? Could Władysław have told Josef what she had said? He hadn't believed her, so would he keep such a ridiculous secret? Her stepmother had raised Maria as her own, but did that mean she would defend her if her own blood's children were at stake?

And what had she said to Josef this morning? What inane things had she told him a century ago, before what she was had become so real—more real than what she pretended to be now?

"Why did you come here?" she asked him, her body tensing for flight.

"We were concerned for your safety. This beast is abroad in the woods here—and I wished to talk with you."

"Talk with me?"

He turned back toward the cottage and spoke in tortured Polish: "Your daughter, may I speak with her?" Maria was suddenly touched by the gesture, the idea that Josef had tried to learn her language. She wondered if he knew that her stepmother spoke the German tongue as well as he.

Her stepmother waved at her brother and said, "Come, Władysław."

Władysław hugged her again and whispered in her ear, "I saw him kiss you."

She and Josef were left alone in front of the cottage.

He stepped up to her.

"What did you want to talk to me about?"

"You have mud on your face." He reached up and wiped her cheek gently with his thumb. "And you've been crying."

It's not mud, she thought, turning away from his touch. "I'm fine." She sucked in a breath and told herself that it was a good thing he was here. He was the one member of the Order she could talk to, and her best chance to convince them to leave, to take their hunt elsewhere.

But she didn't know how to do that. Not when they had dead men to account for.

They were out to kill him, she thought. *Darien just defended himself.*

"What did you want to talk about?" she snapped, more harshly than she'd intended.

He placed his hands on her shoulders. "I am going to leave the Order."

"What?" She spun around. "You can't!"

"Maria?"

"T-this . . . it's your *vocation*. You chose to serve God. How can you—"

"The whole purpose of probationary membership is to determine the initiate's devotion to this service. I have found myself wanting."

Maria stared at him, unable to form a fully coherent thought. This man had given up a title and an estate to serve the Order, and now he wanted to give that up as well? All she managed to say was "Why?"

"Service in the Order means that I am asked to ignore my own conscience, my own heart, in obedience to my master and the pope. There was a time when I thought I could."

Maria caught her breath when she realized how he was looking at her. "Your heart?"

"I have already disobeyed my master directly, beyond what you know. But I wanted to protect you."

No. This couldn't be happening. She couldn't be leading such a man away from God. She couldn't bear that on her conscience after everything else. "Please, reconsider what you're doing. Don't throw it away."

He smiled at her. "You have a generous heart."

"No." She shook her head. "You have no idea how selfish I am."

"You've occupied my thoughts ever since I first saw you—and nothing you've done or said has led me to think less of you."

"Don't say this—"

"I care for you, Maria. More than is proper for a monk."

"Please—"

"If God wished me to serve Him in the Order, He would not have placed you in my path."

She backed away, clenching her fists. "No! Stop it!"

"I love you, Maria."

The words were a slap in her face. Her thoughts screamed for him not to say such a thing, not to think it. "Stop talking!" she yelled at him. She shook her head again, and could feel the anger, the frustration—every confused emotion trying to let loose the beast inside her. In the back of her skull she heard her bones creak, and she felt the first knives of pain stabbing her joints. She clutched at her heart...

She wasn't wearing her cross!

"No! No! No!" she screamed. Not now, not in front of Josef. She couldn't—

"Maria?" He reached out for her, and she knocked his hand away.

Doubled over, she held back the change her traitorous body was trying to force upon her, fueled by fear, anger, and confusion.

"You know nothing of me, Josef. What I am." She looked up at him through the hair that had fallen in front of her face. Something of the wolf had found its way into her voice, turning it rough and growling. "If you care for me, go back to the Order. Lead them away from these woods."

"Maria? What has happened to you?"

She shook her head. Nothing had happened to her. She was what she was. She had simply found out the truth. "If you care for yourself, leave and never think of me again."

She drew in shuddering breaths to calm herself. This was not how things should be going. She couldn't be repeating Lucina's mistake. She was not so lonely. She had her own mate waiting in the woods for her.

So why did it feel like her heart was breaking?

She felt his hand on her cheek, brushing the hair out of her eyes. "I'm leaving the Order because I cannot abide another telling me my own heart."

"Please—"

He lifted her chin so she could look at him. His face was less perfect than Darien's—leaner and more marked by time. But she saw the same determination, and she saw a warmth that Darien lacked.

"You shouldn't," she whispered.

She could strike him, like she had Lukasz. Push him away. She could turn around and run, forgetting any plans to try to cleanly close off the human chapter of her life. She could do any one of those things, but she didn't.

Instead she looked into his eyes and felt her heart race, and she didn't move a muscle as he bent to kiss her.

She wanted him. More than anything else, she wanted Josef. Even after what Darien had shown her—the strength, and the freedom, and the joyful savagery—what she had always wanted was someone who loved her. And for all Darien was, she doubted he could ever give her that. All Darien knew, all he truly cared about was the beast that lived inside her. Josef knew the person she was—or at least the person she wanted to be . . .

Yet as she kissed him, and as his touch warmed depths of her body she was unaware had gone cold, she wept. Because, whatever he had said, if Josef knew the truth, he wouldn't be able to give her that, either.

Still, as wrong and as deceitful as it was, she let him embrace her. She needed him right now. Not the animal that sated its lusts in the woods. Maria, the woman—the human being—*she* needed him. That part of her needed someone to hold her, to comfort her, and not to ask why.

XXIV

Darien woke and stretched, feeling a sense of contentment he hadn't felt since he was a child. The universe had reorganized itself again, and he had a proper place within it. After years of being a single creature on the outside of man's castle, tearing at the monuments of their hubris—after so long defining himself solely in opposition to his enemy—he had something of his own: a life, a family, a mate, all outside the world defined by the desires of men or their God.

The earth where he had slept was still strong with her scent, and he breathed it in, growling in pleasure. He felt honestly happy for the first time since the Order had slaughtered his family.

He let out a small yip to let Maria know he was awake, to come back to him. There were still so many things to show her, so many stories to tell. The evening was crisp and cool, and the night promised to be excellent.

Where was she?

As he came fully awake, he remembered her stroking him. He remembered her naked human form cradling his head. She had told him to go back to sleep.

He padded over to where they had cast off their human clothes. She had taken hers . . .

Where had she gone that she needed to dress like *them*?

Darien felt his mood go cold, still, and dark. Like the sky before a great storm, his mind was suddenly very quiet. She wouldn't go back to them, not after what he had shown her.

He had *mated* with her. No one else. *Her*. He had waited for twenty years to find his own kind. She couldn't give that to him and then leave. She couldn't.

He nosed the leaves where her clothes had rested, trying to think of some other explanation, some excuse. A flash of silver glinted from the leaves, and he saw her cross.

Yes, he thought. *She's not returning to bondage.*

Then he licked his muzzle as a host of new possibilities filled his mind. She had gone back to punish them. They had been the ones to trap her, chain her in silver without any knowledge of the strength within her. What they had done to her, in some sense, was worse than what the Order had done to him. The Order had destroyed his family, but these wretched humans had spent years destroying *her.* Forcing her to deny what she was until she didn't even know what she was denying.

He ran, drinking in her scent. He would catch up with her, and he would help her wreak vengeance on these fools who would have her chained. They would both taste of their traitorous flesh, and he would take her again on a bed made of their bones.

Darien knew that something was very wrong when he heard her crying. He stopped in the woods, just out of sight of the house where they had imprisoned her. He heard the sobs and tried to convince himself that they were the sounds of remorse or pain from the ones who had wronged her.

But he knew her voice.

He crept forward, keeping to the shadows between the trees, stopping only when the cottage came into sight. When she came into sight.

This is not possible . . .

A murderous growl formed in his chest, and his lips curled back in a demonic snarl that threatened to split his muzzle in two. His mate, his bitch—after she had given herself to him—stood in front of the cabin of her captors, sobbing in the arms of some man. And not any man, but a monk of the Order.

One he recognized.

His forepaws creaked as his body began twisting itself for combat, and he dug his growing fingers into the soil. He would tear the monk apart, rip the flesh from his bones while he still lived. The man would watch as Darien fed on his liver. The Order had taken one family from him. They would not take *this.*

Maria broke from the embrace and looked toward the forest, as if she heard him.

Darien froze, staring at them. At *him.*

Do you feel it, man? Do you feel the eye you nearly stole looking back at you?

As he watched, he saw Maria's nostrils dilate, and her face turned right to him. She knew he was here. As he watched, frozen, she placed a hand on the man's chest, gently pushing him behind her.

You foolish bitch! His anger screamed at him to attack, but he had not lived two decades alone against the Order by allowing his rage to lead him. He could take this man now—he could slaughter him whatever Maria might do to protect him—but that wasn't what he wanted. Not this man's suffering, not his death. That was coming soon enough, regardless of what Darien did now. He wanted *her.* He needed her to see what these creatures called men truly were.

She had run back to this house, to this man, only because

Darien had *told* her, but he hadn't *shown* her. Darien slowly backed deeper into the shadows. However much he wanted to taste this man's flesh now, there were more productive outlets for his rage.

Maria cried against Josef's shoulder, letting loose all the pain, frustration, and confusion. He didn't ask her any more questions, and for a time she was able to forget that she was not the same Maria he knew. She sucked in sobbing breaths, smelling Josef's scent, so unlike Darien's. She wanted to lose herself in him, to be the woman he thought she was—to have a life, a family, a husband: all the doomed dreams of the mother who had birthed her.

Such thoughts only made her weep more. She cried until her breath burned against the rawness of her throat.

Then she smelled Darien. Her muscles seized as she thought she heard a low growl.

No, not here.

She broke from Josef's arms and spun around to face the woods. She smelled him strongly now, and she thought she saw movement beyond the trees: a flash of yellow fur, a glint of a pale blue eye.

"Maria?"

She pushed Josef behind herself and stared out at the woods, heart pounding, waiting for her wolf lover to charge out of the woods to challenge her.

Just as Lucina had challenged her father.

Please God, not that.

"Maria? What is it? Is there something out there?"

There were no more sounds, and after a few moments, his scent was carried away by the evening breeze. "Nothing," she said finally. "I must have imagined it." But she knew she hadn't.

"You know what is out there, don't you?"

She turned around and faced him, prepared to lie. But seeing his eyes, she couldn't. "Y-yes."

"You knew it before I told you anything, before I gave you that dagger. That's why your brother carries it now. He needs it more than you do."

He knows. He knows what I am. She felt her stomach sink. Josef knew what she was, and she wouldn't even have the cold comfort of being the one to tell him.

"I came here to save you."

"S-save me?"

"Yes. You have a chance to repent of your sins. There is even a bishop present to grant you absolution. Please, you must abandon your pagan practices. Tell us where the shrines are, where you leave your sacrifices."

She stared back at him in total confusion. Her pagan practices? She was a Christian. Whatever else she might be, she knew that much. She had been baptized. She attended Mass, confessed her sins.

"Maria, my heart has been weighed by suspicions since you showed me your father's cross. It was not until after you confronted me that I understood what this must be, how a good woman like you could be involved in such evil." He took her shoulders and looked into her eyes, an expression of heartbreaking concern across his face. "This creature, it is not your God. It is a satanic deception meant to lead you from salvation."

Her eyes widened as she realized how fully Josef had misunderstood. "Please, I'm not . . ." She trailed off, not knowing how to correct him without making things worse.

"I see it, Maria. You *know* this thing. That is why you spent this morning trying to convince me of its humanity, isn't it? It is why you know of wolves when I mentioned no such thing to you. You sensed it here just a moment ago, didn't you?"

She hesitated for a long time before finally saying, "Yes."

"You're trying to protect it."

Maria felt tears burning her cheeks. Even in error, he came too close to her heart. All he was mistaken about was *why*. "You don't understand. I want this to stop."

"I know," Josef said. "When you disappeared, you sought it out, didn't you?"

"Please—"

"Did it explain why it slaughtered your lord Bolesław and seven other men?"

"They were hunting him."

"Did it explain the villages it has laid to waste? Forty men, women, and children left to rot on the steps of their own church?"

She wanted to deny it, but she had seen Darien's eyes. She had heard him. Yes, he had reason, but the reason was so deep and grave that she could see Darien using it to justify *anything.*

In her confusion, she had to force her heart from turning completely away from Darien's brutality, because, after this, he would be all she had—all she ever would have. She hugged herself and shook her head, telling herself that she really wasn't a wicked person.

She must have said it out loud, because Josef answered, "I know you aren't."

She looked up at him.

"I was watching your face when you saw the evidence of its slaughter; I saw the betrayal in your eyes. Even if this thing is the god of your ancestors, even if you sacrifice to it, this wrath was not what you were asking of it, was it?"

"No." She wasn't even certain what it was she wanted from Darien anymore. Or Josef. Or herself. She did know that she didn't want more people hurt or killed, and that included Darien. In her confusion, she finally said to him, "If you lead them away from here, away from him, the killing will stop. I know it will."

"Maria," he said, lowering his voice, "does your family know what you're doing?"

She opened her mouth, but nothing came out.

"They don't, do they?"

"I—"

"You gave your brother the dagger because you realize that they're in danger."

"No." But he was right: for all she'd been drawn to Darien, she didn't trust him. Couldn't trust him. Especially with her family.

"You *know* that this beast is nothing that will be turned aside by an offering." Josef released her shoulders. "Come back with me, make things right with God. Make them right with yourself. I see in your face—you know you're on the wrong path."

"I can't go back."

"Please. If Brother Heinrich discovers what you've done, he won't be merciful. If you don't come forward and seek sanctuary with the bishop of your countrymen, I don't know if I can keep protecting you."

"If he discovers— You haven't told them?"

"If I had, I wouldn't be here."

Guilt compounded on guilt. She looked up at the darkened sky and felt as if the world were caving in on her. "No, you cannot sacrifice yourself for me, lie for me, when you have no idea what I've done."

"What *have* you done?"

"I—" She couldn't tell him. She couldn't tell him of the animal hunger, the lust that burned within her. Worse, even though she wanted more than anything to turn him away, she had sensed Darien watching, and she knew that if Josef walked the nighttime path back to Gród Narew, Darien would—

"I'll go back with you," she said. It would give her time to think. Perhaps the bishop *could* give her absolution. If not, once Josef was safe in the fortress, she could slip away during the night.

She knew the place intimately enough. Then she would find Darien, and if the Order would stay here, she would lead *Darien* away. They could go east, away from the frontiers of the monastic state, past the point the Germans would ever dare explore. "Just let me say good-bye to my family."

⌖

Darien returned to the clearing in the dark of night, his rage now cold and hard as a stone. He would mete out a grand vengeance—both to the Order and to the wretches who had imprisoned his mate, turning her against him and her kind. In the process he would show her the true face of the humans she lived with. She would have no choice but to reject them.

As distasteful as it was, he retreated into human skin and dressed in the clothing that allowed him to walk within the humans' world. When he took her away from this place, they would shed these rags. Then they would both forget everything of the human world.

But only after he exacted his last payment of flesh and bone from the Order here, and only after he had proved the worthlessness of humanity to her.

Once his human mask was in place, he reached down into the leaves and dug up the cross Maria had left behind. "These chains were so important to you," he said. "Fitting that they will finally free you."

XXV

When Maria stepped into her family's cabin, her mother and three brothers were waiting for her. All of them looked at her, and she felt the weight of their stares.

"You're no longer wearing your father's cross."

Her hand moved unconsciously to her heart to touch it, but it wasn't there. "I lost it in the woods."

She saw the pain in her stepmother's face, and it was all the sign she needed that she had crossed a line that she couldn't recross.

Władysław had stopped smiling, but it was clear that he didn't yet understand. "We can go and look for it in the daylight."

Maria shook her head. "I don't need it anymore."

"What do you mean?" Władysław said.

Her stepmother stood. "Your sister is leaving."

Maria nodded. "I'm going with Josef. I'm not coming back."

Shock froze her brothers' faces, Władysław's most of all. Her stepmother looked at her with a crooked smile and said, "It happens, doesn't it? Children leave home."

"It isn't safe for me to stay," Maria said.

"What danger are you in?" Władysław asked. "I'll protect you."

"Your sister doesn't need your protection," her stepmother said. "I don't think she's concerned for her own safety."

"What?" Władysław looked confused.

Maria met his gaze. "I told you what I was."

"No," he said. "You were playing me for a fool. You still are. But that joke's gone too far." The silence that followed pained her, but Maria said nothing to break it. Władysław turned to her stepmother. "Mother, tell her to stop these lies."

"Your sister is not a liar." She walked up to Maria and said, "Your father knew that this would happen someday. There's another one, isn't there?"

"Someone like me," she said.

"Someone like you?" Władysław echoed, his voice weak and distant.

"His name is Darien."

"But," her stepmother said, "you are leaving with Josef."

"No," Władysław said. "You're saying that this Darien—he's responsible for the killings? The Order, they're hunting him, aren't they?" He grabbed her arm. "You're saying you're this thing—but this other one, he's the killer, the one with blood on his hands?"

"They would kill him otherwise." Maria spoke the words, but they rang hollow in her own ears.

"And what would the Order do with you? This Darien draws their wrath. Is he that much to you that you wish to draw it as well?" Władysław's grip on her arm was hard, bruising, as he shook her. "Is he more kin to you than your own family? I won't allow you to go. You aren't going to indulge in these madwoman's tales before men who would take you seriously enough to set you to fire."

She wanted to scream, but Josef was outside, and she didn't want him to hear the words, even in a language he couldn't understand. Instead, her voice came out in a harsh whisper that took on the growling aspect of the wolf: "My brother, I am *not* human. And you *will* let me go."

His eyes widened and his grip loosened.

"Release me." The words came out in a snarl, and he snatched his hand away as if she had burned him. "Mother is right. I am no liar. And if I remain here, you are all in danger—if not from the Order, then from Darien."

"Maria?" Her stepmother was in tears. "You don't have to choose this path. We're your family."

"You said Father knew this day would come."

"But like this? Your brother is right. If this Darien has taken so many lives, do you want to join him?"

"There's no choice left for me, Mother. All I can do now is keep myself from Lucina's fate." Maria felt her own tears, and she touched her stepmother's cheek. "I won't hurt anyone just to be with those I love."

Then she turned away and left her home.

She walked with Josef in silence. She watched the dark shadows of the woods around them. The shadows beyond the reach of Josef's lantern seemed more ominous than they had ever been to her before. She should flee into the dark, she thought, disappear. If Josef weren't here, she would. If she were certain that he would be safe.

Is that why she was here?

She didn't know anymore. She didn't know who she was, or what she was. She only knew that she was afraid. Afraid for herself, afraid for Josef, and afraid for her family.

She was afraid for Darien, too—even as she listened for his footfall, sniffed the wind for his scent, and scanned the few columns of moonlight that broke the shadows for any hint of yellow fur or the glint of a pale blue eye.

Josef himself seemed lost in thought.

She kept thinking of the woman she had been, how she might have received Josef's declarations. It seemed some sign of how far she had fallen that she couldn't imagine how she would have reacted before tonight, before meeting Darien.

It began to dawn on her how pale he looked.

"Josef, are you well?"

"I am fine." But she heard an edge to his voice that made him a liar. She placed a hand on his shoulder and realized that she smelled blood.

"Josef, your wounds—"

"They are no matter."

She spun him around to face her.

"Maria—"

She pulled up his surcote and placed her hand against his shirt. He gasped, and she felt a dampness through his shirt. "You're bleeding."

"I can make it."

"You're a fool if you think that. And I'm a fool for not noticing sooner. You're going to lie down here, now."

"I don't think that's necessary."

She grabbed his hand and pressed it against his shirt. His eyes widened, and he gasped again in pain. "Do you feel that? You've pulled your scar open. You need to stop moving and put pressure on it, now."

Josef nodded and swayed a little. She helped him to a clear spot by the side of the road, and by the time he rested the lantern on the ground and lay down, she was bearing most of his weight. "Perhaps you're right," he said.

She pulled his surcote and his shirt up, exposing the dressing on his stomach. "God help us," Maria whispered. The dressing glistened moist and black in the moonlight.

She undid the dressing and looked at the wound.

Josef groaned.

"Please, don't move. The top of the scar has pulled apart. The blood's flowing freely, but not fast. If we stanch the flow, you'll be all right." She grabbed the bottom of his surcote and started tearing strips from it. The thick fabric tore easily in her urgency, but the only comment from Josef was "I won't be needing that anyway."

She bound him up and kept her blood-soaked hands pressing on his stomach. Her only comfort was the fact that this was only as bad as it seemed because Josef had been bullheaded enough not to stop when he must have felt his wound tear.

"So," he said after some time had passed, "when do we resume our journey?"

"When you stop bleeding, or a cart rolls by on the way to Gród Narew."

After another long pause, he said, "You have a good heart."

"You don't know me."

"Don't I? I'm dragging you to testify against yourself. Wouldn't it have been easier just to let me bleed?"

"Be quiet. Save your strength." She was astounded that he had any left. How much of a search had he gone on with her brother? How long had he been bleeding before he'd even looked ill?

"Josef," she asked, "if I hadn't been hiding something, if I wasn't what I am, would you have come for me?"

His eyes had closed, but he whispered, "I love you, Maria."

Her heart ached. "Josef, you shouldn't say that. You don't know what I am. I don't even think you know Darien."

When he didn't answer, she looked down and saw that he was asleep.

⊕

Darien spent much of the night observing the comings and goings of the watch on the walls of Gród Narew. There were more men on the walls than he remembered from his prior journeys to this place. Watching for him, he suspected. Still, they were men, and relied too much on their eyes.

The ground that had been cleared before the skirts of Gród Narew was designed to withhold concealment from an army, not an individual. Even in human skin, he could come close to the wall unobserved just by keeping to the opposite side of the stone fences that defined the surrounding pasture. The closer he came, the less the guards' gaze drifted toward him. They believed they would see any threat as it emerged from the distant woods, paying little thought to the ground at their feet.

He approached on the side of the fortress opposite the moon and the main gate, and by the time he had reached the closest of the stone fences, he was deep in the shadow cast by the outer wall. Between him and the bottom of the wall were about thirty paces of bare grass.

He cleared it in fifteen, with no alert from the guards above.

He listened, and even with his dull human ears, he could hear the men walking the wall above. The log-and-earthwork wall towered above him, seven or eight times the height of a man.

He flexed his fingers and reached up.

This would be easier in his true body, but that was what they watched for. Besides, he wore Maria's cross.

So he hooked fleshy human fingers into the flaws in the log skin of the wall and pulled himself up. He scaled it, jamming into gaps so small that his fingers bled. With the silver cross so close to his skin, the wounds were slow to heal, but Darien accepted the pain. He welcomed it. He hated this body that was so like his enemies', so it felt right that it should suffer like he would make them suffer.

His fingers continued to slide across rough wood and bark, and he forced them into the cracks, pushing deeper and harder. By the time he reached the top of the wall, he had lost most of his fingernails.

He hung on the edge, in the last of the moon-cast shadow, listening to the movements of the guards. Their steps were slow and lazy, and after a few moments one passed in front of Darien, oblivious to his presence.

He could tear this place apart.

But that wasn't why he was here.

He waited until the guard's heavy footfalls left him to join another, farther down the wall. Darien heard the beginnings of a whispered conversation and took the chance to chin himself up enough to look over the edge of the wall. Forty paces away, two guards talked while looking out over the vista commanded by Gród Narew. In the other direction, thirty paces away, a third guard walked away from Darien, equally intent on looking for threats coming from his quarter of the woods.

Darien pulled himself up silently and alighted briefly on the walkway between the two sets of guards. He flexed his aching hands until the joints creaked, pausing just long enough to see if he was being observed.

No alarm came; he vaulted off the inner edge of the walkway and into the darkness below.

Darien slipped through the darkened alleys of the human stronghold, choking on the smell of men that filled the air. He slipped past oblivious guards, weaving his way around until he found the stables.

The smell of equine prey was a relief after the stench of humanity. It also reminded him dimly of the man who had attacked Maria; he remembered his smell better than his face.

Horses shuffled and nickered as he slipped inside, but none panicked. They might feel uneasy at a stranger's presence, but, wrapped in a man's skin, he wasn't a subject of fear. He might have ridden one had he chosen to.

Instead, he walked through the sawdust in the darkened stables, passing the rumps of a dozen horses. The moonlight reached in just enough to show the floor and the outline of the nervous horses.

At dawn, this end of the aisle would still be wrapped in darkness. He looked up into the rafters, which were nothing more than an ink-black smear of shadow. He climbed up into the darkness.

He found a perch on a long timber that was broader than he was. He felt his way along until he was above the aisleway. Below, the dim moonlight through the doorway seemed to glow like a spectral bonfire in contrast to the dark where he crouched. He removed his clothes by touch, laying them neatly on the timber next to him, until he was barefoot and naked.

Last he removed Maria's cross, setting it on the timber on his left, opposite the clothes. In response, his fingers started itching. "You will see what men are, Maria."

Then he sucked the blood off his fingertips as his fingernails grew back.

XXVI

Josef woke to birds chirping. He yawned and blinked a few times. Above him, leafy branches framed a threatening red-gray predawn sky. Dampness coated the skin on his upper body, chilling him. For a moment he was unclear about where he was or what had happened. He had gone to find Maria, talked to her, and started their return to Gród Narew.

Had he fallen asleep?

He raised his hand to wipe the fatigue from his eyes and stopped. Blood streaked his hand, and the image raised so many horrific possibilities that his mind recoiled.

He started to sit up but felt a weight holding him down.

He looked down at himself and saw one of those horrific possibilities made flesh. Maria was draped against him, her hands on his stomach, her head by his thighs. Her arms were coated with blood, and blood stained the bandages around his wounds.

Had the worst happened? Had the false pagan god called its vengeance on its servant?

Then he saw that she breathed.

The memory of the night returned to him slowly. The sudden fatigue, his near collapse, Maria shredding his clothes.

"Christ have mercy," he whispered, and said a short prayer of thanksgiving that the beast had not found them asleep in the night.

He was naked from the waist up, and what didn't serve as a new dressing on his wound had been shoved under his head as a pillow. She hadn't made any such provision for herself. She slept with her cheek resting against his thigh, her black hair obscuring her face except for her half-open mouth. He could feel her breath, even through his breeches.

He remembered kissing her.

Her hands were still tangled in the dressing covering the wound in his belly. Even now, where gore didn't streak her skin, her knuckles were a bloodless white. He reached out and touched her hand, and she jerked, lifting her head, shaking the hair out of her eyes. She blurted something in Polish, and Josef told her, "I seem to have survived."

"God forgive me, I fell asleep—"

"No one can stay awake forever." He squeezed her hands.

"No, he's still out there."

"Maria, we're fine."

She looked down and shook her head. "You are far from fine. You almost spilled your life out for lack of attention."

"I am blessed, then, that you cared to mind me." He let go of her hands. "And perhaps you might unclench your grip and see if the wound has sealed itself again."

She looked down at her hands, still holding down the bandage at his stomach. She nodded and grunted a little, and Josef could swear he heard the sounds of bones creaking, as she unclenched her hands and pulled them apart. For a moment it looked as if she had hurt her hands, the skin bruised, the fingers dislocated and swollen. But it must have been a trick of the light, because she shook them both once and Josef saw no more sign of injury other than his own blood crusting the skin.

She felt around the place she had been holding down and,

after some investigation, told him the bleeding seemed to have ceased.

"Good," he said, pushing himself up from the ground. "We can return to the fortress."

She placed a hand on his shoulder; it was distractingly warm against his chilled skin. "You shouldn't be walking around."

"And the alternative? Remain here?"

"You could pull that wound open again."

"I appreciate your concern." He bent over to push himself upright, and Maria grabbed his arm and draped it over her shoulders.

"If you won't rest," she said, "let me help you." She hooked her arm behind him, holding his back as she lifted. She moved slowly, gently, and with a reserve of strength he didn't expect. He reached his feet and felt a wave of disorientation that made his knees wobble underneath him. But she kept him upright.

"Thank you," he said.

"I will not let you kill yourself."

He tried to lift his arm off her shoulders, but she grabbed his wrist with her free hand.

"I can walk by myself," he said.

"And you can walk with my assistance."

He didn't have the energy to debate her on the point.

The sky remained threatening, but the rain held off as they approached Gród Narew. Since it was still before dawn, the gates hadn't been opened for the day. However, there were guards emplaced who saw them slowly climbing the main road up the hillside, and by the time they reached the walls, the gates were opened for them to enter.

A half dozen men grouped themselves around Josef and

Maria, and as they asked question after question in a language Josef couldn't understand, he began to realize how awful he must have looked—shirtless, stomach bound by gory bandages, bloodstained breeches, skin pale as death, supported by a woman half a head shorter than he was.

Maria answered their questions, and a pair of the guards ran off while another pair led the two of them deeper into Gród Narew.

"They're fetching the doctor for you," Maria told him.

"Do I need a doctor?" He felt his stomach tighten for reasons quite aside from his wound.

"You cannot think otherwise."

"No," Josef said. "But I have seen too much of their ministries to think gladly of the prospect."

"Think of it what you will. Your wounds will be tended to."

Josef closed his eyes and allowed her to lead him. In his mind, Nürnberg was too close—the smell of death, the cries of the lost, and the physicians who calmly advised abandonment of the afflicted before they themselves fled to the countryside.

A cloudy dawn came slowly over Gród Narew, the sky boiling red and gray. The overcast light in the stables barely exceeded the moonlight from the previous night. Darien was still crouched in the rafters, waiting. He licked his lips when his prey arrived. A young stable hand, sandy-haired, maybe sixteen, carried a pair of large sloshing buckets into the aisleway.

The boy did not look up. And when Darien was certain that the boy's gaze was turned in the right direction, he gently pushed the cross and chain off the timber with his foot. It fell glittering to the aisleway in front of the boy.

The boy's eyes widened in surprise, and he set down the

buckets as he walked to where the treasure had fallen upon a pile of manure. He picked the cross out of the pile, holding it up by the chain to catch the weak dawn light.

Above him, Darien's bones stretched and creaked, and his muscles writhed, and his teeth became sharp and long in his growing muzzle. The horses, until now dim to the danger in their midst, began rearing and stomping in a cacophony that sent the stableboy spinning around to see the source of their terror.

Drool slid from Darien's slavering mouth, dripping from his tongue to land on the boy's left shoulder. The boy looked up to see Darien falling down upon him, and if he had time to scream, it was lost beneath the cries of the terrified horses.

Josef remembered little of the next hour or so. He was placed on a table in an unfamiliar room. Men came and went. The doctor or his assistant forced him to drink wine flavored with bitter herbs until his stomach was near bursting and his vision became cloudy and unfocused. They talked much, but he understood little. Maria held his hand.

They placed a leather-wrapped block of wood in his mouth as they tore the bandages free and washed his wound, and he thought the pain of that was intolerable. Then they used a needle to close the wound again.

She held his hand through it all, even when he clenched it in pain.

When the doctor had finished, he bent over Josef and said in butchered German, "You be fine." The words came out in a breath that stank as if the doctor had taken several doses of his own medicine. He slapped Josef's shoulder and said, "Strong."

He chuckled and left. For the moment, Josef was alone with Maria.

Josef reached up to touch the clean linens that now covered his belly. The doctor's assistant had washed him only as far up as his sternum, so a line separated clean skin from the mud and blood spatters on his chest.

"Leave it be," Maria said.

He looked up at her; her face looked pale. She had sat there, watching the whole thing, and it had probably been all the worse for her, without pain and alcohol to take her mind off it. "The doctor said I'd be fine."

"God willing," she said.

He leaned his head back down, because the wine made his head swim. "I think I'm more ill from the cure than the wound."

"You rest, Josef. Please? I will go talk to the bishop."

"I should see you there, explain—" He started to push himself up from the table, but she placed her hand on his chest.

She leaned over him, her face above his so that her hair brushed his cheek. Her eyes shone with reflected tears. "Whatever happens," she said, "please don't risk yourself again. Not for me."

"I—"

She interrupted him by lowering her mouth to his. Her lips were sweet, and soft, and trembled slightly as she cried. She raised her head and laid a hand against his cheek. "You cannot love me, Josef."

"Maria—"

She placed her fingers on his lips, and he saw an expression of wrenching sadness on her face. "More than anything, I want that. If I were the woman you think I am, I'd fall into your arms and gladly go wherever you led." Her thumb traced his lower lip. "But if I did that, it would be an unspeakable cruelty."

"But—"

"Promise that you will forget me," she whispered.

"I can't—"

This time he was interrupted by a familiar voice from the doorway. "Who is this woman, and what is she doing with my man?"

Maria straightened up and turned toward the doorway, allowing Josef an unobstructed view of Komtur Heinrich. His master bore an expression of pure malice, directed right at Maria.

The Pole Telek, the new lord of Gród Narew, walked in from behind Heinrich and looked at Maria with an expression of grim but unfocused anger. "She is a servant, Brother Heinrich."

"Then why is she acting the harlot?" Heinrich snapped.

Some of Telek's anger seemed to find a focus in Heinrich. "She was the person I charged with taking care of your knight here."

"Taking care—"

"His wounds. His meals."

"You had a woman do this for a monk?"

"Sir—" Josef began.

Heinrich pointed a bony finger at him and said, "Silence. Nothing from your lips, Josef. I see what has turned you from the Order, and I have no heart now to hear of your sins."

"Brother Heinrich," Telek snapped, "we only have so many servants that speak your tongue well enough to be of use."

"And you took no consideration of our vows, our commitments to God?"

"This is not a monastery."

"So you ply my men with whores and prostitutes?"

"*I am not a whore!*"

Josef's breath froze in his mouth as he heard Maria's words. Her voice sounded strained, hurt, but her eyes glared at Heinrich with a dangerous fury.

Heinrich drew back for a second—the shock of a man who was never corrected by his lesser. Then, even though his voice changed little in tenor or tone, his face turned the ruddy color of barely repressed anger. He took a stride across the room. "You will not contradict me, woman!"

Heinrich backhanded her with his closed fist. Her head jerked to the side, and Josef felt blood spray across his naked chest. He pushed himself upright as Telek stepped forward and grabbed the Komtur's shoulders. "This is quite enough!" Telek said as he pulled Heinrich back.

Maria spat blood from her crushed lip and said quietly, "Is this how you serve God?"

Heinrich raised his hand again, but Telek grabbed his wrist. Maria stood unbowed, glaring at Komtur Heinrich, waiting for him to strike her again.

They were interrupted by a breathless guard bursting into the room, yelling in Polish. Josef understood none of the guard's babbling except for the name "Telek." However, Josef could see the reactions in the faces of those around him. Maria's eyes went wide, and her blood-streaked mouth hung open. Telek's jaw set firm, and he tightened his grip on Heinrich's arm.

"You should come, Brother Heinrich," Telek said. "We may have need of your expertise."

Heinrich, who knew a fair bit more of the Slavic languages than Josef did, had obviously understood enough to distract him from correcting Maria. "Take me there," he said.

"What has happened?" Josef asked.

"He's here," Maria said, her voice as quiet as death.

Telek led Heinrich away, but as they left, Heinrich said, "Do not leave that woman alone with him. He is yet a member of the Order, and until he is released he will behave as one."

Telek snapped something in Polish, finishing with a dismissive wave at Maria.

Maria looked down at Josef and gently touched his arm.

"What's happening?" he asked.

"I have to leave you," she said. "Please stay here and heal. Find a safe life without me."

"Maria—" His voice died in his throat. He looked up into her face, bloodied from Heinrich's blow. His fist had split her lip and left a long cut on her cheek—at least that's what he had seen after his master struck her. As she looked down at him now, her lip wasn't swollen or bruised at all. Except for a smear of blood, her lip was untouched. Even the tiny cut on her cheek seemed much smaller than he remembered from a moment ago.

And as he looked up into her face, he saw the cut on her cheek shrink, then completely disappear. "Your face," he whispered.

In response, her hand went to her chest, between her breasts. It was a gesture he had seen her make many times, touching the silver cross she always wore.

But she wasn't wearing it now.

The guard stepped next to her and said something, and Maria nodded as the man led her away.

Josef stared after her.

"This cannot be," he whispered. "God, please show me that this isn't so."

When no answer was immediately forthcoming, he slowly sat up and climbed carefully off the table.

XXVII

Telek led Brother Heinrich though the alleys of Gród Narew, toward the stables. As he passed the guards, he shouted orders to alert the Duke, to rouse all the able-bodied men available, and to gather the resident Germans.

In between, he told Heinrich, "You are going to order your men to lead teams to search the fortress and find this thing."

"You are not one to command me."

"This is my demesne, and it would do well for you to do as I wish."

"Must I remind you that the Duke himself has given us let to go abroad and perform our duties as we see fit?"

They reached the stables, where a dozen armed men waited for them. Telek turned to Heinrich and whispered in German that only Heinrich could understand, "The Duke doesn't know that this beast you hunt is something you brought upon us. *Yet.*"

"What are you accusing me of?"

"No accusations," Telek said. "I only point out that our Duke is not yet familiar with the work of Brother Semyon." Telek felt the satisfaction of seeing Heinrich's reserve break. Heinrich's eyes widened, and his mouth opened slightly. *Yes, that doesn't just threaten your mission, does it? If your secrets are made known, you'll face discipline by your own masters, won't you?*

He allowed Heinrich a moment to fully understand his threat; then he added, "You would do well to understand that I *will* see my uncle avenged."

He walked up to the guards in front of the stables and they parted to let him pass. As he moved into the aisleway, the smell of blood caught in his throat. The stable hands had taken the horses out to pasture, so it was silent in here except for the buzzing of flies.

It took a few moments for his eyes to adjust to the dim light. As Heinrich walked up next to him, Telek began to resolve abstract piles in the sawdust into parts of a human body. The boy had been torn apart—arm here, leg there, head over there. Blood soaked the sawdust in the aisle, turning it black as tar in the dim light.

The two of them stood in silence for a long moment. Above them, the thatch roof began to rattle with rain.

"We will do what we can to assist you," Heinrich said. "As you ask."

"Thank you," Telek said. He walked up to the boy's remains, and looked into the sawdust. Bloody tracks led away—massive pawprints. "You will advise our men how to fight this thing. How to attack it even if you do not have the boon of a silvered sword."

Heinrich knelt beside one of the boy's arms. It had landed next to one of the timbers supporting the roof. Telek saw something clutched in its hand. Heinrich opened the hand and lifted out a silver cross and chain. He held it up and looked at Telek. "Of course we will help you in the hunt for this demon. Perhaps you can help me, and say if you recognize this trinket."

⌖

His name was Oles.

Maria hadn't known him well, but she'd known him, if only as someone who suffered as much from Lukasz's arrogance as she did. As the youngest boy working in the stables, he was the one most put upon by men like Lukasz, who could hold their heads up only when pushing someone else's face into the mud.

But now Oles was dead. She had heard the rycerz's man reporting that the boy had been torn apart in the stables by some sort of beast.

Maria knew exactly what sort of beast that would be, and the thought of it almost paralyzed her. Why would he hurt Oles? The boy was nothing to Darien. Even had he carried a silver sword, he was less a threat than the elk they had slaughtered in the woods.

She remembered Josef's words: "*Forty men, women, and children left to rot on the steps of their own church.*"

Was that truly what Darien was?

And if so, then what of her?

She had seen the look on Josef's face as he had stared at hers. Rycerz Telek—*Wojewoda* Telek—and Brother Heinrich had been too preoccupied with the news of Oles to notice her wound healing, but Josef had seen it. He had seen evidence that her ties to the wolf were deeper than any old pagan worship, and infinitely harder to erase.

She didn't know what she was going to do, but she needed to find Darien before anyone else was hurt. Once they were outside, Maria took a step in the direction of the stables. The guard with her grabbed her arm. "Where do you think you're going?"

Does he know as well? "I have duties to tend to." She blushed at the insincerity in her voice.

"Perhaps, but did you not hear? We have a beast running loose within the walls. You should not roam around unescorted."

She looked at him: a young squire of the szlachta, earnest and brave, without a clue about what he faced. *You are in more danger than I,* she thought. "I suppose so."

"Besides, the way to the kitchens is shorter in this direction."

"Yes," she said, "it is."

⌖

Rain fell against the fur on Darien's back as he crawled slowly against the thatch roof of one of the buildings next to the stables. He crouched above his prey, watching the men scurry below him, the smell of their fear growing.

He waited until he saw the old man wearing the black cross of the order enter the aisleway. Then Darien withdrew, crawling silently just below the ridgeline of the roof. His handiwork would be seen by the eyes that needed to see it. Now he had to find his mate.

The rain was cold and misting, and a low fog had begun crawling in from the lowlands around the fortress. He dropped into the gray mist as it gathered between two buildings. He crouched in the narrow space between two windowless walls set barely as far apart as his shoulders.

He saw men run past the mouth of the alley, their smell much stronger than their fuzzy outlines. They yelled at people in the buildings to bar their doors and close up their shutters.

That's right, he thought. *Fear me.*

Humans might hunt him down, might slaughter his kind in the name of their God. But in the end, it was they who feared him.

He crept to the end of the alley, sniffing the air for his mate's scent, and he caught it, stronger in the direction of the main stronghold. He licked his lips and stepped out of the alley.

In moments, a trio of guardsmen turned the corner in front of him. Even smelling of fear as they did, they hadn't expected to meet the object of their fear quite so soon. When Darien came out of the mist, practically upon them, all three wore an expression of disbelief. The one closest to him never had an opportunity to do anything else. Darien's clawed hand tore across his throat. The momentum from Darien's blow sent his bleeding corpse spinning to fall on its back in the road.

Pain flared as one of the men struck at him, cutting a deep wound in his side. But these men weren't of the Order, and didn't carry silver weapons. Darien blocked the next blow by grabbing the man's wrist hard enough that he heard bones break. His prey screamed, but Darien silenced him by biting through his throat.

When the second man dropped at Darien's feet, the third man had disappeared. However, the smell of his terror lingered, and Darien heard his panicked footsteps running for the main stronghold.

Darien licked fresh blood off his muzzle and followed. The man did not get very far.

Josef followed the paths he thought led to the main stronghold. He suspected that this was where the guardsman would have taken her. His belly ached, and his feet were unsteady from the doctor's medicine, but he forced himself on. He needed to catch up with Maria. He needed to talk to her. He needed to hear her explanation before Komtur Heinrich—

His thoughts were interrupted by the sound of a dozen marching feet. As if summoned by his fears, he saw Brother Heinrich, Telek, and six other men striding across his path, headed toward the stronghold themselves. No one spared him a glance.

He had no choice but to follow, pushing himself as much as he dared. But he still gradually fell behind. He managed to keep up with them only because the first scream gave them pause, and then Telek and Heinrich carried on a heated discussion in German mostly muffled in the mists.

He heard Telek's words: "... as I say, or we can discuss Brother Semyon..."

The name gave Josef pause. It belonged to no one in his convent, nor anyone in the Order's hierarchy that he had heard of. The group moved on quickly after that, and he watched as they slowly faded into the mists ahead of him.

He heard more screams and growls, sourceless in the fog, seeming to come from everywhere at once. His breath burned in his throat as he realized that he didn't have so much as a dagger. Half naked and wounded, he lurched through the fog, which erased his vision of anything more than ten paces from him. Fear took hold of him, its touch in the clammy grip of fog and rain on his skin. He could feel the specter of death following him more closely now than at any time since he had left plague-ravaged Nürnberg.

The fear was for himself only in small part. Josef had lived on borrowed time for years, his own mortality a familiar companion. The terror in his heart burned for Maria, for what might happen to her. For what she might be. For what she might do. He didn't fully understand what he hoped to accomplish, but he needed to find her.

⌖

The misting rain wrapped Gród Narew in a blanket of gray. It muffled sound and kept everything beyond the closest buildings invisible. The man leading her maintained a confident pose, striding with purpose, leading her by the arm, but Maria could sense his panic swelling. She felt it in the clammy hand on her wrist, saw it in the lack of color in his cheeks, and she realized that she smelled it; the man's odor made her uncomfortably aware of the monster curled barely dormant within her breast.

"Do you know where—where the attacker went?"

"The pawprints stopped at the entry to the stable."

"Stopped?"

"We had no trail to follow."

Maria held out a small hope that Darien had left, that he hadn't trapped himself behind the walls. But they had just reached the gate of the main stronghold when a scream dashed those hopes—a scream that was ripped short with a horrid liquid gasp.

A low growl followed, and she knew it was Darien's.

Why are you doing this?

The grip on her arm strengthened, and her would-be protector said, "We must get inside." He pulled her through the inner gate, through the walls around the main stronghold. These walls were newer brick, rather than the old wood and earth of the outer walls. The way inside hung open, and her guard called up at the men standing in the watchtower overlooking the gate.

"What are you waiting for? Close the gates!"

"Sir," the voice came down, "unless you bear the authority of the Duke Siemowit or Wojewoda Bol—Telek—"

"You fool! Don't you hear it out there?"

"—the captain of the watch at least?"

"The captain of the watch is by the stables putting pieces of a sixteen-year-old boy into a basket. *Close these thrice-damned gates!*" Another grotesque scream punctuated the man's statement, closer now.

Maria backed toward the stronghold, staring out at the main path toward the gate. The air was a gray mist, so much so that she seemed to look out a portal upon Limbo.

Another scream, a deep throaty growl, and the man above them lost any hesitation. "*Close the gates!*"

Even as he called out, and men ran to push shut the thick doors, Maria saw a shadow move through the gray mist. The man with her drew his sword and pushed her behind him. "It's coming."

"No," she said. She could hear the sound of many booted feet through the mists. It wasn't Darien. Not yet.

The man in the tower above called down, "Hold!"

The men on the door stopped moving as the figures of Bolesław's nephew and Brother Heinrich emerged from the fog, leading a half dozen other men. They filed through the partly open gate, Telek in the lead. Once they were all through, the man above called down, "Do we seal the entrance, Woje—"

"Of course!" Telek bellowed.

The men by the door resumed their work. Maria saw a bit of commotion by the door, but she didn't see what, because Brother Heinrich had stepped in front of her and her temporary guardian. As Telek shouted something to his men, Heinrich called to Telek in German, gesturing at the man in front of Maria: "You should tell your man to fall back. That steel sword will only annoy our adversaries, unless he has the luck to completely cleave the neck or heart with his first blow."

"Adversaries?" Telek responded, "There's more than one now?"

Someone shouted something by the gate, but Maria was focused on the object that dangled from Heinrich's bloodstained hand.

How could this man have her cross?

The central stronghold of Gród Narew emerged from the fog in front of Josef like a massive pagan cenotaph to hungry gods long dead. The gate hung before him, a half-closed maw. He reached it just as the last of Telek's men slipped through.

He tried to follow, and one of the men at the gate shouted a challenge at him.

"Let me in," he shouted back in German, doing his best to repeat it in his limited Polish vocabulary. The men blocked his way as his fellows kept closing the gate.

Of course; these men didn't know him. Josef had spent nearly his entire stay here bedridden, and his surcote, which identified him as part of the Order, was in shreds.

There wasn't time to make the point. He dove through the closing gap, only to be grabbed by the man blocking his way. The man shouted something in Polish and Josef heard the slide of steel. Josef struggled until he heard the door shut behind him; then he allowed the men to push him up against the door, a sword at his throat.

Telek saw the struggle from the other side of the crowding Polish armsmen and shouted something that made the sword lower and their grip loosen. Telek turned around as Brother Heinrich called out something. Now that the men had stepped back from him, Josef could see where Heinrich was, and who was with him.

"*Maria!*" Josef called out.

She wasn't paying attention to him, or to anyone by the gate. She was staring at Heinrich, eyes wide and mouth half-open.

"Maria," he said again, his voice now more a plea to God than to anyone here. He'd seen what held Maria's attention: her silver cross dangled from Heinrich's hand.

XXVIII

How could this man have her cross?*

Maria stared at it, and her first impulse was to grab it from Brother Heinrich's bloody hand.

But the disrespectful impulse was unlike her.

Or unlike the Maria she had been.

"You recognize this?" Heinrich said. "Perhaps it is yours?"

Maria backed away from him until she felt the bricks of the inner wall press into her shoulders. The man who had escorted her still had his sword drawn, but the point was lowered and he was looking from her to Heinrich to Telek.

Telek stepped up next to Heinrich. "Brother Heinrich, can you explain your sudden interest in our servants?"

She heard someone calling her name and turned to look back toward the gate. Josef. *No! Why is he here?*

"Just this one. See her face?"

She took a step toward the gate.

"What about her—"

She didn't hear the rest of Telek's words, because Brother Heinrich's fist slammed across the front of her face. She felt the bones of her nose give way as she inhaled choking mouthfuls of her own blood.

"Maria!" Josef yelled, pushing through the knot of confused men by the gate.

"Whore!" Heinrich yelled at her as she fell to her knees, spitting up blood. "Harlot! Succubus!"

"Brother Heinrich!" Telek grabbed Heinrich's shoulder and pulled him back. "What in the name of Heaven do you think you are doing?"

Maria heard the sound of metal being drawn, and she looked up at Heinrich and Telek. Heinrich was pulling his sword from the scabbard at his hip; he stopped only when Telek grabbed his wrist. "Look," he told Telek. "She cannot conceal what she is."

Heinrich stared down at her with a gaze as cold and impassive as death, while Telek's eyes slowly widened. Josef yelled, "Don't touch her," but his voice seemed very far away.

In her face, Maria felt her bones twist and her flesh flow in a tiny painful echo of her changes. She didn't need to touch it to know that her nose was healing. She felt it immediately when the blood stopped flowing and her sinuses cleared, and she could breathe in the scents of fury from Heinrich, and fear from Telek.

"Christ preserve us," Telek said.

"She is a demon." Heinrich freed his wrist from Telek's grip to continue drawing his silvered sword.

Her heart pounded, and she felt her bones creak and her flesh begin to burn with the imminent change. Her mind might be frozen, but her body was not, and it cared to live.

She crouched, and the way sensations spun in her head, Heinrich seemed to move very slowly, lifting the sword.

Like a rearing elk, she thought.

Suddenly Josef was there, between her and Heinrich, holding Heinrich's sword arm. She felt the beast within her about to burst forth, and she couldn't stop it.

Heinrich yelled, "Josef! She is a deception sent to tempt you away from your vocation!"

Maria sprang from her crouch, at a gap that Josef's struggle had made between Heinrich and Telek. She felt hands reaching for her still-human shoulders, but they only grabbed her clothes. The grip couldn't stop her movement once her feet touched ground. She ran off toward the stronghold, pulling her assailant after her until she heard the sound of tearing fabric. Then her attacker fell to the ground, holding the greater part of her surcote.

⊕

Heinrich yelled as Josef pulled at his sword arm, but Josef still had enough strength to hang on. He struggled to restrain Komtur Heinrich as Maria leapt past them.

"Let go, you fool!"

Telek grabbed at her as she passed, but she moved almost too quickly to follow with eyes, much less hands. Still, the large Pole managed to grab the back of her surcote. But the force of Maria's movement was such that it pulled the heavy man off balance. Telek took a single stumbling step before falling down, his hands filled with torn fabric.

The scene distracted Josef enough that he didn't see the man who landed the blow on his back.

Pain shot through his midsection, flaring brightest in his newly stitched wounds. He lost his grip on Heinrich's sword arm, and his master spun around, facing into the stronghold.

"After her!" he commanded.

Something slammed into the gate.

Everyone turned to face the barred entrance. Outside, a man yelled, screaming in Polish. Someone moved to unbar the gate, and three of his fellows grabbed him and pulled him, protesting, away from the door.

On the other side, the man screamed again. Something slammed the door once more, and the screaming stopped. A low growl replaced it—a growl that made Josef's stomach shrivel into a hard little ball.

Heinrich turned to face the door. "Have your men retreat into the stronghold."

"What?" Telek had just pushed himself upright. "One creature—"

"These walls are no barrier to it!"

"Brother Heinrich, I don't think—"

Another scream came out of the mists, this time above them and to the right.

"Men," Telek ordered, "to the stronghold! Seal the doors!"

Josef was caught up in the retreat through the massive door into the stronghold. While men maneuvered to shut the doorway, Josef kept pushing through the crowd, into the Polish fortress proper, following the path Maria had taken. His Komtur and Telek showed no more interest in him.

Heinrich yelled, "Where are the rest of my men and their weapons?"

"I sent orders to them to assemble and arm themselves in the great hall."

Then Josef passed beyond hearing.

Where had she gone?

He slowed as he passed a corridor that crossed the main entry hall. His fist pressed against the tightness in his stomach as he tried to guess which way Maria had gone. She had been moving so fast, she could be anywhere.

Down one corridor, he heard a woman screaming. He grabbed a sword from an armorial display and ran off in that direction.

A few steps into the stronghold's halls, her broadening shoulders finished the job that Telek had begun on her clothes.

She tossed aside the rags her clothes had become, whipping her head around and looking for some escape.

She ran through halls she had known all her life but that now seemed unfamiliar. Everything seemed small and twisted—the colors wrong, surreal, unnatural through her wolf eyes. The place was rank with human stench: cookfires and sweat, sex and piss, ale and unwashed linens. The walls closed in on her, amplifying her fear, driving her forward.

A woman stepped into her path, and Maria recognized her: Lucja worked in the kitchens with her. Lucja looked in her direction and screamed in terror. Maria instinctively reached out to reassure her, but Lucja saw only a black-furred forelimb reaching for her and fell to the ground in a faint.

Maria watched her fall, and looked down at herself. Here, in Gród Narew, her new half-lupine, half-human body was much more monstrous. The lean, muscular body, the shaggy black pelt, the massive paws and clawed hands all belonged in the depths of some primeval forest. Such a thing as her did not belong here.

She stepped over Lucja's unconscious body and ran on.

Josef passed the shreds of Maria's surcote and her other clothes a few paces from a fallen servant. The woman was sprawled facedown on the floor, and despite the obvious—she had brown hair and was clothed—Josef's first fear was that he was looking at Maria's body. It only took a second for him to understand that both conclusions were mistaken. The woman was not Maria; nor was she dead, or even injured.

She began rousing even as Josef approached and knelt by her. As she recovered, her eyes widened and she sucked in a breath for another scream.

"It is all right, miss," he said to the woman, hoping she understood German.

Unfortunately, she didn't. She started screaming at him in her Slavic tongue so quickly that he doubted that he would have understood her even if he knew the language. He shushed her and said, "I'm German. Please, just go hide somewhere."

"German," she repeated. She stared at him for a moment, then grabbed his shoulders and said, "*Wolf!*"

He thought, *It's inside,* even though he knew that the creature in here was not the same one.

He pointed back the way he had come, yelling, "Hide!" Then he ran off to follow Maria. Behind him, the woman called after him, "Wolf! Wolf!"

Ahead, he heard more screams and growls.

No. Please God, no.

⊕

As she ran, trying to escape the alien human world pressing down on her, Maria heard noises in the distance. A growl followed by a scream.

Darien.

The screaming came from outside the stronghold, and it was hard for her to determine a direction. She stopped at an intersection near the kitchens to try to focus on where the growls were coming from. She stood for a moment with her head cocked, fighting the disorientation and the panicked urge to run.

Someone near her screamed. She whipped her head around to see another servant she knew—an old gray-haired woman emerging from the kitchens. The woman stared at Maria, dropping a basket of root vegetables and scattering orange-white tubers across the floor. Behind her, through the archway into the kitchens, things clattered and people gasped.

"No. Please." The words left her mouth, distorted by the lupine muzzle but recognizable. The plea turned the woman's shock into terror, and she ran. In the kitchens, Maria saw all the other servants, people she knew, running from her.

She felt her eyes burn.

Then fire slammed through her side—a flare of pain, sharp and quick. She clutched at herself and saw a steel blade poking through her abdomen. Blood coated the shining blade, glistening in the lantern light. She looked down at it in shock and watched as it was withdrawn from her body.

She growled and turned, clutching the hole in her gut. As she did, the blade swung at her, glancing off her shoulder, slicing a strip of skin and muscle from her upper arm and slamming the flat against the side of her head, making her left ear ring.

Then she saw her attacker. "Josef?"

He stood before her, panting, wielding a sword, bringing it up to swing at her neck. She raised a hand and grabbed the hilt, stopping his swing with an impact that hurt her wrist. He stank of blood and panic and rage. Sweat glistened on his upper body, and his biceps trembled as he tried to wrest the sword from her grasp.

She had lost him. She had lost *everyone.*

"I'm so sorry, Josef," she whispered. His eyes widened, as if he hadn't expected the monster in front of him to speak. "Why didn't you stay away?"

"Maria?" The grief in his voice tore her heart apart.

She let go of the sword and stepped back. Josef shook his head but didn't swing at her again.

"I didn't want to hurt you," she said, her own words sounding monstrous in her ears.

"No!" Josef shouted. "Stop talking!" And he swung at her again.

She dodged the blow, and the blade struck the brick wall behind her, shedding sparks and stinging clay shrapnel. He swung again, and she knocked the blade aside with her arm, opening a massive gash that sprayed blood across both of them, but only for a moment.

She started backing away from his mad swings. His face was a mask of rage as he tried to cut her down.

"Please," she pleaded, "stop." She didn't fear the blade anymore. It was steel, and even when it landed a blow, the wound sealed within moments. What frightened her was the glaze over Josef's eyes, as if the man she knew had disappeared completely.

As she backed between the long tables where the meals were prepared, Josef's sword came down, swinging left and right. She ducked and backed away as the blade slammed into the tables next to her, scattering onions, cabbages, and radishes, and sending pots and dishes flying.

Behind her, the last of the servants escaped out the rear entrance to the kitchens.

In front of her, past Josef, she heard the sound of booted feet and mail. The arch into the corridor suddenly filled with armed men wearing surcotes bearing the black cross of the Order. Two of them had crossbow bolts nocked.

"Brother Josef! Clear us a shot!"

The Germans were armed with silver, and she knew her horrible new body would not shrug those bolts off. The only reason she still lived was because Josef's insane rage blocked their aim. But she was nearing the end of the tables, backing toward the blazing hearth. In two steps, she would have no choice but to move left or right, or allow Josef to close on her.

She needed to shield herself.

As she stepped back past the end of the tables, she ducked to her right, grabbing the end of the table and lifting. The monster was strong, but the weight of the table—twenty paces long—sent pain shooting down her arms, her legs, and her back. As she lifted, she tilted it toward Josef and the Germans. It knocked him back, and she felt two crossbow bolts slam into the table's surface.

She toppled the table into their path, then ran for the rear entrance.

⌖

It spoke his name in Maria's voice, and Josef went mad.

This monster had deceived him—. No, that was a lie. He had deceived himself. He had always known, but the Devil had seduced him into not wanting to know. Now all the blood that this thing—that *she*—would shed was upon his hands. He had defied his vocation, and he had violated the memory of his dead betrothed by thinking—

He attacked blindly, furiously, with no thought of defense or of the wound in his belly. He swung at her, pressing the black wolf thing back, inviting a counterattack. Wanting one. In the complex storm of emotions, he wanted her to strike out, to punish him. He had sinned so gravely that he didn't deserve to survive. Something in him felt that her claws might tear this blot off his soul.

And if she attacked him, it would justify the rage.

But she didn't. She backed away from him, dodging his blows, her too-human eyes showing a grief and loss he didn't want to recognize.

His brothers were screaming at him and the monster was ducking under the long table to his left before his rage ebbed to the point where he realized that he was driving back a demon with nothing more than a steel sword.

He should be dead.

The table came up, shedding bread, baskets of vegetables, and an earthen jug that shattered in a pungent explosion of vinegar when he deflected it with his sword. Then the broad surface of the table angled toward him and he scrambled back—dazed more by the thoughts running through his head than the blockage of his path.

He backed into the arms of his brothers in the Order.

He should be dead. She could have disemboweled him a dozen times, but she hadn't as much as struck out to knock him down. They had chased her into the heart of the stronghold, into the midst of unarmed servants, and the only blood shed had been hers.

The horrifying thought was that the beast he had seen was still Maria, which meant that everything else he had known or thought he had known was wrong.

God help me.

Other knights ran around the edges of the kitchen, avoiding the mass of timber blocking the center of the room. "Josef, are you all right?" asked one of the men holding him upright.

"I am fine," he lied, bracing against the pain in his gut to follow his brothers.

XXIX

Maria ignored the screams and the panicked flight of the people in her path. She had to get out of this place, away from these people. In the confined spaces of the stronghold, she couldn't outrun the booted feet that chased her. Their pursuit drove her higher into the stronghold.

Toward the sound of Darien's growls.

Five stories up, she pushed through a door, out into open air rank with the smell of blood. She stood on a causeway that looked over the inner wall of the castle, meant for defenders to fire arrows or drop debris down on an attacking force.

But that attacking force had made it up here. She stepped out onto the narrow balcony and the pads of her feet made small tearing sounds as they stuck to the blood-soaked floor. Three swords were cast down at random, one still grasped by a naked forearm that had been torn free at the joint.

She turned to face the growls—down the causeway, toward the opposite end of the stronghold.

He stood there, his back to her, rippling muscle and blood-soaked fur, his gore-drenched muzzle snarling, claws tearing the life from the remaining defender.

"Darien!"

The man in Darien's claws lived long enough to scream as he fell over the wall.

Darien turned to face her, a grotesque lupine smile slashing his face. "You have returned to me."

"What are you doing? Stop it!"

"Stop? Did anyone yell stop as they put my family to the fire?"

She stared at him, her breath burning in her throat. The mist chilled her skin, even under her fur. She breathed deep and could smell the extent of the slaughter. She could distinguish the blood from five, from ten, from a dozen different men.

"You have me," she growled at him. "There's no need to go on with this."

He licked his gory muzzle and said, "For what they've done to me, for what they've done to you, everyone in this place must die."

Then Darien leapt at her.

⊕

Josef was at the rear of the cadre of knights as they chased the monster up through the halls of the stronghold. He slowly fell behind, hampered by his injury. Every fifty steps or so he paused to check himself, to make sure he hadn't again torn open the wound in his gut. But despite the throbbing, the new stitches held.

She had held him together throughout the night.

He forced himself not to think about that. It had all been a deception. She was a creature of Satan.

Then why was he still alive? And why had they passed a score of men and women, all panicked and yet unharmed?

Why did she flee?

She was a creature of Satan, but she had worn a silver cross. She called herself Christian.

As he caught up with his brothers on the other side of an

arched doorway, a breeze blew in, carrying the chill misting rain, the smell of blood, and the sound of growls. He saw a pair of brother knights step out, swords drawn, as a low monstrous voice said, "Everyone in this place must die."

The two men in the lead did not have an opportunity to use their weapons. A yellow blur leapt across the open doorway and one man went tumbling, screaming, over the wall. The other sailed backward through the open doorway, scattering the brothers and falling at Josef's feet to stare up at him with half a face. Josef bent down to grab the silvered sword from the dead knight's twitching hand.

Josef stood as the scattered brethren tried to close the gap in front of the door. Even with the silver weapons, they were at a disadvantage against the blood-drenched demon. It stood, blocking the diffuse white light from the doorway, just a pace beyond the threshold. The doorway was meant to be defensible in a breach, so it was small—shorter than the lupine silhouette beyond it. One knight could charge though it, but the choke point made a swinging attack impossible, and a charge at the thing, point first, would be suicidal even with a silvered sword.

The creature was also smart enough to recognize that passing the constricted threshold would be its own suicide. With six swords at the ready, even its speed and strength wouldn't prevent a mortal wound.

Two seconds into the standoff, Josef knew in his heart why he had lived, and why God had spared him. He changed his grip on his borrowed sword and screamed at his countrymen, "Make way!" as he charged at the beast.

⊕

As Darien leapt at her, Maria crouched, expecting him to take his bottomless fury out on her. But he passed above and to the right, landing behind her. She spun to follow his motion and saw two knights of the Order, swords raised at her back.

Darien landed between them. One clawed hand swung up between one swordsman's legs, lifting him up and over the outside wall in a single motion. The other arm came down in a brutal backhand that clawed through the other's face as it knocked him back through the open doorway.

A half second later, she heard a sickening crunch from below that silenced the falling knight's screams. She felt the impact in the pit of her stomach. She had seen death, and she had seen the aftermath of battle, but neither compared to the sickness that filled her heart at such casual brutality. Darien had struck at these men with no more concern than he had attacked the elk.

Less.

The world froze except for her racing heart. Darien faced the shadows beyond the door, and her tongue dried in her mouth. If *he* was what she was to become, how could she deny Josef's claims that she was a soulless demon?

Two words broke her paralysis. From inside, she heard Josef cry, "Make way!"

In response, Darien spread his arms as if to greet him.

"Enough!" Maria screamed. She leapt at Darien, slamming him into the floor past the doorway. "Enough of this!" She landed on top of him, her clawed hands digging into his blood-spattered fur.

She looked down at him from above. He snarled and snapped and pulled his legs up under her. His paws slammed into her gut with a tearing impact, sending her tumbling back, tripping over something, clutching handfuls of bloody golden fur.

The eight parallel gouges in her stomach were sealing shut even as she sprang to her feet. Her eyes widened when she saw what she had stumbled over. Josef had been knocked to the ground by her passage. On his knees between them, he was attempting to push himself up with one hand, holding his sword with the other.

Darien glared at her with a fury beyond even what he had shown the Germans. *"I say what is enough!"*

Darien raised a forearm to strike Josef down, and Maria leapt at him again, this time slamming him into the crenellated wall at the end of the balcony.

He growled at her, their cheeks touching, so that she could feel his lips move along the whole length of her muzzle. "Fool. You think they might return your mercy? He raises his sword against you yet." He pushed, and they rolled sideways until she was the one pressed into the wall. Past Darien's shoulder, she saw Josef readying to strike.

As the sword came down, Maria pushed Darien back so that they rolled again, Josef's stroke missing Darien's head to slam ineffectively against the wall.

Please, Josef . . .

"They would have your head as well as mine." He pushed her off him again, this time with enough force that she slammed into the stronghold wall before her feet touched the ground.

She landed as Josef swung another blow in Darien's direction. Darien moved quickly out of the way, and Maria saw Darien's jaws open, about to come down on the back of Josef's unprotected neck.

In the chaos of pain, growls, blood, and fur, Josef was aware of one thing: the black-furred monster was Maria. Whatever else he knew, or thought he knew, the black lupine demon was still her.

Still the woman he loved.

The knowledge stayed his hand when they grappled and she

was in harm's way, but once the golden one pushed her away, he had no hesitation—the golden one was unquestionably Satan personified in tooth and claw.

Only his swing came too late, slamming his sword with jarring force into the wall. He felt the impact in his wounded gut. He swung again, his sword missing where the wolf's head had been. His arms still followed through on the ineffective stroke, and he felt carrion breath on the side of his neck, and saw gaping jaws and a lolling tongue in the corner of his eye.

Something unseen slammed into his back, knocking the sword out of his hand.

As he hit the blood-soaked floor, he thought he heard that satanic maw snap shut. He tried to roll over and get up, but a massive black paw stepped on his chest, pressing him to the ground.

Maria crouched above him on impossibly large canine legs, a hideous snarl creasing her muzzle as she faced the larger wolf thing.

"Do not take what is mine, bitch!"

"He is not yours. Not if you want me."

"You are mine!"

A feral growl rose, and the words she spoke were barely human: "Only if I say so, Darien."

"You can't defy me like this!"

"You can have me or these men." She shifted her weight so that her foot left Josef's chest. She straddled him, paying him no attention at all. He fumbled for his sword.

"Step aside." The golden monster, the one she called Darien, was focused completely on her. Disturbingly to the point of arousal.

Her growling voice had lowered to little more than a whisper. "Do you love their blood so much more than mine? Or do you just doubt that you can take me?"

Darien gave vent to an inarticulate howl. If any sense was borne within it, it was inaudible to human ears. Maria moved, and Josef rolled to grab his sword. He lifted it, but she was already running the length of the balcony, away from him. She passed right by Darien as if to taunt him. He grabbed for her, but she moved even more quickly than he.

Josef's surviving brothers ran from the open doorway, one crossbowman falling to his knee next to Josef. Even as he brought the weapon to bear, Maria stood upon the wall overlooking the front of the stronghold. Josef watched the man take aim, and his heart pulled taut and still like a skin of a drum.

The man fired.

And Maria leapt.

The bolt embedded itself in the wall where she had stood, and Darien followed her over.

Josef scrambled to the wall and looked down at where the two monsters had landed. The ground was nearly invisible through the mist, but through the gauzy shroud of gray he saw a quick black shadow move, climbing over the inner wall and vanishing into the invisible buildings of Gród Narew. Close behind, a larger, lighter-colored shadow followed.

He saw a pair of crossbow bolts sail after the moving shadows, but to no effect.

Josef leaned against the wall, letting the brick merlon support his weight, the surface cold, rough, damp with condensation, and in some spots sticky with blood. His dead comrade's sword hung loose in his hand, trembling slightly. He stared into the gray mist and prayed to God for strength and for wisdom.

If they are both servants of Satan, why do they fight?

Why had she saved him? And not only saved him but drawn the beast Darien away from this place? Why didn't she kill, like he did?

"What work of the Devil has been wrought here?" Heinrich's

voice came from the doorway. Josef didn't turn to face him, because he doubted he could look at his master straight on. He was only probationary anyway, soon to leave the Order. The question wasn't directed at him.

One of the surviving knights related the battle. Josef half-listened to the details. The knight spoke truth, though the knight's truth put more weight on Josef's attack than was warranted, and omitted the wolves' conversation.

But perhaps the knight hadn't heard it for the growls.

Of course, Brother Heinrich had a pat answer for the monsters' behavior: "Two demons fighting over whose life and whose soul to claim."

Josef clutched his stomach and tried to tell himself that the pain he felt was only the wound in his belly.

He winced when a hand came down on his naked shoulder. "You've acquitted yourself well, Brother Josef."

Josef turned to look at Heinrich to tell him that he was no longer part of the Order, but something in those hard gray eyes stopped him.

"You will come with us, this last time at least."

"Where?"

"To track this new beast home."

XXX

Maria had snatched Josef from Darien's jaws, praying that she knew enough of her bestial lover's heart. She had taunted Darien, pushed him, testing his dominance to the point of fury. To the point of arousal.

When she leapt, she knew there was no question that he would follow.

Her actions were moving so far ahead of her thoughts that the ground was racing to meet her through the mists before she fully understood what she had done. Every instinct in her body screamed that she had just committed suicide.

God help me was the only prayer she had time to compose, as she drew her legs up and closed her eyes.

She slammed into the ground on all fours with an impact that felt as if it shattered every long bone in her body. She rolled to the side, groaning, realizing that was probably the case. She could feel her skeleton moving, realigning, her muscles snaking to pull the damage back in line, the pain exploding and then evaporating in an orgasmic release.

She made it to her feet just as she heard Darien thud to the ground next to her.

He chased her over the inner wall and through the empty alleys of Gród Narew. In the mist, it seemed as if the whole village were dissolving into nothingness.

For her, it was. There would be no coming back here, not after Darien's massacre.

She climbed the outer wall of earth and logs, scrambling over it as if it were only a deadfall in the forest. She paused, crouched on a high point to make certain Darien followed.

He emerged out of the mists, running on all fours now, intent on nothing but her. At first, she feared that he wouldn't be able to follow her up the wall in his wolf form, but the inside of the wall sloped enough, and he leapt onto it with so much forward momentum that, even with a wolf's forelegs, he could scramble to the top.

She waited until his forepaws touched the walkway where she crouched; then she vaulted over the side. As she fell from the wall, she called to the rest of the wolf to claim her, and she landed square on four paws. When Darien jumped after her, she had already run halfway to the edge of the woods.

She led a race through trees that were a black reflection of her previous day with Darien. The woods had dressed as an anteroom of Hell, cloaked in a chill fog that stole light and color, decapitating the trees and erasing the world more than twenty paces away. Whatever lived here had fled or stood mute in the face of the two demon wolves charging through their midst. The only sounds she heard were paws pounding through the mulch of the forest floor and the ragged panting as they ran.

She heard him, she smelled him, she could *feel* him as an angry presence behind her. She knew that, eventually, he would have to catch her.

But she had resigned herself to that fate. He was her kind, and he was right; she *had* given herself to him already. In her own heart, where the old human Maria still clung to herself, there was something irrevocable, inviolate about what she had done. A promise between him and herself, and to God, tying them together.

And even if she could break that bond, it was the only power she had to keep him from continuing the slaughter. She had to lead him far away from all this.

After it seemed they had run for hours, she heard a growling cough followed by the breathless words "Maria. Stop."

Something in his voice, some semblance of reason, made her slow. Inside, she tensed, expecting that this would be the moment when he took her.

"Maria," he repeated.

She slowed and padded to a stop, turning to look in Darien's direction. She smelled his exertion, heard his panting, but he was invisible behind the veil of gray that wrapped the forest.

"We belong together," he said between breaths. "You know that."

"Then stop this killing!"

"Why, Maria? Why are they more sacred than the elk we slaughtered?"

"They are people!"

"Yet they would kill us for what we are."

"Of course they want to kill you, Darien! How many of them have you murdered?"

"They want to kill you as well."

Maria stood briefly mute at Darien's horrible logic. Then a growing realization made her ask, "How did my cross find its way there?"

There was a long silence, where all she heard was Darien's breathing.

"*Tell me!*" she growled into the featureless gray.

"You needed to understand."

She felt her own rage building. "*Understand what?*"

"You ran back to them! I couldn't let that happen."

"You left it on purpose, to make me into a murderer in their eyes." And right now, her mind did drift toward murder.

"Once the humans knew what you were, you'd be doomed. It was better you find out now, when we both could punish—"

"You don't know anything! Just because some humans hurt you, you think they *all* deserve the same fate? My human family knew all along and..."

Her words trailed off.

They wouldn't...

Of course they would.

She turned and ran, no longer listening to him.

How long had she played this game with him in the forest? An hour? How long would it take Heinrich's men to find her family?

And what price would the Order want from someone who'd raised one of their demons?

Josef walked through the next hour as if through a nightmare. He spoke little and moved as if another intelligence directed his legs. He faded in and out of awareness. He wore a borrowed shirt and surcote that he did not recall being given. He also carried a scabbard on his belt, probably from the same anonymous source. He didn't remember descending from the stronghold, but he now stood with his few living brothers by the gate leading out toward the rest of Gród Narew.

The mist refused to burn off with the advancing day, and the cold and damp clutched at him like the hands of a drowning man, pulling him back down toward unconsciousness. Brother Heinrich commanded the more able-bodied men to open the door, and a voice called "*Hold!*"

Josef turned slowly, feeling the motion in his abdomen, wondering idly, with the unconcern of the dreaming:

Am I bleeding again?

Telek stood in the doorway of the stronghold, at the head of a mass of men bearing on their tabards the odd devices of the Poles: multiarmed crosses, horseshoes impaled by swords and arrows, and glyphs less comprehensible—all red and blue, gold and white. They outnumbered the Germans easily four to one.

"What is this?" Heinrich said.

"You will lead us to this beast," Telek called back.

"This is our charge, Rycerz Telek Rydz. We are called to fight this agent of Satan."

"As my uncle calls me. And, Brother Heinrich, you have not shown great skill in containing this *animal.*"

Even in his limbo of pain, fatigue, and disorientation, Josef had the lucidity to catch the emphasis on Telek's last word.

"Do not presume—"

"Presume? You are not in Prussia, you arrogant monk. You walk in our lands, and if we say, 'Put your weapons down and strip the armor from your backs,' you will do so and be glad of the chance to march barefoot back to your own lands."

"You have no right to command us. The Duke—"

"Duke Siemowit has charged me to deal with this. You would do well not to challenge my authority here."

Heinrich took a step forward. "You would lead your men against the Devil armed only with steel?"

"'They are a beast like any other, but one that can at will disguise itself as a man. Also, like any beast, they are deadly to man when wild and untrained,'" Telek said.

Heinrich took a step back.

"I have a good memory for things I've read. Do I recall Brother Semyon's words correctly?"

Semyon? That name again.

"Those letters are only for the initiated. You cannot understand!"

"I understand that this thing is no more demonic than a rabid dog. And according to your own Brother Semyon, if we take its head, with or without the aid of silver, it will be done with. Healing or not, a man with a pike should hold it at bay for the length required for my men to complete the task." He glared at Heinrich. "Now, where is it you're intending to go?"

Josef followed Poles with pikes and battle-axes and the Order, with their silvered swords and crossbows. The Poles marched, and the Germans and Telek rode. Josef sat astride a Polish warhorse, his knuckles white on the reins, every step sending jolts of pain through his gut.

But at least the pain kept him awake.

He tried asking his master once who Semyon was, but the only response was: "A brother knight in the Order, long dead."

Brother Heinrich's curt response fed Josef's already growing doubt. When Maria had challenged him—had asked him if the monsters he hunted ever talked, if they did things any worse than men did—his response to all such questions had been that these things were soulless demons.

Doubt had come first when he'd realized that she was asking for her own sake. Now, with Telek's statements, doubt had taken an equal footing with faith.

Josef had believed they were demons solely because of the words of his masters in the Order and the creature's actions. Now

Telek gave Josef reason to doubt his masters' words; he could quote another knight of the Order upon the creature's earthly nature without Brother Heinrich contradicting him.

That left the beast's actions and Maria's question: Were they worse than the actions of men? He had seen and heard much evil done in the wake of the great pestilence, and the burning of Jews in Strasbourg had not been the worst of it.

If he was left to judge based on actions alone, how could he judge these beasts to be demonic?

How could he judge Maria when her only crime was being this thing?

How could he judge her family?

The mixed group of marching Poles and mounted Germans drew to a halt in front of the cottage of Maria's family. Her brother Władysław walked out to meet them as Telek and Heinrich dismounted.

Josef's heart sank because he saw no way that this could end well.

XXXI

Darien chased after his mate.

His bitch.

He wanted to hold her, hurt her, force himself inside her and pin her to the ground until she whimpered his ownership of her. He had told her—he had *shown* her—the fact that she had nothing else. He was all she had. And still she pushed away from him.

He called to her again, to tell her of the uselessness of man. How they would kill her just for the sake of what she was. She didn't listen, didn't understand, saying how he had somehow made her a murderer in the humans' eyes.

Don't you understand? You were a killer in their eyes as soon as you shed their ugly pink skin.

"You don't know anything!" she howled at him. "Just because some humans hurt you, you think they *all* deserve the same fate? My human family knew all along and—"

"I don't know?" He could barely form words, the rage choking him as badly as it had back at the stronghold. She could say that? She, who'd suckled at the human teat, who had never slept in a true den, nesting in the skins of her kill. She had never smelled the burnt flesh of her own kin. How could she? "How dare you!"

He snapped and leapt at her, to take her down and show her the pain he felt. But she had already run away.

He caught her scent, and tasted fear within it.

He growled and chased after her again.

He caught up with her, her black silhouette suddenly appearing out of the mist; she was standing still, facing away from him. He prepared to leap at her, driven by a confused mixture of rage and lust, but something held him back. It might have been the fear in her scent—fear that, he realized, had nothing to do with him.

He slowed and saw the tension in her, the fear bristling on her back as if she had sprouted spines, the muscles on her flanks so taut they might have been carved from stone. Her jaw hung open in a silent growl as she stared forward, ignoring him.

As he padded up behind her, he felt a flare of renewed anger when he recognized where they were. These were the woods surrounding the cottage where she had been kept as a human. Would she always return here? Would she always search for these human chains to bind her again? How could she not understand what they were?

He needed to grab her by the neck and make her see . . .

Then he was in sight of Maria's cottage and saw that, for once, fate was with him.

In front of the cottage stood a score of men or more, the knights of the Order and the more colorfully dressed Polish footmen. He could smell and hear more men than he could see through the fog. The knights had dismounted to surround Maria's human "family."

The German leader yelled something at the large Polish

knight with him. He waved and gestured at the woman who stood at the focus of the knight's attention. Darien felt his muzzle turn up in a near smile. He could not have asked for a clearer demonstration.

Especially when the woman said something and the German struck her with the back of his hand, dropping her to her knees. Maria recoiled as if she had felt the blow herself.

Darien started talking in a growling whisper: "You see now? They cannot abide you. You are predator, they are prey."

"No," she whispered, her voice crumbling into a gratifyingly submissive whimper. "My parents loved me."

"See how even their own kind turns on them?"

The German drew a dagger and held it up to one boy's throat. He screamed at the woman, demanding that she admit her sins and tell them where Maria was.

"This is why we must kill them all," Darien said.

But she was no longer listening to him. She had started walking, changing as she went, and Darien watched her as his satisfaction slowly turned to horror.

They were going after her family.

She stopped, frozen, watching as Heinrich shouted questions at her mother. The scene so stunned her that she could barely breathe.

"Where is this monster?" he yelled at her. "Where is this agent of Satan you've concealed?"

"My daughter is not a monster."

Heinrich struck her mother, and Maria flinched from the blow. *Have I done this?*

Darien stood with her, whispering that she was a predator, a killer. A monster.

She wanted to deny it. She wasn't Lucina, bent on bringing death and pain. Her parents had loved her, whatever her origin.

Heinrich grabbed Władysław's arm and pulled her brother forward, bringing a dagger up to his throat. "You are *all* complicit in concealing this thing! Do I need to demonstrate the seriousness of this to you? Confess that you've harbored this demon . . . "

Darien whispered that they must kill them all.

She was the predator; they were prey. Seeing the German hold her brother, she could easily imagine her jaws crushing the life from Heinrich's throat. She could tear out his belly and feast on his steaming entrails.

She *could* kill the whole wretched lot of them. They needed to die, and it was her purpose to slaughter them. The wolf conceded that Darien was right, and that she truly lusted for the blood of these men.

All these thoughts gripped her, and she knew she was damned.

Because if Darien was right, then so was Heinrich. A monster such as she had no place within God's creation. Josef was right, and she was a soulless demon spawned from Hell to deceive the righteous.

To deceive herself.

She prayed for strength even though she knew that for her to do so was probably a blasphemy. She walked out of the woods, pulling the demon wolf back inside herself. When she stepped upon the road across from her home, she was clothed only in naked human flesh.

If he hadn't already known that something was deeply wrong, Josef understood it when Maria's stepmother looked into his eyes. When she said that her daughter was not a monster, she said it to Josef, even though it was Heinrich questioning her. But if Komtur Heinrich noticed the direction of her pleas, he didn't care to acknowledge it.

Josef looked around and saw fear in everyone's eyes. The Poles held back in the wake of Heinrich's anger, watching the German interrogate their own without a whispered objection. Even Telek seemed loath to challenge Heinrich now.

Josef wondered if everyone was trapped in the same nightmare paralysis he felt. When Heinrich struck the woman, Telek finally moved, saying, "Brother Heinrich, that is enough."

Josef wondered if he was the only one who heard Telek's voice. Josef's master certainly didn't acknowledge it. Instead he pulled the oldest of her sons to him, holding a dagger to the boy's throat.

Telek stopped moving toward Heinrich. "Enough! Lower your weapon, Brother Heinrich." He placed a hand on the pommel of his sword. "You have exhausted what leave I have given you."

Now people seemed to hear Telek. Josef felt the shift in attention, the Germans moving hands toward their weapons, the Poles turning to face the small knot of Germans.

A small bead of blood rolled down the edge of Heinrich's dagger. "I will not allow these peasants to hide the work of the Devil!"

"Those are *my* peasants." Telek pulled his sword so that an inch of steel was visible. "Will you test my vow to protect them?"

"Do you defy God with these unrepentant wretches?"

"Let the boy go."

"I—"

Heinrich's words were cut off by a familiar voice.

"Please, let them go."

Josef turned toward the road and saw Maria, just close enough to be visible through the mist. She stood on the road, naked, her arms clutching herself against the cold in the barest pretense of modesty. Even though she was half-hidden in the fog, he could tell that she had been crying.

"They've done nothing wrong. It's me you want, isn't it?"

For the space of several heartbeats, nothing moved. Everyone stared at the young woman pleading with them. Even the Wolfjäger knights didn't move; they had spent their vocation hunting monstrosities of claws and teeth, fur and muscle. Never once had their quarry approached as a sobbing young woman pleading for her family.

It was enough to give even Heinrich a moment's pause.

But only a moment's.

"No, Maria, run!" her mother yelled as Heinrich called out an order: "*Shoot her!*"

Of the two crossbowmen, one seemed reluctant to shoot a naked woman, but the other, near Josef, raised his crossbow without hesitation. Josef grabbed for his brother knight's arm just as the man fired. Josef felt the tensing of the man's arm muscles under his hand.

Josef wasn't quick enough. He saw, with unnatural clarity, the impact of the bolt into the flesh of Maria's left shoulder. Without so much as a layer of clothes to retard it, the silver-tipped bolt tore completely through her. She grabbed the bloody wound and fell to her knees with a cry.

And a horrifying howl tore through the forest around them.

She stood before the men of Gród Narew, the Germans of the Order, and her family. She felt the fate of her true mother, Lucina, bearing down upon her, a weight on her soul. There was no escape from what she was, but she could not join in Darien's bloodlust. She believed in God and Christ, which meant that she could no longer believe in her own redemption.

So she did all she could do: she offered herself up to the agents of God in a sacrifice for the sins of her family. She called on them to stop, to take her offer, and no one moved.

Then Heinrich, still pressing a dagger to Władysław's throat, yelled over her mother's cries, and one of the Germans fired. Pain tore through her left shoulder. She had the odd thought that a crossbow bolt should feel like a stab wound, not like the near-crippling hammer blow she felt.

She clutched the wound as the pain drove her to her knees, pain worse than that when Josef had impaled her with a sword.

Of course, she thought. *That blade wasn't silver.*

She heard Darien howl.

"No!" she screamed. "Let this be!"

Josef was struggling with the man who had shot her, but the agonized lupine howl froze him in place. The scream came from the throat of Hell itself, as if Darien had been struck by the same bolt that had torn through her shoulder. Heinrich finally lowered the dagger from Władysław's neck and started yelling orders too quickly for her to understand.

Then the forest exploded behind her, branches and shredded underbrush scattering across the road. Darien fell into the ranks of Poles before they could bring their weapons to bear.

The Germans tried to close on the beast, but the Poles were in the way, blocking their attack.

"No," Maria whispered, gritting her teeth from the pain.

A knight fell back from the chaos, the broken shaft of a polearm run through his chest. A Pole fell to the ground, clutching an arm that now ended short of the elbow. One of the footmen from Gród Narew tried to take the beast's head with an axe, and Darien grabbed his neck in his massive jaws and shook his head from his body with a few quick snaps.

Josef stayed by her family, sword drawn, pushing them back toward the side of the cottage, away from the massacre.

Still clutching her shoulder, Maria rose to her feet.

Pikes snapped like toothpicks, and Darien knocked the Polish defenders aside, to attack the knights of the Order who still stood.

"No!" she screamed.

A silver sword rose, and the wrist holding it met lupine jaws, tearing free of its owner with just a flex of Darien's neck.

Maria ran.

Heinrich screamed to God and charged the wolf monster. Darien backhanded the attacking knight, shredding his surcote and sending him tumbling and bloody into Maria's path.

She jumped over the man as she charged Darien. His gold fur now rusty with blood, he stood in front of the cottage, looming over the scattered bodies of his attackers. The surviving Poles fell back, pikes lowered as if they expected a cavalry charge.

Josef was the only knight left within Darien's reach. He held his sword one-handed, the other arm clutching his belly as he stood between her family and the beast. Darien held up a blood-crusted hand to strike him down.

Maria tackled Darien. The size difference between the wolf monster and her still-human body was huge, but no more so than the difference between her own monster and the elk, and she attacked him in the same way, diving at the knee of one outthrust leg, forcing it to bend, toppling him into the open door of the cottage. Even though she felt the pain of re-forming bone and twisting muscle, she didn't yet have claws to slash or fangs to shred, but as Darien fell, she heard his own weight do the damage for her. She heard and felt tendons tear, and the cracking of the canine ankle joint as it bent underneath him.

Darien howled as he slammed into the floor of the cottage. A clawed hand swung out and grabbed her, claws sinking into the flesh of her stomach. He lifted her up, holding her in a slime of her own blood. She felt a blinding flare of pain as he pierced a kidney.

Then he threw her.

Maria slammed into a window on the far side of the cottage, blowing the shutters aside with her back. She felt her ribs crack as she crashed through, falling facedown into her mother's herb garden.

The pain in her ribs, her kidney, and her shoulder all flared in time to her pulse. Her muscles joined the throbbing agony, moving, slithering under her flesh to twist her bones into their new shapes.

She pushed herself upright in a spasm of relief, the hole in her shoulder the only pain that didn't evaporate with the force of her change. She ignored it.

She stood, a low growl leaving her muzzle.

In front of her, she saw her brothers running around the side of the house, then clustering around their mother as if they could protect her. Maria's stepmother chanced to look in her direction, and her eyes went wide. She stopped moving. Władysław tripped over her and fell to the ground.

In the moment they stared at each other, Maria realized they knew who she was. Like her father staring into Lucina's eyes.

Josef was on their heels, screaming at them to move.

Then Darien pounced on him.

XXXI

Josef hastened to get Maria's family to safety, his mind reeling with the image of Maria, still human, naked and bleeding from a crater in her shoulder, holding the beast's twisted leg in a crushing embrace. The vision still seared his mind as Maria's mother stopped in front of him, tripping her own son.

Josef cried, "Move, curse you all, move!"

He turned to see what had stopped them, then spied another monster standing behind the cottage.

Maria.

Her half-wolf, half-human form stood upright, growling lowly. The fog sapped the highlights from her black fur, leaving a lean silhouette broken only by the white glint of teeth in her muzzle and the flash of her too-human eyes.

Then a weight slammed him into the ground with a familiar snarl. He could smell its fetid breath as it washed against the back of his neck, and he turned to see death's golden-furred jaws clamp down on him.

Then a black shadow fell upon the beast's head.

The monster on him howled as a black muzzle tore into its jugular, spraying Josef with blood. The creature stood and threw the smaller black wolf off its neck. The black one slammed into the side of the cottage with a spine-snapping impact.

Maria slammed into the side of the cottage.

Josef fumbled for his sword and tried to swing at the beast, but the blow had no force from his prone position. The silvered weapon bounced off the thick fur on its flanks, leaving little more than a shallow cut. The monster didn't even notice his attack. Instead, it crouched and jumped after Maria, the spurting wound in its neck already sealed.

It landed on her with growls worthy of a rabid Cerberus.

Maria slammed into the wall of her one-time home and felt flashes of pain as several bones, many in her back, broke with the impact. But she found it easier to think through this pain. Her body, miraculous monster that it was, was already pulling the broken pieces together, making them whole.

When Darien leapt upon her, she could move enough to bring her legs up, raking across his abdomen, pushing him away. She scrambled to her feet as he attacked again, dodging a bite. She felt his claws rake her, but it wasn't enough to stop her. She spun around and jumped onto his back, sinking her jaws into his neck, digging her claws into the sides of his chest to hang on.

Her mouth filled with fur and blood, and the smell of his torn flesh overwhelmed everything else. He screamed and bucked and slammed her into the wall, fracturing more of her bones. In response, she buried her claws and teeth deeper.

He shook and moved toward the road, and she found her grip slipping as his body shifted underneath her. She scrambled for a better hold.

Something slammed into her thigh—a crushing blow that flared pain worse than any of Darien's attacks. Her whole body jerked in response, and she fell off Darien into the pine mulch of the forest floor.

She blinked, disoriented, seeing the trees clawing the gray mists above her. She tried standing, but her right leg collapsed under her. She looked down and saw a crossbow bolt sticking out of the meat of her thigh.

She reached to pull it out, but Darien charged out of the mists, fully a wolf now, his jaws clamping down on her left wrist, tearing flesh and pulling her arm back, nearly dislocating her wounded shoulder as she fell to the ground.

Maria yelped as she slammed down, yanking her arm away, barely managing to keep her hand. As she rolled over to her knees, Darien spun and seized her wounded shoulder in his jaws.

The agony in her unhealed shoulder made her cry out again. She grappled him as he dug into her torn flesh, every shake of his head knocking the breath from her body.

She forced herself upright against him, pushing up, her right leg trembling under the burden. Darien's wolf was large enough to keep himself locked on to her shoulder even as she stood, forepaws dug into her chest, trying to force her back down. He pushed against her, and she found herself stumbling backward until a tree blocked her path.

She felt dizzy, and suspected that demons couldn't lose *all* their blood. Her left arm dropped to the side, nearly useless with Darien chewing through her shoulder, and her right leg trembled, ready to give way underneath her.

Her right hand, knotted in the fur of Darien's neck, tried to pull his jaws away, but she couldn't pry him off. Close to blacking out from the pain, she looked down and saw Darien's appalling excitement, blood-red and throbbing, only a handsbreadth from her.

Desperate, she reached her right hand down and grabbed his testicles, hooked her claws into the flesh, and squeezed.

Darien's entire body went rigid, and his jaws opened in a breathless gasp, letting her shoulder slip free. Her back slid down the tree against a slick of her own blood as she twisted her hand, making him feel the pain she did. When he fell from her, she tore her hand away, castrating him in a spray of fresh blood.

Then she ran, limping, deeper into the forest.

She knew he would recover from the insult, just as the wound she had chewed into his neck had healed.

She panted as she limped into the ghost-gray woods. She was horribly handicapped now. Darien outweighed her and was stronger. The only advantage she'd had over him was speed, and the bolt embedded in her thigh had cost her that. But she had to stop him somehow. Otherwise he would just keep killing and killing and killing...

She had distracted him twice now, focused his attention on her, but that couldn't last. She knew that the next time he caught up with her, he would either kill her or leave her in such a state that she'd be unable to do anything to stop him.

She couldn't do anything *now*. She didn't have the strength to sever his neck the way he had done so casually to the people he had attacked.

Behind her, she heard Darien's howls, and in it she heard a cry for her own blood.

Why wasn't she healing? He had only bitten and clawed her, but the savagery he had done to her wasn't repairing itself. Blood poured from her ragged shoulder, and her left arm hung limp, hand dangling from a flayed wrist. But none of that had been done by silver. The only wounds that shouldn't heal were the wound in her shoulder and the bolt in her leg...

God in Heaven, the bolt!

Darien howled, closer now.

She half-fell, half-leaned against a tree. The silver tip of the bolt in her leg was preventing her body from healing. She reached down and gripped the shaft with a shaking hand.

The pads of her inhuman, half-lupine hand were slick with smears of Darien's blood, and she couldn't find a grip. Her hand slid off, firing an agonizing spasm down her leg that dropped her to the ground.

"Please God, don't let me bleed to death because of this." She rubbed the gore off on the fur of her leg and gripped the bolt again. She gasped. "At least not before I end this."

She pulled, tearing the bolt free. She felt it rip from her flesh, the pain echoing through all her wounds, her shoulder and arm trembling as her body finally began to repair the damage. She tried to push herself upright, but her wounded leg gave way beneath her.

She rolled onto her back and groaned, feeling as if all her strength was leaking away through her shoulder and leg. As if her body itself was collapsing, draining away. She grabbed her leg, trying to hold herself inside.

Her hand held on to the wound—a wound in soft, hairless flesh.

"Please, God, no," she whispered. She glanced down at herself and saw her body: the same human body she had grown up with. The wolf had abandoned her. "No, no, no!"

She tried to push herself up, tried to call the beast back before Darien—

As if the thought had called him forth from Hell, Darien sprang from the fog—furious, intact, and covered in the blood of a dozen people. His forepaws twisted into clawed hands as he landed on top of her, painfully slamming her naked shoulders into the root of a tree, holding her upper arms to the ground.

He stared down at her with a distorted lupine face, the fur of his cheeks matted black with blood, panting foul gore-tainted breath. Threads of drool dripped onto her face, her neck, her breasts.

"Maria," the wolf growled, bending down so his face was a hairsbreadth from her own. "This will stop now."

She struggled, pushing against him with her arms and her one good leg. But even if she hadn't been weakened, she never would have had the strength to dislodge him.

"No place to run," he whispered into her ear, the clotted fur of his muzzle brushing against her cheek. "My mate, my bitch."

She felt the wolf's unsheathed manhood burning against the naked flesh of her leg, and she screamed at him: *"No!"*

Not like this, not ever again.

"You can't refuse me," he said. "You don't have the strength. You don't have the will."

She pushed against him with her leg, but it was like trying to hold up a toppling tree. She tried to kick his newly healed testicles, but the sole of her foot slid on still-bloody fur, and then a massive paw came down and slammed her ankle to the ground, pinning it.

He grabbed her face, cupping her chin, squeezing her cheeks in a furred inhuman hand. "Do you enjoy the pain?" he whispered.

Her free right arm pounded on his back. With his hand holding her jaw shut, she couldn't even scream anymore.

He forced his muzzle down in a perverse kiss as he forced himself between her legs. Her hand flailed ineffectively against him until she felt something on the ground next to her.

Her fist seized on the crossbow bolt as he lifted his face from hers and rammed himself inside her, tearing her open. "You were always meant to be mine."

"No, I wasn't!" She brought the bolt up over her head, and his eyes widened as she brought it down with all the strength she had left, impaling his pale blue eye. It hit some resistance as his body

spasmed in shock; then it tore free from her hand as he pulled his head away.

The sounds from him were incoherent—half howl, half scream: the growling voice of Hell itself. With a jerk, he tore the bolt out of his face, leaving a dark crater hemorrhaging blood. And unlike the wound she had bitten in his jugular, it didn't heal.

"You. A-are. M-mine." His voice slurred and growled, so much the wolf now that she may have imagined the words. He trembled oddly, and his right arm dangled limp at his side. But his left hand wrapped itself around her throat, crushing her windpipe, stealing her breath.

"You. Are. Mine." Blood poured from his ruined face, and his muscles twitched asymmetrically. And as her consciousness faded, she prayed that she had spent the last of her life giving him a mortal wound.

XXXII

As the monster ran for the woods, Josef got to his feet in time to see one of the surviving knights of the Order take aim with a crossbow.

"No," he called out. "You might hit—"

The man didn't listen, and Josef's fears were confirmed when he saw the bolt sprout from Maria's thigh before the pair of them disappeared into the forest.

Behind him, Maria's mother sobbed, "My daughter!"

Władysław cradled his mother and looked at Josef with an accusing stare more cutting than any words.

"I will do what I can to save her," Josef whispered.

He ran toward the road. As he passed the front of the cottage, a mailed hand grabbed his shoulder. "What fool thing are you doing?"

He turned to faced the barrel chest of Wojewoda Telek Rydz.

"My duty."

Telek hooked his head back toward the road. "To him?" A few of the uninjured Polish guardsmen were tending to the Komtur's wounds. He lived, but appeared unconscious. Josef looked about and saw that half the men had fallen injured, and half who had fallen were unquestionably dead. He was one of only four men of the Order still breathing.

"To God," he said carefully. "I made a vow to protect the innocent."

"There's no honor in suicide, lad."

"Is there honor in blocking my way?"

Telek lowered his hand and said, "Take some men with you, so you have some chance."

"No," Josef said. "You cannot leave the wounded here alone. Take them into the cottage, where it's defensible." Then he ran, before Telek could delay him any longer.

From behind him, he heard the Polish knight say, "Godspeed."

God help us all, Josef thought.

⌖

He ran through the forest, following gouges the beast had left in the forest floor as it ran. The woods were silent except for an occasional demonic howl that seemed to echo from everywhere at once. He passed a horrid scene where blood and fur and bits of flesh were smeared thick on the ground and the trees.

From there he followed an unmistakable trail of blood, and the howls became louder, more urgent, more horrible.

But worst was when he heard a human voice—Maria's voice—screaming, "*No!*" Followed by what had to be the voice of Satan come to earth—a pained, manic howl that sounded as if it should rend the very flesh from its throat.

He came upon the hellish scene and nearly howled himself.

The beast's fur was red and black with clotted gore across the whole of its body. It snarled, the left side of the face toward Josef, dominated by an empty, bleeding eye socket. It cared nothing for

Josef. Blind to him, it was focused on the tiny white form underneath it.

It was crouched over Maria's limp human body, horribly violating her as it kept one hand wrapped around her neck. It choked her, slamming her head into the ground.

Josef couldn't find the breath to scream. He ran, swinging his silvered sword, bringing it down on the beast's neck.

But he didn't have the strength or the momentum to sever the monster's neck. He managed only to tear a gaping wound, exposing the monster's spine but not severing it. The creature reared, dropping Maria's body, and turned to face him.

It made a predatory sound deep in its throat, dragging its right leg as it turned and raising its left hand toward him. Half its face was ruined, and it stared at him with a single, hideously human eye. The left half of its face, under the ruined eye, turned up in a fang-bearing smile that could chill death itself.

Then it sprang at him—faster than a man, even in its horribly crippled state. It was all Josef could do to lift the point of his sword, only to have the hilt jerk free with a wrist-snapping force.

The fetid jaws opened to tear out his throat as they fell upon him. He felt the teeth against his skin, and the hot outrush of breath, the slither of its tongue against his Adam's apple.

But the jaws did not close.

He looked up, pain flaring in his wrist and arm as the full weight of the thing pressed him into the ground. He stared up into the bloody crater that had been its left eye. No breath, no motion. Dead.

He sucked in a breath, calling out, "Maria!"

Please, God, do not let her be gone. Please . . .

"Maria!"

He heard someone grunt, and the corpse pinning him shifted. For a panicked moment he thought the monster was coming back to life; then it rolled off him. It landed on its back next to him, a silvered sword impaling it through the neck upward, burying itself deep inside the monster's skull.

Above him, Maria stood gasping for breath, sweating, covered in blood. She wobbled on her wounded leg and fell to her knees next to him. "Josef," she whispered, placing her hand on his chest. "I'm glad it's you."

He reached up with his uninjured hand and grasped hers.

She closed her eyes and lowered her head. "Please be quick."

He sat up, wincing at the pain in his stomach and his wrist. "Be quick?"

"You came to kill us, didn't you?"

He touched the side of her face and said quietly, "Him. Not you."

Her eyes opened and she looked at him almost as if he had offended her. "I am a monster, just as he was. A soulless demon. You said so."

"I was wrong."

"Do you mean to torment me now? Do you know what I could have done—"

"What have you done?"

"I could—"

"Maria?" She looked at him, her eyes moist with tears, skin pale from loss of blood. "What have you done? How many lives have you taken? How many men have you left crippled or dying?"

She shook her head. "None yet. You have to stop me before I do. Before I become like him."

"You aren't going to become like him."

"How can you say that? You've seen what I am."

"I can say that because I've seen *who* you are."

Her lip trembled and she half-leaned, half-collapsed into his arms. He held her with his good arm as she sobbed into his shoulder, "I don't want this."

"It's over," Josef said. "The monster is dead."

"I'm a monster, too. The Devil has taken me."

"Have you killed innocents? Have you renounced Christ?"

"No, but I—I—gave myself to Darien. He took me and I *wanted* it."

He held her tighter. "Are those worse than the sins of any man?"

"I'm a servant of the Devil."

"I am unarmed."

"What?"

"A true servant of Satan would finish me in my weakness. If you believe you are evil, if you *are* a monster, why don't *you* kill *me?*"

She let him go and stared at him in horror. "Josef, I couldn't."

He smiled. He placed his fingers on her lips and said, "Do you wish God to forgive you?"

"Y-yes."

"Then He will."

⊕

Maria's heart raced as Josef led her back through the forest. He had explained how this was necessary, but still the fear grew thicker inside her even as the fog burned off around them. She told herself that fear—any sort of fear—was ridiculous now. She had been prepared to die.

But the fact that she hadn't died made each moment afterward precious, and she clung to each one as tightly as she clung to Josef's good arm.

He was, again, naked to the waist. This time his shirt had gone to bind her wounds, and she wore his cross-bearing surcote to cover herself. The embroidered head of a black wolf rested over her left breast, defaced by Darien's blood. She kept glancing at it, feeling as if it meant something but unsure of what.

Josef couldn't carry anything in his right hand. The wrist wasn't broken, but it had been severely dislocated, and it had swollen black and purple. Since he supported her with his good arm, she had to carry the skin.

Darien's skin. Not all of it, but enough from his head and face to show that the beast was dead. It clung to her fingers in a way that made her wish that she was horrified at the violence done to him, but she couldn't even bring herself to feel regret at his demise.

Josef led her out of the woods in front of her cottage. For a moment, the scene almost seemed normal, before she smelled blood and heard shouts from inside her home, and saw the glint of a crossbow from between two slightly open shutters. She tensed, waiting for the shot, but someone called out, "Hold!"

She stood there with Josef, her feet sinking into the mud of the road, the black soup of it squeezing through her toes. And as they waited, Josef whispered, "Forgive me for what I'm about to do."

I've already forgiven you for trying to kill me.

Still, the tension made her tighten her fists. Her free hand dug into the greasy underside of Darien's pelt, and the one across Josef's shoulder clutched the broken head of the crossbow bolt until it cut into her hand.

Let this work, she prayed, hoping that Josef was right and God still cared for her.

The cottage door opened, and Wojewoda Telek stepped out, his sword drawn. He walked forward, stopping a few paces from them.

"It's over," Josef called out. "The monster is dead." He nudged Maria and she tossed Darien's skin at Telek's feet.

Telek prodded the skin with his sword, then lifted it so that the outline of the giant wolf's face was recognizable drooping from the point. Maria bit her lip, because she recognized Darien in the sagging, empty skin.

Telek held the skin up so that the people in the cottage could see. Maria thought she heard a muted cheer from someone inside. Still holding up the skin, Telek turned back toward them and said, "Step away from her."

Maria swallowed. She wanted to tell Josef not to sacrifice anything more for her, but before she could speak, he flatly said, "No."

"There were two beasts," Telek said. "One blond, one black. You hold the other."

"You're wrong," Josef said. He spoke loudly, as much to the men inside the cottage as to Telek. "This woman is an innocent in all of this."

"Innocent? These things can pose as human, even as a woman. Her cross was found in a slaughtered boy's hand."

"Yes, Wojewoda Telek, and where was *she* when that boy was killed? You and Brother Heinrich are yourselves witnesses to her blamelessness in that death."

Telek opened his mouth to speak, but he obviously had not had a chance to think about the matter. He shook his head and said, "Explain, then, how it came to be there."

"Lost when she was caring for my wounds in the woods or bringing me back to Gród Narew. The boy found it during his duties. And I ask you this: Why would a disciple of evil, a demon cloaked as a man, spend her life wearing a cross made of silver? Would the Devil bind himself like that? Would this monster stand mute and powerless before these accusations while I stand here unarmed, and you stand holding only steel?"

Telek lowered his sword and looked at Josef. "Perhaps—"

"Lies!" The door slammed open, and Heinrich stumbled out of the cottage holding a long silvered sword. Half of his face was covered in bandages, and his chest was bound tightly, but he ran toward them as if in full health. "Lies and deception!" he cried.

Telek stepped into his path and leveled his skin-draped sword at him. "You will stop and lower that weapon."

Heinrich pulled up short, but he didn't lower his sword. "That woman is a vile temptress, an agent of Satan. You saw yourself how she healed. You saw her change—"

"Did anyone see this girl grow into a slavering monster?" Josef countered.

Maria tensed, expecting someone to call out, to say they had watched her transform into the black-furred beast. But no one did.

Heinrich looked up into Telek's face. "You grabbed her. You must have."

"Brother Heinrich," Josef said, "before God, can you bear witness against this woman? Can you say that you saw her become this demon?"

The sword lowered slightly and he looked around, and for the first time she could see something like uncertainty in the half of his face that was not covered by bandages. "Someone must have seen this," he said. No one answered him. "She jumped, naked and wounded, on this monster—"

"A monster that was threatening her family. And you mention that in testimony to her evil?"

"I saw her heal!" Heinrich said finally—the only unarguable evidence he had left.

"Wojewoda Telek?" Josef asked. "Do you have a plain dagger to lend me?"

Telek looked back over his shoulder, frowning and furrowing his brow.

"Please?" Josef added.

Telek pulled a steel dagger out of a sheath on his belt. He held the hilt up to Josef. Josef looked down at his wounded wrist and said, "Perhaps you would be good enough to do this for me?"

"Do what?"

"Cut her."

"*What?*"

"Take her arm and draw blood," Josef said. "You claim she is this demonic beast. Cut her with anything but silver and she will heal, as Brother Heinrich says."

Telek shook his head.

Maria held out her naked left arm, shaking slightly because of the wound in her shoulder.

"Are you afraid she is not what you think she is?" Josef asked.

Telek flipped the dagger around in his left hand, still holding the sword in his right. He hesitated a moment, then quickly drew it across Maria's forearm. The blade was sharp, and she barely felt the cut, but it quickly welled up with blood. It began to sting as the blood dripped slowly down the skin of her arm.

Maria squeezed the crossbow bolt with her good hand, the silver point digging into her flesh.

Telek stared at the cut; it refused to heal.

Heinrich lowered his sword at last.

"Satan has been deceiving us," Josef said. "He has deceived us with blood, chaos, and confusion. He deceived you, Brother Heinrich, with your own anger. You saw this woman, whom I love, as leading me astray—so much that you did not see how your own wrath led you astray. Satan would have you kill an innocent woman and believe your duty done."

Heinrich's sword pointed at the ground. He looked at Maria, and she could tell that he did not truly believe Josef's words. But his expression said he was beaten, as if he couldn't quite understand how to fight them. She could see the weight of his wounds bearing upon him, and she felt a strange sympathy for this old man, understanding what he had lost here.

Telek sheathed his dagger and walked up to Heinrich, slapping the flat of his sword, and what remained of Darien's face, into the monk's chest. "Take your prize and leave my lands." There was little trace of sympathy in Telek's voice.

"The black one is still—"

"Brother Heinrich, that black-haired beast did not trouble us before you arrived. I suspect much the same will continue after you leave. You came here hunting your wolf, and you have your wolf."

"We have a duty to hunt all—"

"As I see it, you can return to your master with one of two tales. You can tell how, after great sacrifice, you found your quarry and defeated it, or you can return telling how you've annoyed the Masovian court, broken the peace, and allowed the secrets of Brother Semyon to be known to all the szlachta in Poland." He withdrew his sword, leaving the gory prize in Heinrich's hands. "I will let you pray for guidance, but I expect you to quit Gród Narew at the next sunrise."

Coda

Wagons came from Gród Narew to carry away the dead and wounded. It was evening before all the men left Maria to her home, her family, and Josef. Her mother dressed her wounds—all but the cut on her arm, which healed by itself as soon as she let go of the silver head of the crossbow bolt she had clutched in her hand.

She fell into an uneasy, feverish sleep on one of her brothers' beds. Over the next few days, her body fought the infection of the silver-inflicted wounds. She faded in and out of awareness, but Josef was always there, next to her bed, holding her hand, wiping her brow, caring for her the way she had cared for him.

In her fever, she found the symmetry of it comforting.

They weren't that different, she thought. They had both been chained, hiding themselves—he behind the black cross of the Order, she behind the silver cross of her father. Yet now that they were free, they had lost their proper places in the world.

But when she tried to tell Josef of her epiphany, her German was not quite up to the task. His response was to gently brush the hair from her face and say, "My place is by your side."

⌖

In her more lucid moments, she came close to hating herself for what he had given up for her sake, but she couldn't bring herself to regret the fact that he had. During one point of clarity she said to him, "You're not going back."

"I told you, I've left the Order."

She looked up at him and whispered, "I'm sorry."

He squeezed her hand and said, as he had before he knew what she was, "If God had wanted me to remain a monk, He would not have placed you in my path."

She still couldn't quite understand how someone could sacrifice so much for her, for what she was. But for all she mourned for his loss, she was grateful to him.

⌖

The day after her fever broke, she opened her eyes and did not see Josef. Instead, the rotund bearded face of Wojewoda Telek loomed over her bed, making her flinch and gasp as if confronted by her nightmares made flesh.

Telek saw her reaction and drew back, and she felt someone squeeze her hand. Turning her head, she saw that Josef was still next to her, and that helped calm her racing heart.

Still, her voice had trouble finding itself. All she could manage was "W-why?"

Telek smiled down at her. "Forgive me for disturbing you in your sickbed, but I came to fetch Josef before the Duke makes his leave of Gród Narew."

She realized he was speaking German for Josef's benefit.

"Is there something wrong? I don't understand." She feared

that some sort of trial might be at hand, the Duke taking his ire out on the remaining Germans in his domain.

"The Duke wishes to reward the hero of these past events; Josef's valor and bravery were witnessed by many. Three times he engaged these monsters by himself, the final time returning with the skin of the wolf. Ennobling a foreigner is almost never done, but the szlachta all agree with the Duke's decision."

Maria opened her mouth, then closed it. She was filled with a mixture of joy and fear at hearing that Josef might find himself elevated to the szlachta. God surely was repaying him for his sacrifices by granting him a position in Masovia. But what did that mean for her? For them?

She looked up at Josef and her vision blurred. "That is good news, Wojewoda Telek."

Josef said nothing, though he looked down at her with an expression that said, *I will not leave you.*

But doubt already squeezed her heart. *Maybe you should.*

"I also wished to speak to you, Maria."

She turned to look at Telek again. He was regarding her with a puzzling expression—not one she was accustomed to seeing on her betters. In fact, it was almost identical to the way he had looked at Heinrich after the Order had crossed the river: wariness mingled with respect, as if he regarded a peer, not a serving girl.

But she had to be misinterpreting that.

"Before Brother Heinrich and his surviving knights left our lands, he did press his case before the Duke—despite my interventions."

Maria sucked in a breath. Telek was talking about *her*.

"Still, the man has little head for politics, and is so convinced of his own righteousness..." Telek shook his head, his mouth curving into a tight-lipped smile. "His most damning accusation came down to the nature of the cross you wore."

"Father's cross?" Maria's hand traveled to the empty space between her breasts, as if she could clutch at a memory. Her breath caught in her throat.

"You see, the Duke was familiar with such a token. His father, King Władysław, had commissioned a dozen such silver crosses and matching chains, to give as rewards to some of the men who had served with him when they pushed the Order back to Toruń, over twenty years ago. The fate of one such cross was the subject of much gossip at the court a few years later."

Telek looked at her, as if she should know of what he spoke. When the silence stretched on for too long, filled only by her beating heart, she quietly asked, "What happened?"

"One of these men, while noble in battle, was less than noble in his own household. It is said that when his wife fell ill after bearing his third son, he took one of his newer serving girls to bed, wearing little but the cross on his neck. When he awoke, both cross and servant were gone, never to be seen again."

Oh, Mother, was that where you were for so long? Maria felt the edges of panic creeping in. Telek was going to bring her stepmother to account for a crime she had committed on Maria's behalf. She couldn't bear the thought—

"Of course," Telek said, "that is unlikely to have been the cross you wore."

Maria's mouth had already opened to protest her stepmother's innocence, to offer herself to justice in her stead, but Telek's words stole her breath.

Josef spoke on her behalf: "Why talk of these tales now? Are you here simply to torment a woman on her sickbed?"

Telek shook his head. "Your concern for her becomes you, but I suspect she can care for herself ably enough." If anything, his smile broadened. "As I told the Duke, it is surely improbable that your necklace is the one from that old story. For many reasons, the most important of which is that the servant who stole it was unquestionably German."

German? It was my stepmother.

"I informed the Duke that what I had seen was most likely a necklace of some base metal, kept at a high polish. And since the object in question was lost during that final battle, Heinrich could not provide any smith's marks that could have shown your necklace's provenance."

Maria's hand still clutched her chest, where her cross had once rested. Telek placed his hand on top of hers. She felt something in his grasp, cold and metallic. He took his hand away and kept looking at her face. "It is a shame that it was lost."

Her father's cross—her *stepmother's* cross—now rested on the back of her hand. She was speechless, not knowing what to say. Josef placed his own hand over it, squeezing her hand beneath. "Yes, it is," he told Telek.

"You might be interested to know," Telek added, "that the Order, as well as the Church, did not always consider these wolf creatures demonic."

"What do you mean?" Maria asked.

"Brother Heinrich carries an interesting history, which I had a chance to peruse. At one time, in fact, these creatures may have been enlisted in the service of God. Or, at the very least, the Order itself."

Josef looked shocked. After a moment, he said, "This was the Brother Semyon you spoke of, wasn't it?"

Telek stood up and placed a hand on Josef's shoulder as he looked down at Maria. "To your Brother Semyon, these creatures were as much of earthly origin as you or I. But to my thinking, it seems that if the Order's history of training and using these creatures has borne ill fruit, it may be because they had the bad sense to take a being that thinks as a man and treat it as less than one."

Maria stared at him with a growing realization. *He knows. He knows what I am.*

"What are you saying?" Josef asked. She could hear the edge of suspicion in his voice.

Telek let go of Josef's shoulder. "I'm saying nothing of import right now." He looked at Maria. "I just hope that, despite your obviously imminent betrothal to this young man, Gród Narew will not be completely deprived of your service. I urge you, in the future, to think upon my goodwill and reciprocate it."

Maria looked up into Telek's face and nodded.

"I'll leave you alone for a moment." He turned to Josef. "Only a moment, though; the Duke's court should not be kept waiting."

As Maria watched him leave the cottage, she whispered to Josef, "He knows what I am."

"He suspects."

Maria shook her head. "No, he *knows*. He saw me heal as well as Heinrich did. He knows, and he . . . he . . ."

Josef bent over and stopped her stutter with a kiss. When he raised his head he told her, "He knows that the black-furred wolf was as much the hero in this as I am, even though Heinrich is blind to it."

Her breath caught at his touch, at his breath on her face, and she thought of Telek's other words.

Betrothal.

She raised her head and kissed him back, lifting her hand to caress the side of his face. Eventually he lifted his head, smiling. "He said only a moment."

She looked into his eyes. "You will come back to me?"

"Always."

"But they'll give you a position, land. I have no dowry; I'm a common woman—"

"You are anything but common, Maria. There is more nobility in you than I've seen in anyone born to the role."

"I am also a monster," she whispered.

"No, you aren't." He said it sharply, as if rebuking her.

She felt her heart thudding again in her chest. Just the possibility that he might really care for her, might really love her . . .

"When we came out of the woods," she couldn't help asking, "what you said before Telek . . . Did you mean it?"

"Mean what?"

Maria swallowed. "You said, 'this woman, whom I love.' Do you still, even after knowing what I am, what I become—"

He placed his fingers on her lips and said, "Stop fretting over *what* you are. I love you because of *who* you are."

Relief filled her. "I love you, too," she whispered.

And when he left to go with Telek, she closed her eyes and imagined that somewhere, Lucina, her mother, had found peace.

ABOUT THE AUTHOR

According to the author, "I went to college at Cleveland State University to study mechanical engineering, but I dropped out when I sold my first novel. Since then, I've had a variety of day jobs, including working as a lab assistant, doing cost accounting, managing health benefits for retired steelworkers, and most recently managing a database at a large child welfare agency. In the same time I've written over twenty novels under various names, of which I think *Wolfbreed* is my best work."

S. A. Swann grew up and still lives in the Northeastern Ohio area, along with three cats, two dogs, a pair of goats, a horse, and one overworked spouse.